beyond these Walls

J. L. Berg

Beyond These Walls

Cover Designer: Okay Creations, www.okaycreations.com

Photography: K. Keeton Design, www.kkeetondesign.com

Editors: Jovana Shirley, Unforeseen Editing, www.unforeseenediting.com, Ami Deason, www.bookglambyami.com

Interior Designer: Champagne Formats

Visit my website at www.jlberg.com

ISBN- 978-1508526520

Other Books by J.L. Berg

when you're ready

ready to wed

never been ready

ready for you

ready or not

within these *Walls*

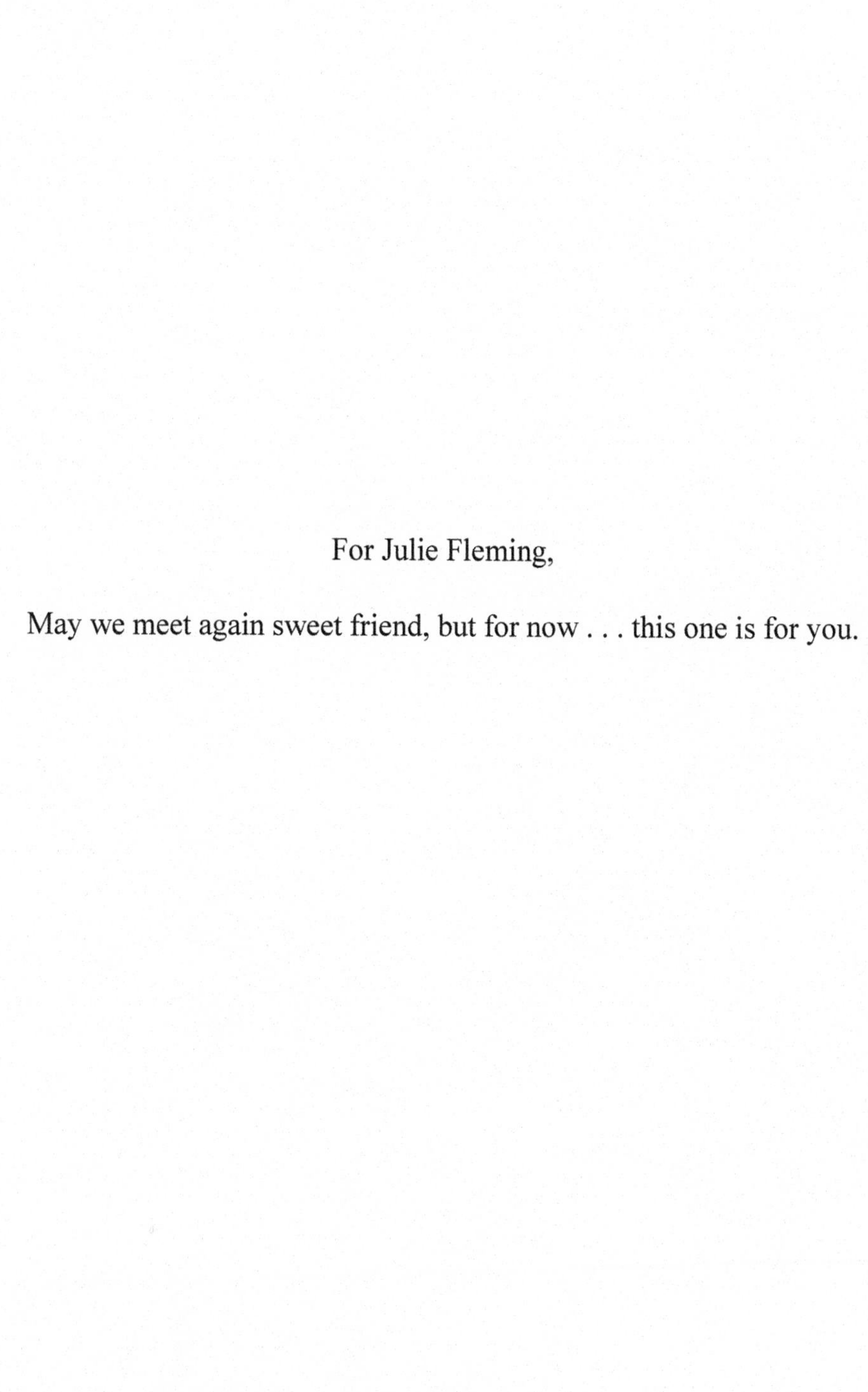

For Julie Fleming,

May we meet again sweet friend, but for now . . . this one is for you.

prologue

THE COOL OCEAN air rushed through the hills, tousling my hair and sending a chill up my spine, as we climbed a bit higher toward our destination.

"How are you doing?" Jude asked.

With his hand firmly wrapped around mine, we traveled through the vibrant green grass.

"Good, really good." I smiled as my hand danced across the tops of purple wildflowers scattered everywhere. I took a deep breath through my lungs, letting the air swirl around my rib cage, and said a small prayer of thanks, knowing there had been a time in my life when a simple deep breath wasn't possible.

"We're almost there. Do you see it?" he asked, pointing with his free hand toward the water's edge.

"Oh my gosh, yes!" I exclaimed.

In the distance, overlooking the ocean was a small church—or the remains of one. Three walls still stood, and as we walked closer, I could see the remnants of the fourth spread across the ground in piles. The roof and floor were long gone, but in its place, nature had taken over. Tiny daisies and beautiful blue sky had woven perfectly through the weathered foundation and walls, creating something that seemed almost part of the land.

Neither of us spoke for a long while. We just stood in the center, absorbing its quiet beauty. This was how I'd always imagined it. When I'd sat in my hospital bed, fantasizing about faraway places and exotic trips to destinations unknown, this was what I'd always pictured in my head.

And here I was, standing in my own dream.

Because of Jude.

I turned, and our eyes met. There, in the middle of the church, surrounded by wildflowers as waves crashed below us, the love of my life dropped to one knee.

"What are you doing?" I asked, my voice shaky and thin, as I looked down at him.

"Exactly what I've wanted to do since the moment I met you."

"I don't know what to say."

"Don't say anything." He smiled warmly. "Just listen."

I nodded as he took my hands in his own.

"I know you think that I saved you, but in all honesty, it was you who saved me. Anyone with the same amount of wealth could have paid for that surgery. It wasn't hard. But you pulled me out of the darkness. If it weren't for you, I would have spent the rest of my life in that hospital, hating myself for the mistakes of my past. You are my light, my angel, and now, I want to make you my wife. Please say yes, Lailah. Please make me the happiest man alive and marry me."

Tears welled up in my eyes as he reached into his pocket and pulled out a tiny black ring box. As he lifted the lid, I felt my new heart skip a beat at the sight of the dazzling ring tucked inside.

Traditional and timeless, it was exactly what I would have picked out. I couldn't help but reach out and run my fingers over the top of the single solitaire set on a thin gold band.

"Yes," I answered softly as happy tears trickled down my face.

I watched as he slipped the ring on my left hand. It was a perfect fit. Happiness and joy shone in his eyes as he stood, scooping me up into his arms. I knew forever with him was exactly where I should be.

"I love you," I said, running my hands through his messy blond hair.

"I love you—hey, did you hear that?"

What? That's not how this is supposed to go.

"Hear what?" I asked.

"I swear, I heard a child cry out. Didn't you hear it?"

"No, I don't think so."

This never happened.

Dread flared to life in my chest as he looked around.

"Come on. Let's go look."

Suddenly, I heard the faint cry of a child. I looked around, but all I saw were hills and miles and miles of green countryside.

Another cry.

"Wait, I think it came from over here!" I pointed and turned right, which took us farther inland toward a group of trees.

I don't remember a forest.

We entered the large cluster of trees, and suddenly, it grew dark. The tall tree limbs seemed to come to life, reaching out for us, as we walked deeper and deeper.

"I think I heard it again," Jude said, moving faster.

His speed approached a run, and I tried to keep up. Huge tree roots leaped out of the group, blocking my path, and soon, we were separated.

"Jude!" I cried, looking right and left.

"Lailah! I'm right here!"

"I can't see you!"

I turned around in circles, the rising panic taking over.

"Jude!" I screamed. Feeling my breath beginning to weaken, I stood frozen in place as the dark walls of the forest began to close in around me.

The child cried out again, and this time, it was a cry of anguish. I suddenly felt torn.

Where do I go? Who do I run toward?

"Jude! Help me!" I managed to say before collapsing.

Seconds later, the darkness swallowed me whole.

one

An Unexpected Visitor

Lailah

"LAILAH," A VOICE called out in the darkness. "Wake up, angel. You're having another bad dream."

The fog began to lift, and I slowly opened my eyes. Looking down at me with an equal mixture of concern and amusement was Jude. A hand gently combed through my messy hair as a smile crept its way across his handsome face.

"There you are," he said.

"Hi," I answered back, stretching slightly as the last lingering bits of grogginess melted away.

"Same one?" he asked, obviously referring to the nightmare he'd awoken me from.

"Yeah," I confirmed.

"You know, if it weren't for the upcoming wedding and the untold stress I know it's having on your system, I'd be a little concerned about the fact that my extremely romantic proposal has somehow turned into a recurring nightmare in which you get swallowed whole by an evil forest."

"Believe me, it's not by choice," I said, a shudder running down my spine at the mere thought of those shadowy tree limbs.

"We could still elope." His eyebrow perked in challenge.

"Our families would kill us."

"Only if they could find us," he answered quickly.

"You've already spent a fortune on it," I argued.

"We've spent a fortune. Say it with me, Lailah. *We've spent a fortune.* You are my fiancée—my soon-to-be wife," he reiterated. "Everything I have is yours—ours, remember?" He pulled me closer to his chiseled side.

I nuzzled in closer and sighed.

"Okay, fair enough. Since it's our money, I must protest against such a blatant waste of our funds. So, no elopement, buddy," I said, pinching his side for effect.

"Ouch!" He laughed. "As long as it all ends with someone saying, 'I now pronounce you husband and wife' I'm fine with whatever you decide."

"You'd really forgo everything and marry me tomorrow?"

Rolling over, he pinned me beneath him, encapsulating me between his strong muscular arms. My fingers instinctively traveled up over the intricate black ink of his arm.

"In a heartbeat. But you're right. Our mothers would kill us if we didn't let them witness this day. So, we will be good, and I'll give you the wedding you've always dreamed of. And then, my bride to be, you and I will spend the next three weeks in . . . oh, right. I can't tell you. It's a surprise."

I shook my head, letting out a puff of air in frustration. "Jerk."

"Such language." He laughed.

"Why does it have to be a surprise, Jude?" I whined, wrapping my arms around him. "Ireland was enough of a surprise for an entire lifetime. You don't have to keep trying to dazzle me," I said.

His head lowered, and I felt the wisp of his lips touch my cheek.

"Actually I do," he whispered. "Every day for the rest of our lives, I'm going to do just that. You deserve to be dazzled, Lailah."

Momentarily stunned by his words, I just stared up at him, lost in his warmth and love.

"Could you at least tell me what to pack?" I asked, a shy grin creeping across my face.

"Mmm . . . no," he responded. Immediately, he chuckled as he watched the look of frustration cross my features. "I could, however, provide you with a guide."

"A guide?" I asked, my face going blank in confusion. "Is this one of those rich-people things? Are you going to stick me with a snooty personal shopper, Jude? Because I'd rather end up with a bag my mother packed—or just a bag honestly."

"Really? You don't want a personal shopper? Because the one I had in mind is perfect for you," he said with a mischievous grin. He quickly kissed my cheek and hopped off the bed to begin his morning routine.

"No," I answered, sitting up fully and firmly crossing my arms across my chest.

Since moving to New York, I'd been forced to grow accustomed to many things—city life, the lack of trees, people constantly wearing black for some unknown reason. But the biggest adjustment was Jude's money.

He'd come to me as Jude, the quiet nursing assistant. What had started out as a simple friendship within the walls of a quiet hospital had blossomed into a love so unlike anything I could have ever imagined. I'd soon discovered the broken man who worked the lonely halls of Memorial Regional in Santa Monica was actually the heir to a multibillion-dollar corporation. Hiding from a past filled with pain, Jude had run from the duties and obligations of his family and hated himself for it.

It'd turned out that I wasn't the only one with scars.

Jude had saved me, in more ways than one, and in turn, I guessed I had done the same. But living with a billionaire was never a life I'd envisioned for myself. Sometimes, when things had gotten rough and sickness had taken over or I had been told that another procedure was needed for my heart, I had often wondered whether a life, any life, would be possible at all.

All I wanted was Jude. Whether he was a janitor, a nursing assistant, or one of the richest men in the country, he would always be the man who had snuck into my room with a chocolate pudding cup in his hand.

"What if," Jude said, his smirk growing wider, "I said that this particular personal shopper was flying in especially for you?"

"That, in fact, makes it worse," I said, making a sour face.

"All the way from Santa Monica?"

My eyes widened. "Grace?"

He answered with an enthusiastic nod.

I jumped out of bed and threw myself into his arms. "Are you serious? When? Where? How?"

We fell back into bed, laughing. "Yes, I'm serious. She's flying in today. In fact, her flight landed a while ago. So, you'd better get your ass in the shower because she'll be arriving at our door in a few minutes. Oh, and she's bringing the baby. You're welcome."

I squealed, hugging him and scattering kisses across his adorable face. "You are amazing!" I exclaimed.

Grabbing my face between his hands, our eyes locked, and I felt him sober slightly. The buzz of our happiness zinging between us reduced to a hum as he pulled me toward him.

"No, it is you who amazes me—constantly, daily, every minute. I love you, Lailah, and I can't wait to make you my wife."

As his lips touched mine, I was the one who was truly dazzled.

"So, you're sticking with green for my dress?" Grace asked as we wandered down the streets of Manhattan.

"Yes." I laughed. "You asked me that last week, you know."

"I know." She sighed, bundling up baby Zander and bringing him a little closer to her chest.

Grace had stumbled into motherhood with little mishap. It had shaken her perfectly planned world slightly—having a creature who cried and slept whenever and wherever he chose—but she and her husband, Brian, had adapted well, and Zander was flourishing. I'd always seen Grace with a girl. She was so feminine and dainty, earning the nickname Snow White at the hospital where she worked as a nurse, but seeing her now, with her charming little boy, made perfect sense. He was the calming blue yin to her bedazzled pink yang.

"But I thought that, maybe after my constant whining, you might have changed your mind," she added, making a goofy face in Zander's direction.

He laughed in glee at his mother's silliness.

"You mean, your constant badgering to change the color to pink?" I asked, looking across the street to a rare cluster of trees.

They had begun to change color, fading from green to a fiery orange, which contrasted starkly against the dark grays of the buildings in the background.

"It wasn't pink exactly. More of a pale blush color. Think of it as a winter pink." She smiled.

"Winter pink? Now, you're stretching it, Grace." I laughed. "You know why I love green."

"Yes, it matches Jude's eyes, which is romantic and beautiful and goes great with the wedding's Christmas theme, but you can't blame a girl for trying."

"I'll give you extra points for persistence," I added, pointing toward the store we had talked about at lunch.

"Yes! That's the one! We should find lots of honeymoon stuff there, huh?" she exclaimed. She was doing that strange thing parents sometimes did where they were simultaneously speaking to an adult and their child at the same time. The conversation was geared toward the adult, but the octave of the voice and the overly expressive facial features suggested otherwise.

It was both weird and adorable at the same time.

The three of us entered the large store and began browsing. It was exactly the type of store I was comfortable in. No one came rushing over to judge how much money I was about to spend. I was left alone to roam through the racks with Grace as we carried on a casual conversation, catching up on our lives.

"So, how is life in the cardiac unit?" I asked.

She held up a long-sleeved sweater with fur trim. I shook my head and laughed as Zander reached out from his BabyBjörn for the fuzzy brown collar.

"Well, we haven't had a prom in a while," she said with a toothy grin. "But it's good," she answered. "A little lonely without my favorite patient, but I wouldn't want it any other way."

"At least you still have Marcus," I said.

"Yes, I do. Having your mother and him around is like having an extra set of grandparents. They are really wonderful, Lailah."

"Well, I didn't expect otherwise."

The next item she held up for my inspection was a ruby-red bikini. My eyes bugged as they fell on the two barely there scraps of fabric.

"First, a sweater built for arctic weather, and now, a bikini? Where exactly is he taking me?"

Her grin widened. "Wouldn't you like to know?"

My face fell slightly as I contemplated my answer. "He didn't overdo it, did he? I mean, he knows he doesn't have to always offer up these crazy romantic gestures. I'll love him no matter what."

She hung the bikini back on the rack and took a few steps closer. Wrapping her arm around my shoulder, she ushered me toward some chairs in the corner of the store. Luckily, no abandoned husbands or boyfriends were left in the store today, so the spot was all ours.

"What do you mean?" she asked as we took our seats.

"I just worry sometimes, after everything that has happened—the heart surgery and his guilt over not being there—that he feels this overwhelming need to make up for it. I don't ever want to be a burden to him, Grace." Feeling like I was confessing a horrible sin, my hands nervously wrung together.

Jude was the most amazing person I'd ever met. Admitting that I thought he could somehow be acting out of guilt rather than a place of love felt like the worst kind of crime imaginable.

"Lailah, I know the two of you have been through more in two years than most couples experience in a lifetime, but please believe me when I say, these grand gestures that you consider so monumental are nothing compared to the love that man has for you. When he called me last week and asked if we wouldn't mind flying out for the weekend, there was nothing but excitement in his voice. I remember the old Jude. He was so filled with remorse that there was no room for anything else. This isn't him. Let him love you the way you deserve to be loved."

I let her words settle between us, feeling them sink in and solidify. It was exactly what I'd needed to hear. The confirmation pushed away any lingering doubts.

I'd spent the first twenty-two years of my life believing my life would be spent within the walls of a hospital room, only to find an entire world just waiting outside its doors. Jude had made that possible.

He'd made *me* possible, and I'd never felt more confident in myself.

But that little girl, the one who never got to experience the thrills of learning to ride a bike or jumping into a pile of leaves, often wondered if those around me noticed the subtle differences between me and the rest of the world. Did they pity me? Did they feel the need to make right the wrongs my damaged heart had taken from me? It was something I'd wondered and struggled with since the scars across my chest had closed up and healed, and life had moved on around them. As time had gone by, these feelings would ebb and flow like crashing waves on the ocean.

And I'd always come back to this one simple conclusion. My family, Grace, Jude—they all loved me for me, and that was all that mattered.

"You're right. I'm being silly—once again."

"It's not silly, Lailah. You wouldn't be you if you didn't worry about others. It's just who you are and one of the many reasons I am proud to call you my friend."

I couldn't help but smirk. "Well, now, you're just buttering me up." I laughed.

"I am. Can we continue shopping? Or at least pretend to? Zander is about to go AWOL with the lack of movement."

"Of course, but on one condition."

"Anything."

"Can I hold him for a bit?"

She smiled. "I thought you'd never ask."

two

Growing Pains

Jude

"WHERE THE HELL is he?" I roared, slamming my hand hard against my desk.

My secretary, Stephanie, cowered in the corner, unfamiliar with my strange behavior, which instantly stilled me.

"Forgive me, Stephanie." I cringed, holding my hands out in a silent plea for mercy.

She nodded and took a paltry step forward. I loosened the tie around my neck in a desperate attempt to allow the free flow of oxygen to my lungs again. Although standing in a room so large that it could dwarf many New York apartments, I felt like I was suffocating.

Is this how Lailah felt all those times when she couldn't breathe because her heart wouldn't allow it?

I gripped my chest and realized that it wasn't my heart that wasn't working. It was my brain. I needed to calm myself and take a deep breath.

Just like my father before me, I wandered to the large windows overlooking the city below and began to count. By the time I reached ten, the blood in my veins began to slow as my breathing returned to normal.

"Find him, please," I said.

Stephanie still stood near the doorway, probably too scared to leave without orders.

"Quickly," I added.

She scurried away as I stood stoic, looking at the street below.

I'd practically grown up in this office. From the time I was a young child, I'd been raised to take over the family business. My father had been a hard man to love. So driven to succeed, sometimes, all he had seen was a way to move ahead rather than noticing the sons he'd left behind.

He'd loved us in his own way. I knew giving everything he had to this company was how he'd shown us the depths of his heart. Standing here and looking out at the same view his own eyes had settled on year after year, I understood that, now more than ever—unlike him—I couldn't let it consume me.

I wouldn't.

There was too much at stake.

I hadn't come this far to fall back into the pits of hell again, and Lailah deserved more than a barely there corporate hotshot who took her for granted.

And that was why I needed some goddamn help.

I began taking another deep breath through my nose.

Stephanie's voice rang through on the speakerphone, "Mr. Cavanaugh, I have him on line one, sir."

Walking toward my desk, I pushed the button to respond, "Thank you. I'll take it from here."

I heard her release the call, and I was introduced to silence.

Taking a seat, I waited until he had the balls to say something.

Finally, a long-drawn-out sigh could be heard on the other end. "Are you giving me the silent treatment, little brother? I thought we'd grown out of that."

"I thought we'd grown out of a lot of things, Roman," I responded.

"Oh, come on. It's the fucking weekend. Don't you have better things to do than call me up at the ass-crack of dawn to rip me a new one?"

The laughter in his voice sent me to an entirely new level of pissed off.

"First of all, it's nearly past noon, jackass. Secondly, this isn't just any weekend. We happen to have one of the most important meetings of our lives today. Foreign investors have flown in from Japan. Does any of this ring a bell?"

"Right," he said lazily. "I thought you and the board had a handle on that?"

Female laughter sounded in the background.

"You are on the board."

"Good point. And what time is this meeting?"

I looked at the platinum watch adorning my wrist. "In less than two hours."

"Well then, I guess I'd better get in the shower. You owe me, Jude."

I heard a high-pitched yelp before the line went dead.

I shook my head in disgust, wondering how my brother had managed to sink further into the cesspool of his own lack of mortality since I'd returned home.

When he'd brought Lailah to me, seeming genuinely concerned for my well-being, I'd thought that maybe he was on a path of redemption. But as soon as I had started to get my own life back on track, his had begun to spiral.

I'd tried to speak to him about it, get through that snarky tough exterior to figure out the reason for his sudden turn, but he wouldn't let me in. He wouldn't let anyone in. I was honestly starting to wonder if there even was a reason or if that brief glimpse of the man I had seen, who could be so much more, had been nothing more than an elaborate act.

After all, he'd gotten what he'd wanted. I'd taken my place in the company and pulled it back from the brink of collapse, and now, he was free.

He was free to be the nonexistent asshole I remembered.

My phone rang, and as I looked down at the number showing up on the caller ID, I instantly felt the anger Roman had caused dissipate.

"Hey, Angel," I said with a smile as I cradled the phone in my hand.

"Hi," she answered cheerfully. "Just thought I'd check in and see how your day was going. I know you have that big meeting this afternoon."

Shaking my head, I let out a puff of air as my fingers came to the bridge of my nose.

"Did I get it wrong?" she asked, suddenly alarmed.

"No, no. You always remember everything perfectly."

Unlike others, I thought to myself.

"Oh, okay good. So, are you ready?" she asked, excitement ringing through the tone of her voice.

"Yes, actually. I spent the morning going over everything, and in a minute, I'll be heading over to the boardroom to do some last-minute strategizing with . . . mostly everyone, but I think we've got it."

"Roman isn't there, is he?" she asked, the exuberance now gone.

"No," I simply answered.

"That . . . well, he's just not a nice man."

My mouth twitched as I tried not to laugh, instantly warmed by her. She was so meek, yet when needed, she could be as fierce as a lion.

Even now, my lioness still couldn't bring herself to say a bad word about anyone.

"Yes, he is, but he's my brother, and unfortunately, that means I have to put up with him."

"Well, I'll be sure to kick him the next time I see him."

A chuckle escaped my lips as I imagined her scrawny frame kicking my imposing large brother.

"You do that."

"Go knock it out of the park, Jude," she said warmly.

"I will. See you tonight?"

"Okay. I'll save you some dessert."

"No, you won't." I laughed.

"I'll try."

"Deal."

"I love you," she said.

"And I love you," I replied before hanging up.

My eyes fell to the picture I kept on my desk. It had been taken at the wedding of Lailah's mother a couple years back, just before I'd surprised her with our trip to Ireland. The water was behind the two of us, and there was nothing but future and possibility in our eyes.

It was how I wanted us to look forever.

"That wasn't so bad?" Roman touted.

We hopped into the back of the chauffeured black sedan that had been hired for the evening. Another car had been instructed to take our dinner guests back to their hotel, so they could rest for their return flight to Tokyo.

"Thanks to me," I muttered as I loosened the knot of my tie. My hand moved down to unbutton the top two buttons of my shirt.

"Not only thanks to you. Who wined and dined their Japanese asses off tonight? That would be me. I showed them a good time—something you sure seem to be lacking these days. Rough waters at home? Honeymoon phase over before the honeymoon can even start?"

His goading did nothing. I simply turned and smiled. "Things are excellent between Lailah and me—in fact, never better. And to think, I owe all this overwhelming happiness to my generous, selfless brother, Roman. Oh, wait . . ."

He deadpanned, no longer in the mood for joking. Instead, he lunged for a bottle of water in the cooler under the seat from the small bar area that had been set up by the car service.

Good, he needed to dry out.

"There was nothing selfless about what I did. You were moping around here like a wounded puppy, Jude. Someone needed to do something to get your ass back into gear, so I did the easiest thing possible. I gave you what you wanted. I just figured it would mellow you out a bit."

"I am mellow," I argued. "With everyone else."

"Ah, so the truth comes out."

His gaze narrowed, and our eyes locked. When I looked at Roman, sometimes, it felt like my future self was staring back at me. We had so many physical traits in common, yet our personalities clashed like oil and vinegar.

"I just wish you would take something, anything, in life seriously."

He patted my back, and his head motioned toward our building as the car pulled up. “Now, that’s what we have you for,” he said.

“Are you coming up?” I asked, opening the car door to hop out.

He shook his head, smiling. “This car is paid up until morning. Might as well use it to my advantage.”

“I’m sure you will.”

I shut the car door, leaving Roman to his vices for the evening, and I focused on everything waiting for me upstairs—a home, a fiancée, and a future.

Lailah was my beacon. No matter how bleak life might get, how rough the waters might seem, I knew she’d always be there to safely guide me back home.

I quickly made my way through the entrance, taking the elevator to the thirtieth floor. This apartment had been my home since I left Santa Monica. When I used to walk through the front door, I’d seen nothing but a prison, a place keeping me from where I wanted to be—with Lailah.

But I’d made a decision. I’d paid a price.

Wanting to save Lailah and pay for the transplant she’d so desperately needed, I’d known I would have to return to the life I’d left behind. I still remember the way my hand had shaken as I wrote my good-bye to her, wishing I could tell her everything I had bottled up in my heart, but I’d known if I did, she would never have gone through with the surgery.

In the painful months that had followed, I’d discovered what it was to lose myself all over again.

I never wanted to feel that again.

Lailah was my everything, and I’d continue to move mountains to make her happy every day of her life.

Exiting the elevator, I made my way down the long hallway toward our door. Turning the handle, I found the apartment aglow with candlelight.

“Lailah?” I called out, my eyes darting around the expansive living room and kitchen.

“In here. Come find me,” she hollered back, her voice coming from the bedroom.

I’d thought I would be returning to a houseful of guests, assuming Grace and Zander would spend the evening with us. Candlelight and a summon to the bedroom were a welcome surprise.

My hand hovered over the tops of the candles, sending the flames into a frenzied dance. The ghostly shadows moved across the walls as I stalked down the hallway. Pushing the door open, I slowly stepped inside the room and found Lailah lounging in a sofa chair by the bed, in nothing more than a light-blue satin bra and matching panties.

"Is that new?" I asked, attempting to keep the pitch of my voice from reaching the next octave.

She smirked and slowly crossed her legs, one foot over the other. "Do you like it?"

"Very much."

"One of the many things I picked up on my shopping adventure with Grace today."

I nodded, walking forward and dropping my suit jacket on the floor. "Remind me to tell Grace how fond I am of her."

"I will." She laughed.

Stepping closer until I was hovering over her, I asked, "Will we be seeing her and Zander tonight?" I bent forward, tracing my fingers over the delicate skin of her shoulder.

"No," she answered softly. "She thought we could use a night to explore my new . . . wardrobe. We're meeting them for brunch in the morning."

"Good."

I offered my hand to her and watched as she rose from the chair to stand before me. With beautiful platinum-blonde hair and baby-blue eyes, she was almost ethereal-looking. Since leaving the hospital with her new heart, she'd gained some much-needed weight, giving her feminine curves and strength. Not a single ounce of frailty seemed to exist in her now.

She was my fierce survivor.

"You are the most beautiful woman on the planet, Lailah Buchanan."

"Soon-to-be Lailah Cavanaugh," she corrected.

I pulled her into my arms. Her bare skin sent fire zinging through my fingertips with every touch.

"How many days?"

"Forty-three," she replied.

"Why did we decide to get married right before Christmas?" I asked, dipping my head toward the crook of her neck.

A low moan escaped her lips as I kissed a path down to her breasts.

"Because I love snow and the color red. Plus it's in between semesters."

"You're entirely too practical," I whispered before placing a single kiss on the light-pink scar running down her chest from her many surgeries.

"That's why you love me." She laughed.

Reaching my hand behind her back, I made quick work of the closure on her bra. I slid the straps slowly down her arms, and the bra fell to the floor.

"I love you, Lailah, for many reasons. Let me show you one right now," I purred in her ear.

"Yes."

I carried her to the bed and made good on my promise for the rest of the night.

three

Change the World

Lailah

I LOVED BRUNCH.

Two meals seamlessly blended together meant I could eat whatever I wanted, and I didn't have to get up at the crack of dawn to do it.

It was one of the best ideas ever—besides introducing chocolate to breakfast foods. Whoever had devised that genius idea deserved a Nobel Peace Prize.

As I happily stuffed another bite of chocolate-chip pancakes into my mouth, I turned to see Zander closely watching me from his high chair. His bright blue eyes followed the movements of my fork as it moved to my plate to scoop up another piece of pancake. A tiny pink tongue darted out and made a wide sweep across his top lip.

"You're cute," I said, "but these are mine, buddy."

He blew raspberries in response and banged his chubby fist down on the plastic tray, sending little round Cheerios flying in every direction.

"I'm going to pretend you didn't do that," I commented as I picked sticky cereal out of my hair.

He giggled, which sent the three adults at the table into a fit of laughter.

"He showed you," Grace said, covering a dainty snort with her napkin.

"So selfish," Jude interjected, shaking his head. "Unwilling to share food with a helpless poor child. Who am I marrying?"

He grinned mischievously as I glared up at him, carefully plotting my revenge.

With cunning stealth, I raised my hand, still full of half-nibbled Cheerios, and quickly dumped them on top of his head. Some instantly fell back to the table, but others made a new home within the tendrils of his sandy-blond locks.

Youthful laughter followed as Zander watched Jude shake the mess from his hair, sending a cascade of cheerios to the floor.

"Such a mess," I said, mimicking Jude's words. "What a lack of respect for the wait staff. Who am I marrying?"

I smiled smugly as I shoved another large bite of chocolate-chip pancakes into my mouth while he laughed.

"You two are crazy," Grace said, dumping a new pile of finger foods out for Zander to munch on.

"It's all those years of a lack of oxygen to her brain," Jude replied dryly.

I turned to him, wide-mouthed. "She said *we* are crazy." I laughed. "Not just me."

"Yeah, I guess I'm a bit mad. But it's your fault. I was totally normal before I met you."

I rolled my eyes as I moved the last gooey piece of pancake around on my plate, trying to lap up every last drop of maple syrup. "Totally," I said.

He chuckled as he sat back in his chair and slowly sipped on a cup of coffee while drawing small circles across my back. The sensation sent chills down my arms, yet the feel of his fingers brushing across the fabric of my shirt made me feel warmer rather than colder because he was touching me, loving me. I never wanted that feeling to end.

"I wish you didn't have to go back so soon," I lamented. I made a small pouty face in the direction of my best friend.

"I know, but I didn't expect to see you at all until the wedding, so just think of this as an added bonus, thanks to your generous man over there."

I turned, sending him a warm expression of gratitude.

"It was purely selfish on my part," he confessed. "I knew I'd be in business meetings all day, and I didn't want her to be alone."

"The fact that you cared enough to fly me all the way across country just so your fiancée wouldn't be alone all day shows just how unselfish you are, Jude."

He shrugged, placing his empty cup of coffee on the table, while he continued to rub my back.

"How did the meetings go?" Grace asked.

"Good actually. Roman managed to pull his ass out of bed in the nick of time, and he threw his megawatt charm into high gear. I think we have a good shot of getting their support."

"That's great! I know you were hoping for this deal," she said, a genuine smile spreading across her face.

"We were. It would strengthen our base, which is exactly what I have been trying to do since I returned. I'm trying to make sure Cavanaugh Investments is around for many more lifetimes and is able to withstand any financial earthquakes that might try to tear it down in the future."

"You're doing a fantastic job—both of you," she added. "Lailah told me she made dean's list last semester."

"She actually told you that?" he asked, raising his eyebrows in surprise. "She hasn't even told her mom."

"You haven't told Molly?" she nearly screeched, staring me down.

"It's not a big deal." I shrugged.

"It's not a big deal to tell your mother, who happens to be a professor and covets education like most people covet chocolate or Louboutin heels? Yeah, I'm sure she wouldn't care at all."

"I just don't want her to make a big fuss," I said.

"Why?" Grace asked, tearing off pieces of her pancake and placing them on Zander's tray.

"Because it's not really that important in the grand scheme of things."

Setting the remainder of the half-shredded pancake back on her plate, her eyes met mine. "Everything in your life is important, Lailah.

Don't you remember that? Have you become that desensitized already?"

"Desensitized?" I scoffed, looking over to Jude.

Folding his napkin, he placed it on his plate and silently observed the conversation.

"Do you remember that naive skinny girl who couldn't wait to get out of the hospital and begin living a life she never had before?"

"Yes."

"Don't forget her," she urged. "She would want you to celebrate everything, no matter how small or insignificant, Lailah. Seeing you grow into your own over the last two years has been amazing. The strength and courage you bring to this world make me proud to call you my friend. But don't let the world change you. Change the world, Lailah."

Her words hit home as I tried to recall the last time I'd pulled out my list of wishes that I'd created over the years while hiding away in that hospital room.

My Someday List was everything I'd wanted to do if given the chance at a normal life. When Jude had discovered it, he'd made it his goal to help me strike out every last wish off that one-hundred-forty-three-item list.

But as the days had gone on, life had begun to settle, and so had I. The worn pages of my journal had become something of an afterthought now that the world had finally exploded around me.

"*Don't let the world change you,*" Grace had said. "*Change the world.*"

"I think it's time for some cake," I announced.

"That's my girl," Jude said softly, signaling to the waiter across the room.

"Make sure he brings some chocolate pudding, too," I added. "We're celebrating!"

"Sure thing, angel."

I might not have been changing the world yet, but while I figured out how, I could at least make sure I shined through.

"You must be the only multimillionaire I know who takes a cab to the airport," Grace joked, shaking her head, as our little yellow taxi pulled up to the curb at JFK.

"And how many multimillionaires do you know exactly?" Jude asked from the front seat.

He leaned over to hand the driver what was no doubt double, if not triple, his required fee—plus, a hefty tip. The man's eyes bulged as he thanked Jude several times and then quickly jumped out to help with Grace's bags.

"Well, two—if you count your burly brother. And I know he wouldn't be caught dead traveling the streets of Manhattan in anything less than a town car."

The three of us exited the cab as Grace cradled Zander in her arms. He was the only kid on the planet who could be lulled to sleep by a New York taxicab. Meanwhile, I'd held on for dear life and prayed we wouldn't end up at the bottom of the Hudson.

"That's because my brother is stuck-up and arrogant," Jude said, smacking her hand away from her suitcase. He took the handle and slung Zander's diaper bag over his shoulder. After heading toward the check-in counter, he turned back around and smiled briefly. "And he also doesn't have an amazing woman in his life, like I do, who still gets a thrill each time she hails a cab."

I laughed, shrugging my shoulder. "It is exhilarating."

"And what number was that?" she asked, swaying back and forth.

We stood in line behind a man in a business suit, waiting to check in at the first-class counter.

"Ninety-eight." I blushed.

Her shoulder lightly bumped mine, and I turned to see her warm smile.

"Keep marking them off, Lailah."

I nodded, turning fully to wrap my arms around her. "I will."

Her bag was checked, and boarding passes were issued. Soon, we were standing by security, delaying the inevitable.

"I guess we should say our good-byes now," she said, frowning.

"Yeah," I agreed. "I'm going to miss you."

"Right back at you, girl. But, hey, it's just five weeks, and then I'll be right back here with my pink dress, ready to party!"

I laughed. "Green! You mean, green dress!"

"Right. Green. Figured I'd give it one last shot."

"Let me kiss my little man before you take him away from me again," I begged.

She shifted Zander in her arms, so I could easily reach his sleepy face. His soft pink lips parted slightly as tiny puffs of air escaped. A small smile tugged at the corner of his mouth as he dreamed, and I couldn't help but smile in return.

"Whatever you're dreaming of, sweet Zander, I hope it comes true. I love you. Never forget the many people in this world who cherish these tiny hands and your sweet face. Be good for your mommy and daddy, and I'll see you soon." I placed a wisp of a kiss on his forehead and repeated the action on Grace's cheek. "Take care, and fly safe. I love you."

"Love you, too."

Jude stepped forward and gave Grace an awkward side hug, so he wouldn't disturb the slumbering bundle in her arms. "Thank you for coming. I truly appreciate it," he said.

"Anytime."

With a sad smile and a blown kiss in our direction, she threw Zander's diaper bag over her shoulder, and then she turned toward the security line and disappeared into the crowd of people.

"You okay?" Jude asked as his fingers intertwined with mine.

"Yes," I answered as we headed back toward the entrance. "I just hate good-byes."

"It's not really a good-bye, you know. It's more of just a see-you-later."

He pushed open the glass door leading to the street and held it as we stepped out.

"Did you steal that from a movie?" I asked, smiling. "It sounds very familiar."

"Maybe. But it made you smile."

"You always make me smile."

There was no need to hail a taxi at the airport since they were lined up like vultures along the curb. We hopped into the first available one we saw, and Jude gave him the address to our apartment.

As we settled in the back, Jude's arm snaked around me, and I turned to watch the city come into view. I'd grown up in California where palm trees and beaches took precedence over skyscrapers and subways. Life was different here, but then again, life anywhere outside of a hospital was different and new.

Whether I was living in an apartment in Santa Monica, blocks away from the sandy beach, or in the heart of one of the busiest cities in the world, it didn't matter as long as I was alive.

Grace had been right this morning. I had become slightly complacent in my new life, trying to fit in, when I should be embracing my newfound existence. When given a second chance, you shouldn't fade into the background. Rather, you should explode like a rainbow of colors dripping down a canvas.

Jude's voice suddenly cut through my deep thoughts, and I looked to him in confusion.

"What did you say?" I asked.

"I asked whether you ever felt deprived because of everything that had happened."

"What do you mean?"

"It's just, today, seeing you with Zander, plus the crazy dreams . . . it makes me wonder if you ever wish for more than just me in this world."

I turned to face him, my hand reaching up to stroke the stubble on his chin. "Are you asking if I want a child?"

He nodded.

"Don't you think we should get married first?" I joked.

A halfhearted smile tried to form, but I could see his mood was still sullen.

"Jude, please don't think I ever feel deprived. This life, everything I have, is more than I ever expected. Before I met you, I fully believed I'd die without one of those wishes on my Someday List ever coming true. But here I am, healthy and strong, making each and every one of them come true because of you."

"But what if you want more—later."

"You," I said, tilting his chin upward so that his gaze would meet mine, "are all I need."

As his lips touched mine, I curled my fingers into his hair. I'd never been surer of anything in my life.

Jude was all I'd ever need.

But as our kiss deepened, the sudden vision of my dream flashed through my memory.

My fingers reached out in the darkness to find him, but he wasn't there.

four

Cooking Is Hard

Jude

"ARE YOU SURE I can't help with anything?" I asked, pressing mute on the TV once again, as the sounds of clanging pots and pans came bustling forth from the kitchen.

"I'm okay!" Lailah hollered back.

I turned around from my place on the sofa to see her moving about in the kitchen like a chaotic housewife. Wrapped in a frilly pink apron—given to her by Grace as a housewarming gift when Lailah had moved in here—she darted from the refrigerator to the stove and then back to the counter where her recipe book rested. Then, she just repeated the process.

Placing my head on the back of the sofa, I grinned. "Positive?"

She stopped mid-step and turned to see me watching her from the couch. A quirky smile spread across her face. "Maybe. Okay, you want the honest truth?"

"Of course," I answered, my head perking up to listen.

"I am in way over my head," she groaned. "Thanksgiving dinner—even for two people? It's hard! I'm not sure what I was thinking."

I laughed, rising from the sofa to join her in our massive kitchen. I never understood why Roman had selected such a large place for me to live in when I arrived back home. I knew he was outlandish, having a place several floors above us that was twice the size of ours, but when I'd entered this house for the first time, all I had seen was empty space.

With Lailah here, it finally felt like a home.

"Can I please help you now?" I begged. "I know men are supposed to sit around, watching football, on this particular holiday, but I'd much rather spend time with you."

"Even if I put you to work?" she asked.

"I have many fond memories of the two of us in kitchens," I said, remembering a similar situation much like this where we stood around a large metal counter and attempted to cook a meal together. It hadn't been a date—at least, I hadn't planned it that way—but it was the first time I'd seen her as something more than just a girl whom I owed a debt.

"I think your culinary skills have greatly improved since then," she commented.

"Thank God for that."

She put me on potato duty while she began assembling the apple pie.

"Remember when we went apple picking last fall?" she asked.

I watched her carefully measure out the cinnamon and sprinkle it over the heaping bowl of apples.

"Yeah. You were so excited that we ended up coming home with an entire bushel." I laughed.

She gave me a doubtful look. "It was not that many. Maybe half. But I kept thinking about that last night as I was doing my last-minute grocery shopping, and I stopped to pick these up. I was enthralled with the entire process of apple picking—the cute little baskets, the fresh air and freedom to pick as many as you wanted. I remember feeling like that a lot during that first year after my recovery. I don't ever want that to end."

I stopped mid-potato and set the peeler on the counter. "Then, don't. Just because you've been apple picking doesn't mean it can't be just as exciting and wondrous the second or third time around."

"I know." She smiled and moved toward me. Her hands were covered in cinnamon and sugar from mixing the apples together, and she had a mischievous look on her face.

My eyes followed her fingers as they slid up my arm and finally disappeared around my nape of my neck, leaving a sticky trail of sweetness behind. She reached my mouth and watched as I parted my lips and licked the sugar off her fingertips.

"Some things just keep getting better," she whispered.

"Lailah," I warned, gripping her hips hard.

Smirking, she placed the tip of her pointer finger on her satin lips, and as her lips closed over it, sucking the remnants of sugar with gusto, the last shred of control I had snapped.

My hands tightened around her waist before lifting and turning to hoist her onto the counter.

"Temptress," I growled. Not giving her a single second to respond, I slammed my lips on hers, demanding everything she'd just offered.

Food was forgotten as clothes were shed, and bodies were joined. Every thrust reminded me that I was the luckiest man alive. Every kiss told me I was exactly where I was supposed to be, and every moan that escaped her lips echoed my heart that beat solely for her.

Everything I had was hers, and I willingly gave it to her, over and over again.

"It's a good thing no one is coming over." She giggled, looking at the mess in our kitchen.

"Well, it would be an interesting story to explain."

It was well past midnight, and somehow, we'd managed to send bowls, food, and flour flying in every direction. Our lovemaking had been dirty and intense, causing a serious delay to dinner plans.

"So . . . pizza?" I asked.

She moved about the kitchen in nothing but my T-shirt. "Yes!" she exclaimed. "You order, and I'll attempt to make some sense of all of this."

I dialed the number to our favorite place down the street, knowing they'd still be open, and I ordered a large with everything. I ran to the bedroom to grab an extra shirt and a pair of boxers that weren't covered in flour.

Once I was quickly changed, I darted back to the kitchen to offer my help with the disaster we'd created.

Lailah had already made great strides, packaging up everything perishable and putting canisters back in the pantry. She had now moved on to cleaning the counters. I took the job of sweeping and picking up whatever random things had ended up on the floor. Each bowl or dish I grabbed reminded me of how she'd looked pressed against the counter and then slung over the barstool. No matter how many times I had her, it never seemed to be enough to snuff out my burning desire for her.

I could spend a lifetime loving her, and I'd never stop wanting more.

Within thirty minutes, we had the kitchen cleaned up, and we were lounging on the couch with slices of fresh pizza.

"Best Thanksgiving meal ever," she said before taking a big bite from the crust of her second slice.

"Absolutely."

Amid flickering candles and cheesy holiday music, we ate pizza and talked about our lives. It was one more memory of Lailah I could add to the growing pile I had stored away in my mind. Each and every one, I cherished like a precious gift, knowing that none of this would have ever been possible if it weren't for that beautiful new heart beating inside her chest.

We finished eating and headed to bed, going through the nightly rituals couples do to prepare for sleep. Once teeth were brushed and Lailah removed her makeup, we settled into bed, pulling the down comforter up around us.

"Want to play a game?" I asked, cuddling into her.

"If that is a sexual innuendo, you've got to give me an hour or so. My heart might be new, but it's not a machine."

I chuckled softly. "No, I meant an actual game."

"Like Monopoly?" she asked, her eyebrows rising with curiosity. "'Cause you know I'm terrible at that one."

"No. I was thinking something a little less structured," I offered.

"Good. I'm not sure my brain can handle much more at this hour."

"Okay, roll over," I instructed.

I laughed as I watched her suspiciously eye me, but she did as I'd asked and rolled onto her stomach.

"Oh, and take off your nightgown," I added.

Her head popped up to look at me as I innocently waved my hands in front of me.

"Just trust me."

She lifted slightly as the hem of her nightgown rose above her head and fell into a heap next to her.

Opening her nightstand beside the bed, I pulled out a bottle of sweet-smelling lotion she loved and dropped a dollop on my palm. Warming it a bit, I began smoothing it up and down her soft skin in deep circles.

"Not that I mind"—she nearly groaned—"but this doesn't seem to be much of a game."

"Just wait," I said.

Using the tip of my finger, I traced a pattern across her skin. "Do you feel that?"

"Yes," she answered, her head tilted toward me as she laid on her stomach.

"What did I just draw?"

"A heart," she replied, a small smile appearing from the corner of her mouth. "Do something else," she said.

This time, instead of a shape, I made letters turning into a word.

"Wife," she whispered.

"Yes." I bent down, kissing the bare skin of her shoulder.

She turned and pulled me close, our lips touching softly like two young lovers meeting for the first time.

She pulled back, enough to slide her hand down toward the hem of my T-shirt before lifting it over my head. Then, the tips of her fingers skimmed my sensitive skin as she traced along the hard ridges of my stomach. Her eyes never left mine as she wrote invisible words along my flesh.

"I love you, too," I whispered, closing the distance between us.

No other words were needed as we came together once more, claiming each other with silent promises, tender touches, and the moving melody of our souls.

five

Doctors and Leftovers

Lailah

"RISE AND SHINE, sleepyhead," Jude called out from the hallway.

He appeared at the bedroom door with a large tray overflowing with food.

"Breakfast in bed?" I asked, rising up to take a peek at what he'd brought.

"Well, sort of. Since we didn't quite get our Thanksgiving dinner experience last night, I thought we might try again."

I frowned. "Please don't tell me corn pudding and stuffing are on that plate, Jude. I might have eaten some weird things in my hospital days, but even they didn't try to feed me dinner for breakfast."

He smirked, setting the tray down beside me. I began to inspect the contents—as well as him.

"This doesn't look half bad," I said as my fingers bent down to check everything out. "But what is it?"

I looked up to Jude and found him grinning. "Well, I found a recipe for a leftover egg soufflé, and then I thought the mashed potatoes would be good, kind of like grilled pancakes."

"But hardly any of this stuff was actually made, so they can't really be considered leftovers, Jude."

He just shrugged and started pouring a cup of coffee for me from the French press.

"How long have you been up?" I looked down at the feast before me, trying to contemplate how long it had taken him to make the individual dishes and then combine them into a soufflé.

"A while. I wanted you to have a Thanksgiving meal."

I steadied his hand and watched his gaze meet mine. "You're amazing. Thank you."

After handing over a steaming cup of coffee, he disappeared into the bathroom. When he returned, he was ready to begin the not-so-pleasant part of the morning.

"Mood killer," I complained.

"You know me—highly punctual and responsible," he said, shaking the box of pills marked off by the days of the week.

"So sexy," I retorted.

Although I had a new heart and was as healthy as I could be, I would never be able to outrun the pharmacist. Transplant patients, whether with a heart like mine or any other organ, had one major fear that ruled their lives—the possibility of rejection.

This heart now beating inside my chest was a stand-in, a counterfeit for the damaged sick one that I'd been born with. At any point in my life, my body could reject this perfect organ and this life. Everything I held so dear could be over in the blink of an eye.

Tossing my head back, I dutifully took my morning pills before diving into my breakfast. "Oh, wow. This is good."

"Yeah?" he asked, scooping a chunk of cheesy soufflé onto his plate.

"Absolutely. And the mashed potato thingies . . . yum," I said between bites.

He laughed at my enthusiasm as he dived into his own breakfast. The comfortable silence settled between us while we ate.

"Are you sure you're okay with going alone today?" he asked after he'd set his plate back on the tray.

I was going back for seconds but nodded as I licked butter off my thumb.

"It's just a checkup, Jude. I have them every month, which seems a bit of an overkill anyway."

He ignored my comment about the frequency of doctor visits and sighed. "I know, but I always go with you."

Briefly setting the plate down, I looked up at him. "I know, and I appreciate it, but go spend a little time with your mom. She doesn't come into the city that often anymore. Take her to Bloomingdale's and get some shopping done. I'll meet you for lunch."

He let out an audible shudder. "I can't believe she chose this day. Of all the days to shop, she had to pick this one."

"Maybe she wants a bargain?" I offered up as a reason his mother would drive into the city on Black Friday, the busiest shopping day of the year, to spend the day with her son.

"A deal? At Bloomingdale's and Saks? I doubt that."

"Well, maybe she just misses you. We did ditch her on Thanksgiving this year—and there is the little issue of Christmas."

He rolled his eyes, rising from his spot on the bed, and he walked toward the closet. I took the time to appreciate his backside, covered only in boxers. He was just as handsome as the first day I'd met him—tall, muscular with a hint of danger swirling around those black tattoos angling down his arm.

"We did not ditch her. I asked if she wouldn't mind if we had dinner here. She chose to stay in the country with friends."

"I know. She told me, and she was actually excited about it. She said it was the first time she wouldn't have to worry about planning a menu in years. Notice that I didn't say *cook.*" I laughed.

"She never cooked, but she'd still make herself sick while planning every damn detail for the holidays. She wanted everything to be absolutely special for us."

"And was it?" I asked, picking my plate back up to gobble up the last of my potatoes.

"Of course. She loved seeing us happy."

"Runs in the family," I said.

"Well, some of us," he commented.

"Give him time, Jude. He might surprise you just yet."

"Maybe, but I'm not holding my breath."

As he returned to the bathroom to shower, my attention turned to the windows near our bed. I couldn't help but look out onto the city and wonder if, somewhere in that sea of people, someone was out there for Roman, someone who could find the man I knew he wanted to become.

The first time I had gone swimming in the ocean was about a year ago. Jude and I, back from our adventures in Ireland, had flown to Santa Monica to visit my mom and Marcus for the weekend.

We'd spent two days with them, enthralling them with stories and pictures of our visit to the Emerald Isle. Of course, I couldn't say no when they'd begged me to share the epic way in which Jude had proposed to me. It had been a lovely weekend, and it had gotten even more perfect when Jude asked me to take a walk along the beach that Sunday afternoon.

We'd dipped our toes in the ocean, remembering the first time we'd been here together.

Suddenly, he'd said, "Let's go swimming!"

"Like right now?" I'd asked, not bothering to cover my laughter.

"Yeah. Why the hell not?"

I'd had no answer, so on that seasonably hot afternoon in September, we'd jumped into the waves, fully clothed in the warm ocean. I'd never felt the surge of water hitting my chest, and I'd had no idea how to duck under an oncoming swell of white water.

I remember holding my breath as we'd dived further into the surf and that wonderful gasp of fresh air that had followed as we broke the surface once again.

Since my heart transplant, I'd experience that same feeling each and every time I visited the doctor.

Sitting in this uncomfortable green chair, my foot nervously bobbing up and down, was like sitting at the bottom of the ocean. I felt like I hadn't taken a single breath of air since I left home.

So far, I hadn't had a reason to doubt anything, yet that was exactly what I did.

Everything was perfect. I was finally living beyond the walls of the hospital. I was in love, and in less than a month, I'd be married to a man who had made all of this possible.

So, of course, I expected everything to go wrong.

I never shared these fears with anyone, especially Jude. I knew it was most likely ridiculous, but I had spent the majority of my life thinking I wouldn't make it past my twenty-fifth birthday. It was a hard notion to shake.

These checkups were like my monthly pat on the back. It was the reassurance I needed to get through the next thirty days, knowing my heart was pumping and nothing was going wrong in my perfect slice of heaven. I'd fought with Marcus—well, everyone—about the frequency of the appointments. Marcus, my lifelong doctor and now stepfather had won in the end though. Every month was excessive, but to be honest, it was nice to know I was still healthy, still whole. It was like playing monopoly and getting one of those jail passes every four weeks.

What were they called?

Maybe I should have added Monopoly to my Someday list.

"Lailah Buchanan?" the young blonde nurse called, peeking her head out from a door across the waiting room.

I stood and walked briskly past the other patients to join her.

She ushered me back to an exam room. "How have you been feeling?"

We settled into the small white room after checking my weight. I stepped up to the table and took a seat, hating the way the paper crinkled and crunched with every slight adjustment.

"Good," I answered.

"Nothing different? No changes we should know about?"

I shook my head as she wrapped a blood pressure cuff around my arm. "Not really. Maybe a bit of additional stress from wedding plans and finals coming up but nothing out of the ordinary."

Her mouth curved into a slight smile as she tucked the tip of the stethoscope into the crook of my arm. "When is the big day?"

"December sixteenth," I replied.

"Oh, wow. That's soon!"

"I know. I can't wait."

She finished her routine of preliminary checks, taking vitals and writing them into my chart.

"Well, I wish you the best of luck. The doctor will be in shortly."

She stepped out, and I was left alone to stare at the walls and pick at my nail polish.

How many minutes and hours of my life had been spent waiting on doctors?

The time lost was something that would most likely make others mad, enraged even. A fraction of my life had probably been wasted away in this exact position, waiting.

Always waiting. In retrospect, it wasn't all that bad.

I was healthy.

And I was alive.

I'd gladly stare at a thousand more dingy white walls and pick apart a million more manicures while I sat waiting for a specialist to come in and examine me as long as the end result was the same.

"Hey, Lailah!" Dr. Hough greeted happily as he walked through the door before taking a seat.

"Hi. Happy belated Thanksgiving," I said. "No Black Friday shopping for you today, I'm guessing?"

His smile turned into more of a grimace. "No, thank you. I'd much rather be here with my patients. Although, I think I'm in the minority."

"Well, I appreciate you coming in, especially on a holiday." I winked.

Dr. Zachary Hough was one of the best cardiac surgeons in the state. This, paired with the fact that Marcus and Dr. Hough had been roommates in college, had made him an excellent candidate to take over my care once I'd made the decision to move across the country. It had been a tricky decision, especially for someone who had just undergone a heart transplant, but luckily, my medical team at UCLA had been willing to make it work, and everything had transitioned smoothly.

Dr. Hough had worked closely with my doctors back home, and he still spoke with them, providing updates and taking guidance if needed. If something were to go wrong, I had no doubt in my mind that he would be able to handle it.

"So, how's the new ticker doing?" he asked, scrolling over the latest lab work results I'd gotten done a few days prior.

"Everything is great," I answered.

"Good."

Silence fell as he continued to read through everything, and I watched in apprehension as his finger thumbed through the pages, tracing over numbers and summaries.

He looked up at me, and our eyes locked.

The walls began to feel like they were closing in, and my breath constricted in my chest.

"Well, everything looks good, kid."

Air filled my lungs as I swam to the surface of relief.

Thank God.

"You're sure?" I asked.

"You ask that every time," he replied, shaking his head back and forth. "You're doing great. Just keep taking your meds and stay active but not too active," he said with a grin. "Stay away from sick people, especially now that flu season is coming. And what is the last thing?"

"Enjoy it," I answered, knowing exactly what he'd say.

"Exactly. Now, get out of here. You have a wedding to plan, isn't that right?"

"Yes, sir. I just got your RSVP. I'm so glad you'll be able to attend."

"Wouldn't miss it for the world, kid," he answered.

I hopped off the table and smoothed out the back of my skirt, only to rise up on the tips of my toes to give the big beast of a man a hug. "Thank you," I said softly.

"Anytime. Oh, and on your way out, tell the receptionist to schedule you for after the first of the year."

"What?" I asked in confusion. I always came once a month, like clockwork.

"You're doing great, Lailah. Go enjoy your honeymoon. We'll be here when you get back."

"Okay."

I made my next appointment for the middle of January and headed off to find Jude and his mother in the midst of their shopping spree.

As I walked down the streets of New York by myself—something I'd never even imagined I would be able to do—I took a deep breath and reminded myself that everything was just fine.

Too much good in your life didn't mean the rug was about to be pulled from beneath you.

I just needed to take a deep breath and trust—trust myself and this new heart beating inside my chest.

SIX

See You Later

Jude

EVERY FEMALE WITHIN a two-block radius saw the sleek black car pulling up to the curb. The second glances and hopeful looks I received when stepping out of the limo, carrying a dozen red roses in my hand, were priceless.

Sorry, ladies. These are not for you.

I'd only met Lailah on campus for lunch a handful of times, but I knew her routine. She was a creature of habit and loved to walk under the Washington Square Arch on Fifth Avenue. Even if her classes were blocks away, she'd always manage to find some excuse to bring her back to this place.

I'd once asked her why she loved it so much.

She'd smiled, her eyes looking off in the distance, as she formed her answer. "I don't know honestly. I think it just reminds me that I'm really here."

I planted myself just under the arch, leaning against the stone, and I waited. It didn't take long before I spotted her, bundled up in a long wool coat. Under a knitted hat, her blonde hair peeked out the sides, falling around her face like straw. She moved gracefully among the crowds of tourists and students with her backpack on one shoulder as she wrapped her arms around herself for warmth.

It took several moments for her to spot me, but I knew the instant she did. Her eyes lit up, and her smile grew wide with surprise.

"What are you doing here?" she asked, throwing herself into my arms.

"Obviously, I came to surprise you. I wanted to be here to congratulate you on another semester finished!"

"Thank you!" she replied. "It feels amazing! But it's not as amazing as getting married! Do you realize that, by this time tomorrow, we will be hitched?"

"Hitched?" I laughed at her word choice.

"Yep, hitched—to tie the knot, to wed . . . I could go on."

"So smart," I commented, holding out the bouquet of roses in front of her. "These are for you, by the way."

"They're beautiful, Jude. Thank you." She took them in her hand, leaning forward to inhale their sweet smell, before taking my hand.

"You hired a limo?" she exclaimed as we reached the curb.

"Well, it is a special day." I grinned.

Shaking her head, she reached her free hand into the pocket of my jacket and pulled me closer. "You're too much, Mr. Cavanaugh."

"Just about right, I'd say." Unable to stand a second longer without her taste, I bent down to kiss her, savoring the warmth and tenderness.

"Just a few more of those left as a single man," she joked.

"Are they different as a married man?" I shot back, opening the door for her.

"Guess we'll have to find out." She leaned forward again, brushing her lips against mine. "Tomorrow," she added with a smile.

"Tease."

She bent forward, putting one foot in the car before freezing. Her head popped back up, looking at me in surprise. "Oh my gosh!" she shouted, fully tumbling into the car.

I laughed, following close behind but with a bit more grace, and I found her in the loving arms of her mother.

"I didn't think you'd be here until tonight," Lailah cried.

Molly smoothed back the light blonde strands of hair around her face. “We managed to catch an earlier flight,” she said. “Marcus has already checked in at the hotel.”

“This is amazing. Now, you can spend the rest of the day with us!”

“Actually, I’m going to have to bow out,” I said as we all settled into our seats.

Lailah’s eyes met mine, as she placed the large bouquet of flowers in her lap. “What do you mean? You’re not working this afternoon, are you?”

“No,” I answered. “Surprisingly, Roman did manage to make it in on time today, like promised, but I do have a few last-minute errands I need to make.”

Her gaze narrowed. “And you can’t do those last-minute errands with me?”

“Nope.” I smiled.

“Hmm,” was all she said.

Laughing, I leaned forward to place my hand on her knee. “You really hate surprises, don’t you?”

“Yes.” She pouted.

It was cute but didn’t sway my decision for a second.

“Sorry, not changing my mind.”

“Jerk.”

“Do you see how she treats me, Molly?” I joked.

The limo pulled up to a random curb about five blocks away from my destination. Lailah suspiciously looked around, trying to guess where I was headed. Molly just shook her head and grinned.

“Stop trying to figure it out,” I whispered before leaning forward to steal one last kiss for the road.

Her lips lingered against mine for a brief moment before I pushed the door open and stepped out.

“I’ll see you tonight.”

She blew me a kiss, and I shut the door. The car pulled away from the curb, and I stepped onto the sidewalk.

“I love you!” Lailah’s voice rang through the city noise.

I turned to see her smiling face, full of life and exuberance, hanging out the moonroof of the limo. She waved her flowers back and forth like a flag.

I cupped my hands over my mouth, and amid the sea of people walking past, I shouted back, "I love you, too!"

"See? You're not the only one who can be surprising!" she yelled before the limo rounded the corner and disappeared.

I chuckled under my breath and shook my head.

No, definitely not. Lailah always managed to keep me on my toes, and there wasn't anyone else I'd rather be with.

With my secret errands done, I returned to our apartment with just enough time to shower and get ready for the rehearsal dinner that Molly and Marcus were hosting in our honor.

We'd decided to forgo the traditional rehearsal the day before the wedding, agreeing that our simple service wouldn't really need to be practiced. Plus, I wanted the first time I saw her walking down that church aisle to be real.

The apartment was quiet as I stepped out of the shower and wrapped a towel around my waist. Lailah had packed an overnight bag and booked a hotel room where her parents and Grace were staying. Grace, baby Zander, and her husband, Brian, had arrived not too long ago, and I'd already received a text from Lailah, saying that Grace had commandeered her for the rest of the afternoon to do her makeup and hair for the evening.

A small smile played across my lips as I walked into the closet to gather my clothes for the evening.

We were getting married tomorrow.

It was still hard to imagine, yet the hours couldn't tick away fast enough. I'd been waiting for this day for what seemed like an eternity. There was a time when I'd believed it was an impossibility, something I could only envision in my dreams.

But now, it was nearly here, and I couldn't wait to place that ring on her left hand and make her mine.

I tossed on a pair of slacks and a light-gray shirt before adding a purple tie and dark gray vest for my bride. She loved seeing me in a vest. I rolled up the sleeves of my shirt, ran my hands through my damp hair, and grabbed a pair of shoes.

I was ready to go in under twenty minutes.

I still had a bit of time before our reservation, but I decided to head out anyway, just in case traffic got tricky or anyone decided to arrive early.

My instincts were right on target as I found myself stuck in a cab twenty minutes later and only six blocks from our apartment. My foot began to nervously tap as I looked at my watch. Finally, I leaned forward and handed the driver a couple of twenties.

"I'll just walk. Thanks."

A brisk fifteen-minute walk later, I made it to the restaurant with the ability to still feel most of my toes, and I headed inside for warmth. I soon found my mother sitting in a cozy chair by the bar with a glass of dark red merlot in her hand.

"Hey, Mom," I greeted.

She rose to her feet to hug me.

"First one here?" I asked, briefly looking around, as I took the seat next to her.

"I believe so. Your brother said he would meet me here for a drink, but I haven't seen him yet."

I kept my comments regarding Roman to myself, and instead, I tried to change the subject. "Did you check in to your hotel all right?"

She nodded and took a quick sip of wine before answering, "Yes, it's quite lovely. Returning to the city does sometimes make me miss our place here, but I do love the quiet of the country."

When my father had died over a year ago, my mother had made the painful decision to sell their city home. It had been years since they lived there, but it'd held special memories, having been the primary residence where Roman and I had been raised. Now that we were grown though and it was just her, she hadn't really seen the value in keeping it. Now, when she visited, she'd either stay in a hotel or with Lailah and me in our apartment. Since we were leaving for our honeymoon the morning after the wedding, Mom had chosen to stay in a hotel near the reception location, like most of the other guests who were from out of town.

"I love the country home," I replied, remembering the many adventures Roman and I had journeyed through as young boys in that great big house over the years.

"It looks marvelous this time of year," she remarked, smirking.

"I know, I know. We'll be back in three weeks, Mom."

She shook her head in mocked disdain, obviously trying to cover the small smile spreading across her face. "Your first Christmas as husband and wife, and you won't even be here."

"It's called a honeymoon. I believe yours lasted a month."

She grinned. "Five weeks actually, and it was divine. You know I'm just goading you. We'll be here to celebrate the holidays when you return. Enjoy every minute, sweetheart."

"We will."

A flash of red caught my eye, and I turned just in time to see Lailah walking through the entrance with her parents a few steps behind. I watched her shrug off her thick red coat and scarf, and what lay hidden underneath was simply magnificent. She was a vision, covered in crimson and lace. The dress she wore hugged her waist before flaring into a flirty skirt down to her knees. Her hair fell in loose waves around her shoulders, and her eyes glimmered with excitement.

So beautiful.

I was up on my feet, moving toward her, before my brain even registered the fact. She was a force that drew me in, and I never wanted to be anywhere else but surrounded by her dazzling light.

"You're here!" Lailah exclaimed.

I reached her side and took her hand. "You look stunning," I said, leaning forward to brush a lingering kiss against her lips.

The corner of her mouth curved as she stepped back. "Just wait until tomorrow."

"Oh, I can't wait."

She glanced around, seeing my mother as she rose from her spot at the bar. They waved to one another, and then Lailah tried to spot the other few remaining members of our dinner party.

"Has Roman arrived yet?" she asked.

"No," I answered bluntly.

"There's still time," she soothed, stroking the sleeves of my shirt in a comforting manner.

"I know. But would it really kill him to care about someone else for once?"

Her fingers found mine, curling and locking us together. "He did, remember? That's why we're here tonight. Because Roman cared about you enough to fly all the way across the country to tell me what an amazing man I'd managed to let slip through my fingers. If it wasn't for him, none of this would be happening right now, Jude."

I sighed in frustration—mostly because I knew she was right and partially because I couldn't figure Roman out.

Why would a man do something so selfless yet manage to pull a complete one-eighty and return to being a full-time asshole the second he returned back home?

What was I missing?

The hostess took us back to our private table that had been reserved for this special evening, and I gave her instructions to send any late stragglers straight back.

Of course, the only late straggler was my brother, but I was trying to be polite.

Sitting next to Lailah among our family and friends, everything suddenly started to become very real, and the tardiness of my brother was soon forgotten.

My hand fell to her knee under the table and squeezed. She turned to me as everyone was busy chitchatting. As our eyes locked, I knew she felt it, too—that amazing feeling that anything was possible because we'd found each other.

Moisture pooled at the corners of her eyes, and as I raised my thumb to brush it away, she mouthed the words, *I love you.*

Just as I began to repeat them back to her, I was promptly interrupted.

"So sorry we're late!"

I turned to see Roman walking toward the table with a buxom brunette dressed in a napkin that she was trying to pass off as a dress. Every head turned as the two passed by, and as they drew closer, I couldn't decide if the attention was due to the napkin-sized dress or the smell of alcohol that seemed to be seeping out of their pores.

I rose quickly from my chair as Roman tried to head toward the single empty seat just to the left of Lailah.

"I wasn't aware you were bringing a date, brother."

His darkening eyes met mine, and his mouth curled up into a

menacing smile. "Wasn't aware I had to tell you, *brother,*" he replied.

"Well, it is common courtesy so that we know how many place settings to have the restaurant prepare for. As you can see, we are a seat short," I said, gesturing to the empty chair.

"I guess Ginger will just have to sit on my lap then. Huh, sugar?"

Ginger—if that was her real name—just smiled and nodded, the silicone in her boobs bouncing up and down with enthusiasm.

Just fucking great.

I sighed in frustration, pinching the bridge of my nose, as I glanced around at our family members nervously looking about.

"No need for that, Roman. I'll go ask the hostess to set an extra seat for your . . . friend."

"Thank you," he remarked as his hands slid around Ginger's waist.

I didn't bother waiting to see where else they might venture to. Instead, I went in search of the hostess.

The anger inside of me was about to boil over, but I knew I had to keep it at a simmer. Tonight was not about Roman. It was about Lailah. All I wanted was to make sure she was happy, and I would not let some random hook-up of my brother's detour that goal.

With the help of a very understanding restaurant manager, room was added to the table, squeezing in another chair, and Ginger was promptly ushered to her own seat.

Within minutes, the entire event seemed to breeze away into the past as conversations began, and excitement peaked. Grace and Lailah made game plans for the morning, deciding what time they should order room service and confirm appointments. Lailah's mom conversed with mine about the weather differences this time of year on the opposite sides of the country. Roman continued to share his love with the two most important things in his life—liquor and hired entertainment.

Dinner orders were placed, and conversations fell into a quiet rhythm as drinks were sipped, and everyone settled in, waiting for food to arrive.

"Are you two packed and ready to leave tomorrow?" Lailah's mother asked, holding a glass of chardonnay in one hand, while her fingers brushed the outer curve of Marcus's thumb.

"I think so, but it would have been helpful if I'd known what to pack. Right now, I feel like I packed for six different trips because I had absolutely no idea what to bring, so I was forced to bring everything," Lailah answered in a huff.

I couldn't help the tiny smirk that spread across my face. "You seem awfully put-out for a girl who's about to go on her romantic honeymoon," I retorted.

"Oh, is that where I'm going? Because I'm not quite sure. We could be doing survival training, for all I know."

"Now, there's an idea." I winked before leaning over to kiss her forehead. "I promise, no matter where we go or what we do, it will be magical. Want to know why?"

"Why?" she asked, her vividly bright blue eyes seeking mine.

"Because I'll be with you."

"I think I just threw up a little in my mouth," Roman muttered.

I shot him a dirty look. Just in time, the waiters arrived with our dinner.

My asshole brother was once again forgotten as we settled into our amazing meal. Since moving to New York, I had made it my personal mission to make sure Lailah learned as much about the city as possible—from the food to the culture and right down to the grimy subway system. I'd known she didn't want to live in a glass box anymore, and I didn't ever want her to feel like I was putting her in one.

There were times when I still worried about her though. When on a crowded street with someone nearby coughing, I'd find myself pulling her away, wondering if she needed to wear a mask more often. She had them, but she loathed the idea of wearing those terrible blue plastic things in public. She would wear one when the situation called for it, but luckily, those had been few and far between.

Keeping her away from infection had so far been relatively easy. Combined with our vigilance, we'd also been lucky. She attended a university where colds, flus, and God-knows-what ran rampant. She'd caught a few minor things but so far, so good.

Her good health had allowed us to travel the city in abundance. We'd been tourists, learning everything there was to offer. Much of it, I'd already seen many times over, but some of it had been just as new to me as it was to her. She had been astonished to know I'd never taken a ferry to the Statue of Liberty. It just wasn't something we'd done in my childhood. I'd seen Lady Liberty standing proud out in the distance more times than I could count, but I'd never actually taken the time to go out and touch her. It had been thrilling.

Of course, everything with Lailah always was.

She brought a whole new sense of adventure to life that I'd never expected.

That was how tonight at this restaurant had come about. I'd seen this place a dozen times on my way to work, but I'd never given much thought to it. One day, Lailah had dragged me in for lunch, and we'd discovered our place. It was quaint and cozy. The food was amazing—fresh and organic—and the chef always managed to think outside the box. We had become regulars from that moment on.

"Hey," Lailah said, looking at my plate of braised pork loin with marked interest.

I couldn't help but chuckle. "Yes, you can have half," I answered, not bothering to wait for the question I'd known she was about to ask.

Her face lit up with glee as she began to cut her chicken in half before setting it on my plate. "Can I have—"

"Yes, you can have half of my risotto as well. But I get half of those potatoes!" I added.

We started our normal ritual of halving everything on our plates and shuffling it around. Lailah could never decide on just one dish, so she tended to always want what was on mine as well. Since realizing this, I'd been more than happy to share—as long as I got half of hers.

I was a big guy. I couldn't survive on half a plate of food.

Looking up, I found Grace watching us with doe eyes. Her lips were puckered into a little pout.

"What?"

"That's adorable—and kind of weird at the same time," she said.

"Shut it." I grinned before stuffing a large piece of potato in my mouth.

Everyone soon finished their plates, and dessert was about to be served. Lailah and I had preselected this course, wanting it to be special and knowing many might try to go without.

"Pudding?" Grace laughed as the waiters set the dishes in front of everyone. "We're having chocolate pudding for dessert?"

Lailah dipped her finger into the dark chocolate creaminess and brought it to her lips. "Yep, we sure are."

Everyone chuckled as spoons were lifted, and people began eating.

"Oh my heavens," my mom said from across the table after taking her first bite. "This is divine."

And it was. It wasn't the store-bought brand the hospital cafeteria stocked that had once brought two lonely people together years ago. We still loved our Snack Packs, especially in bed, but for tonight, we wanted something special, and the chef had given us just that.

Taking my first bite, I glanced over just in time to see my brother spoon-feeding his escort. Her tongue slithered out like a snake, the tip seductively caressing the silky chocolate. My brother looked on with a lustful dark expression.

Now, I was the one who wanted to hurl.

And my appetite was officially gone.

Lailah, having already finished her bowl, took a few bites from mine before everything was cleared off the table. As conversations ended, jackets and coats were returned, and everyone was bundling up for the cold weather outside.

We all headed slowly for the entrance. Lailah and I trailed behind, our joined hands swinging between us. As we reached the door, we paused to stand face-to-face.

"I guess this is where we say good-bye."

"Not good-bye," she corrected. "That's the great thing about marriage—never having to say good-bye."

"Then, what do we say?" I asked, grasping her hands in my own.

"See you later." she winked, reminding me of the wisdom I'd once given her not so long ago.

"Okay." I smiled. "See you later, Angel."

She grinned, reaching up to briefly kiss my lips. My arm caught her waist and held her, deepening our once chaste kiss, until catcalls sounded around us.

"Come on, Jude. Save some for the wedding!" Marcus called out.

We pulled apart, and a smug grin plastered across my face as our foreheads touched.

"I think that's your father's way of saying that it's time to go." I chuckled.

"I'll see you tomorrow, Mr. Cavanaugh."

"I'll be waiting."

I watched her begin to walk away. Her fingers lingered, holding and grasping on mine, until we were finally forced to let go. The door swung open, and I felt the chill from outside hit my face as she and the rest of the crew staying at the hotel walked through it before heading down the street. My hands went to my pockets, seeking the warmth they'd lost when she left. I never noticed my brother still lingering in the corner.

"How about a celebratory drink? One final hurrah before the last nail gets pounded into that coffin of yours tomorrow."

I turned to find him watching me, his dark eyes skeptical and leery.

"Where did your date go?" I asked, stepping toward the bar, figuring that was enough of an answer for him.

"She had to . . . work."

"Hmm," was all I said.

We settled into two stools and ordered—whiskey sour for Roman, Coke for me.

"Why did you bring her?" I asked, turning toward him, as I ran my hands through my hair in frustration. "You knew it would piss me off. So, why do it? Do you really hate me that much, Roman?"

His expression hardened. "You know, not every-fucking-thing in this world revolves around you, little brother." He stood swiftly, swaying slightly, and he stepped away from the bar. "I think I'll go find someone else to drink with tonight. Drinking solo wasn't exactly what I'd had in mind."

He threw down a twenty for the drinks we had yet to be served and bailed, leaving me confused and alone at the bar.

Our drinks arrived moments later, and as the bartender set them down, he looked around and asked, "Your friend all right?"

"I have no idea," I answered honestly.

With Roman, I never did.

seven

Rise and Shine

Lailah

"RISE AND SHINE!" I announced, spreading the heavy curtains apart to let the golden sunlight stream into the previously dark hotel room.

The large space was immediately flooded with blinding bright light from the world outside, and I turned to see two unhappy people gazing up at me from the beds across the room.

"You know, when I agreed to this sleepover, I assumed it would include sleep—or at least more sleep than I usually receive during a normal night at home with an infant and a husband who swears he doesn't steal all the covers. He does, by the way."

I giggled softly as I looked over at my poor sleepy friend. I tried covering my mouth, but it in no way hid the smile peeking out. "It's my wedding day!" I said happily. "We've got things to do!"

"Sweetheart, you know it's only"—my mother glanced over at the alarm clock on the nightstand separating the two beds—"five in the morning!" She let out a groan as her head hit the pillow.

"The hairdresser won't be here until noon!" Grace nearly cried, pulling her pillow over her head in an effort to turn off the sun.

"Yes, but I thought we could get breakfast and then maybe, um . . . I don't know." My voice drifted off.

"You couldn't sleep," my mother guessed, her lethargic mood transforming into a warm smile.

"No. I'm too excited."

"Well, let's all get up then," Grace said begrudgingly.

I skipped across the room and wrapped her in a tight hug. She returned the gesture, and I felt her mouth curl into a smile against my cheek.

"You know, there isn't another female on the planet I would get out of bed for this early—or one who could get me into a green dress."

I pulled back and met her gaze. "It will be stunning—I guarantee it—even if it's not pink."

"Okay, but if not, you have to promise to do all of this over again—in pink."

I laughed as my hands wove with hers, and she gave them a tight squeeze.

"Deal," I answered.

"So, what's on the agenda first, boss lady?" she asked, covering a yawn with the back of her hand.

"Well, why don't you go jump in the shower, and I'll order room service?"

"Okay, but make sure you order at least a gallon of coffee. No, make that two. And let me know if my phone chirps while I'm in the bathroom. Brian said he had a handle on things, but I'm still waiting for that panicked phone call."

"Has he never had Zander alone?" my mom asked. She was now sitting up in bed with a warm robe she'd grabbed from her suitcase wrapped around her.

"A few hours here and there but not overnight—and vice versa. I've never been without him this long. I know he's just down the hall, but it still feels weird to wake up and not jump out of bed to check on him."

I smiled, seeing the way my best friend had changed over the last two years. Her heart had doubled in size from becoming a wife first and then adding the role of a mother. She breathed out love from every pore in her body, and I felt nothing but pure joy for her happiness.

There were times in my life when those I loved had been timid, nearly scared to share with me the joy they felt in their own lives because of the situation my sickness had presented in my own life. What they hadn't understood was that seeing excitement, hearing about their accomplishments, was what helped make the rough days and nights a bit more bearable.

I had known my life would never be like the nurses who had befriended me or the patients I'd met who eventually left and moved on. But knowing them and becoming a part of their lives, for even a brief moment, had helped ease the loneliness and given me a window to the outside world, making the walls around me feel just slightly thinner.

Now that I was free, no longer a slave to the heart that had held me captive for so long, my friends and family would freely share their ups and downs with me, and it was a wondrous feeling.

It felt normal.

And being normal was all I'd ever wanted.

"Well, so far, no texts and no missed calls," I said, holding up her iPhone in its bedazzled pink case. "So, I think your knightly husband is handling the infant just fine. Go get in the shower, and I will order us food!"

"And coffee!" she reminded me as she marched into the shower.

I picked up the phone receiver, pressed the number for room service, and waited until someone picked up.

"How may I help you, Mrs. Cavanaugh?" the person asked on the other end.

I stumbled momentarily, having never been called by my soon-to-be surname. The room had been booked under Jude, so I guessed it was just naturally assumed I was the Mrs. to the Mr.

Mrs. Jude Cavanaugh.

It was surreal and surprising.

It was completely amazing.

I quickly came back to reality and placed our breakfast order. I asked for enough food to serve an army—or at least the entire floor. I felt a little guilty for waking everyone up so early, and I wanted to make it up to them. So, after hearing the total bill that would have once made me faint, I thanked the man and hung up.

"We should have food in about thirty minutes," I said, turning to sit on the bed opposite from my mom.

She looked at me with soulful eyes, tears leaking out of the corners.

"You're getting married today," she gushed. "I never thought I'd see the day."

"You're crying on me already?" I said, springing from the edge to cross the wide gap separating us.

I sat down beside her, and she gathered me in her arms. It didn't seem to matter how old I'd gotten. Nothing beat the feel of my mother's embrace.

"All those years we spent in the hospital—when I sat beside your bed and watched you recover from one surgery after another with nothing but the same bleak future for you to look forward to—I hoped and prayed that a day like this would come. No one in this world deserves happiness more than you, my angel. No one."

Wetness trickled down my cheeks as her words seeped into my heart, etching themselves into my very soul.

"I love you, Mom."

"Oh, baby, I love you, too—so very much."

"Did you know that many brides find it difficult to eat on their wedding day?" Grace asked from across the room as she pushed a black olive around on her plate. Her hair was up in large barrel curlers, and she sat cross-legged on the freshly made bed.

I smirked, trying to remain perfectly still, as the gorgeous brunette behind me continued to tug and pull at my long mane, promising to turn it into bridal perfection.

"Well, that's just plain ridiculous," I replied, carefully bringing a slivered strawberry up to my mouth from the plate sitting on my lap.

Grace laughed, setting her plate down beside her. We'd basically done nothing but eat and lounge around the hotel room for hours. When she'd said we had nothing to do, she'd meant it. There was absolutely no reason any of us had had to wake up at the crack of dawn this morning. The wedding ceremony wasn't being held until six in the evening, which meant that today was going to drag on endlessly.

And it certainly was already.

My eyes darted over to the alarm clock, and once again, I sighed.

"Sweetheart, just relax. The day will be nothing but a memory before you know it. Try to enjoy every second," my mom reminded me.

I smiled and let my shoulders relax. "I'm trying. I just can't wait to see him standing at the end of that aisle."

A knock sounded at the door, interrupting our conversation, and Grace suddenly jumped up to answer it.

"Password." She giggled.

"It's me," a male voice said from the other side.

"I don't know any *me.* You need to be more specific!" she joked.

"Grace, I'll tell everyone I see tonight the real name that appears on your birth certificate. Don't make me do it!" Brian's voice came through loud and clear.

"You wouldn't!" she squeaked.

"Oh, I would, babe."

"That's just evil!"

"Your name isn't Grace?" I asked, suddenly intrigued.

"Yes, it is! Well, it's my middle name. Never mind!" she scoffed, opening the door to let her sneaky husband in. "You have my son. You should have just said that from the beginning," she cooed, holding open her arms to take a babbling Zander.

"And miss all that? Never." He grinned. His hand snaked around her waist, gripping the fuzzy fabric of her robe, and he placed a tender kiss on her cheek.

Zander watched the exchange between his parents with interest as his tiny fingers pressed against their faces.

"So, what brings you here, handsome?" she asked, stepping away to sit down on the nearest bed with her new adorable little bundle.

"I was charged with a task, and I've come to deliver it."

I looked at him and shook my head. "Oh, no. Please tell me he didn't."

"I don't know what the question is, so I can't answer that."

"Did he get me something?"

Brian's wide grin was answer enough.

"He's incredible." I sighed.

"Did you really expect anything less from Jude?" my mother asked.

"No. That's why I gave Dad a gift to hand over to Jude today as well." I smiled, slightly shrugging my shoulders up before remembering I wasn't supposed to be moving.

The stylist was so good that I'd almost forgotten she was there.

"I was told to deliver this," Brian said, pulling a small box out of his pocket and stepping forward to place it in my small hand, "before your makeup was done."

A small laugh escaped my throat. "That man thinks of everything."

"I'll leave you ladies to your primping." He turned to his wife and child. "Come on, son. Let's give Mommy a few more hours of pampering."

Zander reached out for his daddy and gave us a wave with his chunky baby hand, and then soon, both were gone.

"So, are you going to open it?" Grace asked eagerly.

She and my mother were staring at me. I glanced up to see that even my stylist had stopped to see what might be hidden beneath the ornate silver wrapping.

With shaky fingers, I slowly lifted the red bow and pulled off the paper. When I opened the box, a gasp escaped my lungs at the same moment tears stung my eyes. I was so glad I didn't have makeup on. It would have been ruined for sure.

A stunning silver heart locket was resting in the velvet box. But it wasn't just any heart locket you'd find anywhere. The heart was made of two interlocking angel wings. The wings opened, and nestled inside was a folded piece of paper with Jude's angular handwriting.

My angel, my Lailah, my love.

"Oh God, I love this man," I choked out.

The room was silent, and as I looked up, I found three women with tears to match my own.

"Please tell me he has a brother," my stylist said between sobs.

I laughed. "He does, but my Jude is one of a kind."

And today, that one-of-a kind man would become mine forever.

eight

Restless in New York

Jude

A QUIET KNOCK echoed through the apartment, and Marcus didn't waste any time in jumping off the couch to answer the door. Seconds later, Brian appeared, following closely behind Marcus.

Brian's eyes met mine, and he slowed slightly. "Still pacing the floors, I see," he said as he adjusted a fussy Zander on his hip.

I ignored his comment and kept with my current plan of wearing a hole in the hardwood before the end of the day.

"You should have planned a morning wedding. Lailah's a mess as well."

My eyes darted up to Brian's, remembering the errand I'd sent him on. "How is she? Is she okay?"

He smiled smugly. "Well, she wasn't dressed when I saw her . . ."

My eyes widened as I took a wide step forward, intent on grabbing Brian's neck, but then I stopped myself when I saw his innocent child between us.

His free hand went up like a white flag. "Kidding. Mostly. Shit, Jude. Relax. I'm just messing with you. She was in a robe, and she was getting her hair done. It's too bad you don't drink, man, 'cause you could use a little something for those nerves right now."

My hands went through my hair, and I took a step back, falling into the oversized chair positioned by the large windows overlooking the city. "It's not nerves. I'm just sick of waiting. I've been up since the crack of dawn. I just want to see her already."

"I get it, Jude," Marcus chimed it. "I waited over twenty years to finally marry the love of my life. The morning of, I was a nervous wreck."

"We should have eloped." I sighed.

"And left me to deal with Molly when she found out? You would have done that to me? After everything I've done?"

A small chuckle escaped my throat. "No, I guess not. But damn, if you could make that clock move a little faster, I'd appreciate it."

He smiled warmly, moving toward the chair where I'd chosen to fall into a useless slump. "Come on, Jude," he said, holding out a cupped hand.

I firmly gripped it, and he pulled me to a standing position.

"Let's go get some lunch and see if we can't talk away some of these hours. Sitting around here will be like watching a pot of boiling water."

Brian sighed. "I'll be right back. I've got to go take back a few snide comments."

I had no idea what he meant, and before I had a second to ask, he was gone.

Marcus's arm fell loosely around me in a fatherly gesture—one I'd seen but never really had the pleasure of enjoying as a kid. My father's love had always been shown in his devotion to the family business, not in physical gestures.

"*One must always provide for his family,*" he'd once told me.

And he had. It had been his number one goal, his life's ambition. Even though I'd missed out on an abundance of hugs and trips to the zoo, my father had shown his love in his own way.

Still, as Marcus looked at me with admiration and pride, like a father admiring a grown child, I couldn't help but wonder what an embrace like this would have felt like from my own father.

"I never thought I'd be eating here on my wedding day," I commented, looking around at the shabby interior of the hole-in-the-wall restaurant Marcus had chosen at random after we'd walked down the frozen streets of Manhattan.

"That's exactly why I picked it. You'll have plenty of time for that hoity-toity crap your mom has set up for later. Let's just relax, play a game of pool, and talk."

I nodded, feeling a bit calmer already, as I ordered a round of beers for Marcus and Brian. I indulged in my usual Coke, but since it was my special day, I added a cherry just for kicks. Seeing my fiancé die after the two of us had partied a bit too hard one weekend had officially ended my partying days in one devastating night. Nowadays, I just didn't see the point.

I'd learned to move past my guilt, the all-consuming raw fear that my every action had caused that accident to happen that night. If I hadn't introduced us to the group at the club, if we hadn't stayed and followed them to their home, if I'd only gone back to the hotel when Megan asked, if we hadn't been drunk . . . there were so many factors, so many reasons, and I'd decided it all came down to one guilty party—myself.

But over time, after much healing, I'd learned that blaming myself would never bring her back, and living in the mountain of regret I'd built around myself would never solve anything. *Would Megan be happy to learn I'd given up my life as well?*

So, I'd freed myself from the shackles I'd sentenced myself to and learned to live again—with Lailah.

But some things never change, and the idea of drinking scared me to death, especially since I'd been entrusted with the greatest gift on earth. If anything happened to Lailah because of me, I didn't think I could live with myself. When it came to her, I could never be reckless.

As our drinks arrived and greasy burgers and French fries were ordered, we made our way over to an empty pool table and began setting up our first game.

"So, seeing as I'll be a married man in a few hours," I said as I rubbed a little blue chalk along the tip of my pool stick, "how about you entertain us with a few stories about my beautiful bride, Marcus? Tell me something I might not know."

His motions mimicked my own as he readied his pool stick, and then he began to collect the scattered balls that had fallen into the pockets from a previous game.

"Hmm . . . let me think," he answered, placing each ball into the triangular form before sliding it up to the silver marker on the table.

Each painted ball rolled and spun around as they made their way across the green felt. He lifted the triangle and centered himself, leaning over to take in the perfect position.

Crack.

The balls flew perfectly across the table, and several immediately fell into pockets.

"Damn, man. Give us a chance." Brian laughed.

Marcus smirked as he walked around to find another angle. "Did she ever tell you that she went through a rather impressive *Twilight* phase a few years back?"

I nodded. "Well, she didn't exactly tell me. It was more like I found the mound of books, DVDs, and even an Edward doll in a box shoved in the back of the closet. Do they really sparkle?"

"I'm afraid so. She made me stay late one night after my shift, and we watched every single one—or at least the ones that were out. When I asked where their fangs were, she hushed me and said to keep watching."

"She's moved on, and now, she makes me watch *The Vampire Diaries* every week."

"Oh, I remember. She pulled me into that a few times. Just be glad they don't sparkle."

"Are we playing pool or turning into teenage girls?" Brian asked, raising his pool stick in the air for effect.

I laughed and motioned for Marcus to continue his turn. He knocked around a few more balls, but none scored, so it was my turn.

"Here's something you might not know. When she was younger, there was a time when she had to sleep with the aid of an oxygen tank. She's always had to use one from time to time, but around when she was seven, it became a nightly ritual."

I frowned, trying to imagine my angel, young and frail, chained to a bed each night, breathing through an oxygen mask.

"After about two weeks, she became so angry—with me, her mother, and even the noisy metal tank by her bedside. At seven, she'd endured more than most had in a lifetime, and I think she'd just decided it was enough. It was one of the few times Molly ever reached out for me for non-medical help when it came to Lailah."

I took my turn, barely interested in the game anymore, and it was soon Brian's turn. Taking a sip from my soda I sat down and listened to Marcus as he continued his story.

"I ended up calling one of my buddies up at the Children's Hospital at Stanford. I knew Molly asking me for help was huge. It meant that she trusted me beyond the realm of a doctor-patient relationship. This was something she was asking of a family member, and I didn't want to mess it up."

"What did you do?" I asked.

"With a bit of borrowed advice from my friend, I showed up at their apartment with balloons and dress-up clothes in hand. Molly opened the door and thought I'd gone insane. I was wondering the same as I entered Lailah's bedroom and found her sitting there, curiously staring up at me. When I told her we were going to meet a new friend, her eyes perked up and darted to the door. They immediately fell when I explained that this friend was someone she already knew but just hadn't been properly introduced to."

"The oxygen tank?" I guessed.

He nodded, taking his second shot, having already sunk a few balls in his first turn. Then, he darted across the table to land a few more. "I explained to her that her oxygen tank was a superhero, and it had a big job to do—to keep her alive. I said that, sometimes, superheroes had to go into the real world in disguise, so I was there to help give her oxygen tank the superhero look he or she deserved. We spent the entire evening decorating that tank and giving it a name. She happily spent the rest of the summer with Oxy the Oxygen Tank. We'd secretly switch the outfit every time the tank needed to be replaced, and she never complained again."

"Oxy, huh?" I grinned.

"Yep. She was seven," he added.

"I like it."

Within minutes, Marcus had crushed Brian and me, and just in time, the food arrived. Brian and I weren't willing to risk a rematch, so we all squeezed back into our booth and began scarfing down what had to be the best burger I'd had in months.

"Damn, you know how to pick 'em," I said to Marcus in between bites. I paused to breathe. Even the fries were perfection—crispy and dark brown with just the right amount of seasoning.

"It's one of my many talents. Hearts and food—that's about all I'm good for." He laughed.

"I doubt that," I said before taking a long drink of soda.

Marcus had been there for Lailah through her entire life, standing by her when her own father hadn't. He'd been the father his brother never could be. Oxy the Oxygen Tank might have worn the tiny cape night after night in that little girl's bedroom, but it surely wasn't the only superhero in Lailah's life over the years.

And now, she'd become the hero of her own story.

After another game of pool where Marcus managed to crush Brian and me once again, we headed a bit farther down the street for a last-minute shave. It had been creeping up to the three o'clock mark, and I had begun to get antsy, but the guys had insisted—saying that if we headed back now, I'd do nothing but dive into my suit and begin pacing back and forth across the floor until we had to leave for the church at five.

They were both right. It would take me less than twenty minutes to get ready. No primping was involved for the groom. I'd just have to throw on a nice tailored coat and tie along with a new pair of shoes, and I would be ready to go.

Another distraction was exactly what I needed.

The place Marcus had chosen was definitely his style more than mine. An old red-and-white striped pole stood proudly outside the ancient parlor that had probably been around since my grandfather roamed the city. As we walked in, I inhaled deeply and got a whiff of aftershave and cologne.

A man sat high up in a chair with his head leaned back. His entire face was wrapped in steaming towels as the barber attended to another man at the counter. The cash register dinged and sprang open, reminding me of a place my mother used to take me to for ice cream when I was a child. Made of solid metal with gold lettering, the old piece of machinery didn't even plug into the wall. It was probably older than all three of us combined.

"Hello, gentlemen. How can I help you?" the elderly barber asked while walking back to his steaming client.

I watched as he unwrapped the towels to reveal dewy pink skin and a relaxed happy face.

"We were hoping you might be able to do a couple of shaves today?" Marcus inquired.

He nodded, pumping the hydraulics on the chair a few times to bring the man down to his eye-level.

"Sure can. Special occasion?" he inquired.

"This man is going to become my son-in-law today," Marcus stated proudly, patting me on the back.

My face curled into a half grin as I felt his fingers gripping my shoulder. I didn't think I'd ever get used to the love this man had for me. I felt undeserving of it, yet I never wanted to let go of a single drop of the overwhelming joy he had when he looked at me with such pride.

"Well, that is quite a celebration. Can't show up at your wedding without a proper shave. Give me a minute to finish up Dale here, and I'll be right with you."

The three of us headed to the old plastic chairs over in the corner to take our seats. I snickered a bit when I saw Brian's eyes go wide as he sat down and felt the legs wobble slightly. Like the owner, everything in this establishment was old, including the rinky-dink chairs we were occupying. I wasn't sure they were used to holding a former high school linebacker like Brian. Hell, even my chair was bowing a little, and I hadn't been hitting the gym nearly as often as I once had.

After several minutes of small talk and flipping through ten-year-old car magazines, the formerly pink-skinned man was now making his way out the door.

"Now, which one of you is up first? The groom?"

Marcus nodded, and I leaped to my feet, ready for my own form of wedding-day pampering. The man ushered me to the barber chair, his eyes darting to my hair. After a cursory check, he must have decided it was decent enough to meet my bride later that evening because he didn't say anything further as he proceeded with just the shave.

"You ever have any relatives come by my shop?" he asked as he grabbed the hot towels from a nearby bin.

"Uh . . . no, I don't believe so," I answered his odd question, arching my brow in confusion.

"It's just, you look like a guy who used to come by here about fifteen years ago. I never forget a client or a face. It's why I've stayed in business for so long. You don't see too many barber shops around New York these days. It's all salons and cookie cutter shops. But not me. I've made it because I remember people, and my clients respect me for it. And you look just like this guy . . . Stevens—that was his name. He came in here once a month for about a year and then disappeared. I never saw him again. But if I could place a bet on it, I'd say you were his twin—or son. Spitting image, I tell you. Spitting image."

"Sorry," I answered. "The only male relative I had around here fifteen years ago was my father, and his last name wasn't Stevens."

He shrugged. "Well, I guess everyone's got a twin."

The hot towel went over my head, and he told me to sit back and relax. For once that day, I actually did.

In just a few short hours, I'd be standing at the end of an aisle as I watched Lailah walking toward me, ready to become my wife—forever.

nine

Angels in Winter

Lailah

WE ALL STOOD back, looking up at it and just stared.

"It's so pretty." Grace sighed, looking over at her sleeping son, who had been delivered to us earlier that afternoon by Brian.

Apparently, my husband-to-be was antsy and needed guy time, and that didn't include babies.

"It's not too fluffy?" I asked as my eyes darted back and forth to the gobs of fabric hanging from the dress as I tried to remember how I'd looked in it during my last fitting.

My hands nervously wrapped around the silken waist of my robe. Spending years in nothing more than T-shirts and sweats, it was hard to gaze up at something so stunning and imagine me inside of it.

"Heavens no. When it comes to bridal gowns, there's no such thing. It's perfect," Grace replied.

When a girl had spent the majority of her life believing she'd never get married, let alone see adulthood, stepping into a bridal salon to pick out a wedding dress was an event to remember. Sure, it was a big day for anyone, but for me, it'd signaled a turning point. I was no longer Lailah, the girl everyone pitied. I was Lailah Buchanan, future wife to Jude Cavanaugh. As far as I was concerned, I was the luckiest female on the planet.

Okay, maybe every woman felt that way as she stepped into a bridal salon, but I was sure most of them knew from an early age that they'd eventually meet that wonderful man and find themselves planning the wedding of their dreams.

I'd never had such lofty plans in my life.

I'd only dreamed of surviving.

And now, I had.

When I'd stepped into that beautiful bridal store and looked around at the twinkle and glitz of pearls and diamonds sparkling from every shimmery corner, I'd suddenly become that little girl who had never gotten to plan her dream wedding.

I'd picked out the biggest, puffiest ball gown I could fathom, and I had spent an embarrassingly long amount of time in front of the floor-to-ceiling mirror, twirling and just looking at myself. Eventually, smiles had become tears and then sobs as I realized what this moment meant.

I'd survived. I had made it through to the other side, and now, I was here, living the life most people took for granted.

My mother and Grace had wrapped their arms around me, nodding, telling me I'd never looked so beautiful. I hadn't bothered with trying on any other dresses. I'd had my bridal moment, or whatever they called it.

And here I was, standing in front of my dress, ready to put it on for real.

There were no more fittings, no more sneaking into the office closet just so I could catch a glimpse of its organza layers and remember what they'd looked like while falling down around my body like beautiful sheets of snow.

This was all actually happening, and now, I just needed to realize I was deserving of it.

"So, are you ready to put it on?" my mom asked, reaching up to unhook the hanger from the top of the closet.

"Yes!" I nearly squeaked in excitement.

They both laughed as I dropped my robe, and I watched as they carefully unzipped the back.

"That's not what you're wearing underneath, is it?" Grace asked, her head doing a double take as she caught sight of me standing in my simple white satin underwear and matching strapless bra.

"Um . . . yes. Why?" I asked, now feeling self-conscious.

My hands moved to cover my stomach, but she batted them away.

"Oh, stop. I'm just commenting on the fact that it's a little . . . well, underwhelming." She smiled.

"And virginal," my mom added with a laugh.

I looked down at what I had on and frowned. "It's white and satin," I answered with a huff. "I got it at the bridal salon!"

"Oh, honey. I knew this would happen. Hold on," Grace said, raising a single finger in the air, issuing a virtual pause on our conversation.

I gazed over at my mother who still held the dress, midway through unzipping it, and she just shrugged. Obviously, she wasn't in on this little adventure. Comments were her only contribution.

I turned to see Grace shuffling through her enormous suitcase, hunched over with her butt raised high in the air, as she dangled on one heel, trying to somehow be ladylike in her emerald-green dress. The view was quite hilarious.

"Aha! Found it," she announced, pulling out a pink bag and shoving it in my direction.

"Pink. Should have known." I rolled my eyes.

"Just the bag." She laughed.

I opened it and found a mass of tissue paper surrounding delicate white lacy lingerie. I pulled it out, feeling my cheeks redden instantly, and I held it up for closer observation. "Is this a—"

"Thong? Yes, hon."

I was fairly sure my gulp was audible. My eyes widened as Grace's laughter filled the room. I looked to my mother, who was joining in on the fun as well.

"I might just have a heart attack right here, new heart be damned," I muttered.

"Oh, sweetheart, it's fine. Very tasteful."

"Okay, but try not to look, Mom."

Her face curled into a smirk as she made a valiant effort to contain the giggles. "Okay."

I quickly changed, swapping my sensible satin boy shorts for the barely there lace thong Grace had bought me. When she had been with me a few weeks ago, I'd purchased a few things for the honeymoon but nothing too risqué and definitely nothing that went up my butt. Jude and I had been together for a while now, but I was still very much a newbie when it came to certain things—and apparently, dental-floss lingerie was something I could add to that list.

In addition to the new sexy panties, Grace had also purchased a new strapless bra for me.

I eyed it warily.

"It's a push-up. Believe me, you'll thank me later."

"Will I still fit? I mean, I was fitted to my dress with this bra on," I said, looking down at my regular non-push-up satin bra.

"Yes, the girls will fit, and they'll look amazing."

"The girls?" I asked, quickly turning to change.

"Yes, treat them with a little respect, Lailah. They're the only two you get."

I circled back around and watched her eyes bug as they zeroed in on my chest.

"Whoa. Tell Jude he can send my thank-you flowers anytime."

I looked down and nearly gasped. "Are you sure this is decent? I mean, they're nearly poking me in the eyes!"

The sound of my mother's snickering filled the air.

"Oh, hush. They are not. You don't have nearly enough down there to poke an eye out. Besides, by the time we get the dress on you, it will be just enough cleavage," Grace commented.

"Just enough?"

"Yes. Church cleavage—not too much, not too little, just right."

I rolled my eyes and maybe snorted just a bit. "Okay, Goldilocks."

Moving across the room, careful to cover my backside around my mother, I stood in front of her as she held my dress and took a deep breath.

"Okay, let's do this," I said.

Our eyes met as she lowered it. I took Grace's hand, and with one foot after another, I slowly stepped into the dress and watched as they lifted it up around me. The bodice came around my waist as they worked to pull the zipper up.

"Perfect," my mother said. "It fits like a glove."

They smoothed out the layers and then brought the beaded belt to adorn my waist. With an expert hand, Grace tightly tied it right at the small of my back, and I turned to see myself for the first time.

"Don't cry," I chanted. "Don't cry."

The dress was exactly as I remembered but so much more. The sweetheart bodice fit snugly, accenting the small curve I'd gained since the surgery. It flared out at the waist, dozens of thin organza layers flowing elegantly to the floor.

"I look like a princess," I said.

"No," my mom replied. "You look like an angel."

I saw her misty eyes in the mirror, and I had to look away to keep from sobbing.

"I think we have a few final touches before we go," Grace said, her voice rough from obvious tears.

Her fingers touched my neck, and I felt the cool touch of metal wrap around my throat. The locket Jude had given me hung neatly on my chest, barely reaching the top of where my scar began. It was visible in this dress, and I'd considered wearing a gown where it would have been hidden, but I'd spent too much of my life hiding.

This was who I was—a survivor.

And today, I refused to hide.

My heart grew louder, beating a bit faster, as the limo pulled up to the curb of the beautiful Gothic church that stood proud and tall against the New York skyline.

As soon as I'd seen it, I'd known this was where Jude and I would be married. After a defeated day of looking at church after church, only to find nothing that had truly spoken to us, I'd almost given up on my dream of getting married in a historic church.

Jude's parents had said their vows in the beautiful Trinity Church, and sure, I wouldn't have minded that either. But that place was gigantic, and to keep Jude's mother from going completely insane and inviting the entire Eastern seaboard, we had tried to stay clear of large venues.

Tired, achy, and sore from walking around half the city, we'd climbed into a taxi. As I'd slumped into the backseat, listening to Jude's easy voice assuring me that everything would work out, I had looked up, and there it was. I'd immediately asked the cab driver to pull over. Grabbing Jude's hand, like a crazy person, I'd dragged him out of the back of the car, and I'd run toward the entrance, not stopping until we'd reached the inside.

We'd put our deposit down that day.

In that moment, it had felt like today would never come.

And now, here I was, in my wedding gown, ready to meet my groom and pledge the rest of my life to him.

It seemed like fairy tales really did come true—even for the little girl who had grown up within the walls of a hospital and never expected anything truly special to ever happen there.

"Are you ready?" my mother asked, taking my hand in hers.

I squeezed it as our eyes met briefly before I looked up toward the top of the limestone steeple.

"Yes," I croaked out, trying to stifle the tears threatening to break through.

The limo door slowly opened, and there was Marcus, standing proud and tall, waiting to help us into the church.

"There are my girls," he said. "How about we get you inside?"

I nodded as he took my hand in his and carefully helped me out of the limo, mindful of all the layers of fabric around me. I stood outside, hardly noticing the freezing temperatures of the early evening setting in, and then I saw Marcus's face.

Moisture rimmed his aged eyes.

"You . . . my God, Lailah. You're stunning."

I fell into his embrace, soaking up love and warmth from the only father I'd ever known. He'd been my doctor my entire life. He might be just a stepfather by society's standards, but to me, he was so much more.

"Thank you," I said, pulling back to look at him.

"For what?"

"Everything. There's too many to list, Marcus. You've been there for me and Mom every step of the way, and I would have died in that hospital a long time ago if it wasn't for you."

He tried to protest, but I knew it was true. Every minute of every day, he'd fought for me.

"My mother might have chosen the wrong Hale brother that night, but she's been choosing you ever since."

He gave a wisp of a smile. "I know." His eyes shifted beyond me to where my mother now stood, his eyes blazing as they found hers.

Her fingers curled around my bare shoulders. "We need to get you inside," she said as her hands began running up and down my arms in an attempt to warm me. She might have relaxed in her ways, but her driving need to protect me still ran strong and true inside her.

I nodded. "Where is he?" I asked, turning to Marcus.

"In the back, far away from any windows. Don't worry. He doesn't want to ruin this moment either."

A few horns honked as we made our way to the entrance, and I couldn't help but turn and wave as people honked, rolled down their windows and yelled congratulations. Luckily, no one told me to turn and run or hollered that marriage sucked. That definitely would have put a damper on the celebrity moment I was having.

Marcus pulled open the heavy door to the church, and my mom helped me enter quickly. After we made sure all of my dress was safely inside, I gave the okay to close the door behind us. Grace had already arrived separately, wanting to make sure everything was perfect. I also believed she secretly wanted my mom and me to have a moment alone together. It wasn't necessary, but I appreciated the gesture. It had been nice to spend the last couple of minutes with my mom while driving down the streets of New York. I didn't know if I would get another chance to just be with her like this before Jude and I left for our honeymoon. I was guessing Grace had known that. She always seemed to know exactly what to do.

"Oh, Lailah, it's beautiful," my mother said, her voice full of awe.

I finished smoothing out my skirt and looked up to see that the church had completely been transformed. It was daytime when Jude and I had visited, and although it had been absolutely dreamy then, we had known we wanted an evening wedding. Having returned sometime later during an evening service had only given a glimpse of what it might look like since the bright lights above washed everything out.

Now, only the glow of what seemed like a million candles lit the room. It was romantic and everything I'd imagined it would be. The glow from the natural lighting flickered and danced against the stone walls and high Gothic cathedral ceilings.

"It's perfect," was all I could manage to say before I was whisked away to the bridal suite.

Guests were starting to arrive outside, which meant I would be walking down that candlelit aisle in less than an hour.

ten

A Night to Remember

Jude

I TOOK A deep breath, touching the new cuff link on my sleeve, as Marcus stood next to me in front of the congregation. The small a cappella choir began, their angelic voices filling the church, from high above where they stood in the balcony.

Grace emerged first, carrying a small bouquet of red and white flowers against her green dress. She looked happy and elated as her head turned briefly to smile at Brian and Zander seated in the crowd. Brian held out their son's tiny hand and waved at her as she walked by before taking her spot to the right of me, leaving a wide space where Lailah would be.

Lailah.

I turned just in time to see her and her mother round the corner. With one arm wrapped firmly around Molly, Lailah lifted her gaze as they both took their first steps down the aisle.

I lost the ability to breathe.

She was breathtaking, exquisite.

Dear Lord, she was mine.

Loose curls fell around her shoulders surrounding her like a halo, her floor length veil trailed behind her like a thin train. Her dress was winter white and fit her personality and body beautifully.

My fingers itched to touch her, to roam over every inch of that silky skin.

It had felt like an eternity since I saw her last, yet it had been less than twenty-four hours. I knew now more than ever—as she walked toward me, escorted down the aisle by her mother—that Lailah was the one I was always meant to be with.

I might have started my life down one path, but all roads had led me to that hospital, to this moment, and to this woman.

It was true—what they said in cheesy romance movies. When the bride entered the church, as she looked at her husband-to-be, everyone else seemed to disappear around them.

As Molly placed Lailah's hand in mine, giving me a tender squeeze on the shoulder, the entire church melted away. I saw nothing but the dazzling gleam of her eyes under the candlelight and the soft tender smile radiating through her as we turned to face each other.

I wanted to whisper something to her, to tell her how beautiful she looked and how much I loved her. *But how could I fit a hundred different emotions and feelings into a single sentence?*

It was impossible, and I only hoped that the vows I'd prepared would do her justice.

The pastor greeted the congregation, and I briefly took a moment to look out and see our family and friends smiling back at us. Our mothers were in the front pew. My mother was already clutching a delicate lace cloth between her fingers, knowing she'd need to blot away the tears that would eventually make their way down her cheeks. After giving Lailah away, Molly had taken her seat next to my mother.

The church was filled. Many I knew, but most I didn't. I had argued with my mother, trying to keep the attendance low, but ultimately, I'd given in, knowing that my professional position and our family name required me to invite certain individuals.

At this moment, I didn't care who was here with us.

As long as Lailah was in front of me, looking at me with that wondrous excitement in her eyes, the church could be filled or empty, and I'd still be the luckiest damn man on the planet.

"As a pastor of this church for thirty-five years, I've married many couples right here, at this very spot. So many, in fact, that I've married some of their children here as well."

He chuckled a little under his breath, and the congregation joined him.

"Many of those couples stick out in this old memory of mine, those who just seem . . . well, special. Jude and Lailah, from the minute they stepped through the door, became one of those couples. Lailah's overwhelming spirit seemed to fill the entire church as she bounced from corner to corner, gasping with excitement over the architecture of this beautiful building."

I smiled, remembering that day. Pastor Mark recalled it perfectly.

Lailah and I had visited half a dozen churches while on vacation in Ireland, many just like this. Nothing had deterred her excitement each and every time she entered someplace new. Life would never dull for Lailah. Each day was a miracle.

"I'd seen such excitement before, but when I appeared and explained our process for being married here, that joy would usually soon dissolve, and many couples would disappear just as quickly as they'd appeared, searching for another church with a far easier process. See, I'm a bit old-fashioned."

I rolled my eyes a bit, which caused Lailah to scrunch her nose and giggle a little.

"I still believe that a couple should know one another before marriage, which is why I require all my couples to go through premarital counseling. When I approached Lailah and Jude with this requirement, Lailah literally jumped up and down and asked when we could start. It was then that I knew I'd found something special.

"I've learned so much about these two since that day. Standing here, presiding over this blessed union, I am beyond honored."

His warm smile, filled with love, shone down upon us. I'd grown immensely fond of this man over the last two months during our weekly sessions as we spent time getting to know him and his views of marriage and life.

"Lailah and Jude have chosen to recite their own vows, a modern touch that this old guy is actually pretty partial to."

He gave me a nod, letting me know I could begin. A flutter of nerves settled into the pit of my stomach as I watched him turn the microphone in my direction, so the congregation could hear each and every word.

As my eyes settled on Lailah, suddenly, everything solidified, and calm found its way around my anxious emotions.

"A time not too long ago, I thought I'd never see you again. I'd wake up each morning, thinking about all the moments I'd told you I loved you, and that would only lead to all the times I hadn't—like those hurried good-byes when I had seriously been pushing my thirty-minute lunch break or the many nights we'd fallen asleep together and never said it. All those missed opportunities to say I love you weighed on me, like pennies slowly filling up a jar until the little copper coins spilled out onto the floor."

My fingers held on to hers as my thumb slowly grazed her hand over and over as I said my vows, "When you came back to me, I felt this overpowering need to tell you just how much I love you, every second of every minute of every day. Sorry, I know that those were probably a rough couple of days."

The congregation laughed as her eyes lit up, and she giggled.

"I was simply overwhelmed. This—what I feel for you, Lailah—it's powerful. Following those first few days after our reunion, I realized that I could do nothing for the rest of my existence but tell you just how much I love you, and it still wouldn't be an accurate measurement of what I feel for you. My love is immeasurable, infinite and always evolving, and you have it, all of it—for as long as I live."

Lailah's lips quivered as she tightly squeezed her eyes closed. Reaching into my pocket, I grabbed the lace handkerchief my mother had given me moments before the ceremony. I gently held it to Lailah's face and dabbed the tears away. Her fingers briefly curled around my wrist, touching the cuff link that rested there, before taking the handkerchief in her own hand.

Pastor Mark looked to her, silently asking if she was ready, and she nodded.

Her voice was a bit hoarse, filled with emotion, as she began to speak, "I could say so many things to you in this moment, including how you saved me in so many ways. But you would just shake your head and disagree, choosing to say the opposite.

"So, instead, I'm going to talk about snow."

My eyebrows rose as several people in the church chuckled.

"Like most West Coasters, I have a weird obsession with snow. It's cold and white, and it falls from the sky. The first time I saw it, I ran outside without even bothering to put on a jacket, and I danced around under snow flurries laughing and screaming like a crazed person. I'm fairly certain I nearly sent you to the hospital." She grinned.

I nodded.

"From that moment on, my reaction hasn't changed much—although I do remember to bring a coat. Being the California girl I am, I had no idea just how much snow could fall from the sky. Living in New York has been a hard and fast education in weather.

"There was a storm, a particularly bad one last winter, and the city had to actually shut down. The snowplows couldn't keep up with the amount of snow Mother Nature was producing, and as I sat on the couch while the lights flickered off and on, I looked out the window, worrying whether we'd have heat through the night. But then, you came and wrapped your warm arms around me, and I realized that nothing mattered as long as we were together. Snowstorms, heart transplants, or anything else the world wants to throw our way, as long as your hand is in mine," she said, looking down at our joined palms, "I'll never fear the unknown."

I was in awe.

As we exchanged rings and I felt her delicate fingers slide that cool metal band into place, I wondered, *Does one man deserve so much? Or am I tempting fate?*

eleven

Mr. and Mrs.

Lailah

JUDE'S SOFT GREEN eyes melted into mine as he placed the simple gold wedding band onto my ring finger. I looked down at it, the tiny white diamonds twinkling under the soft glow of candlelight.

I'd imagined what it would look like on this day, standing here with Jude in front of our friends and family.

It felt solid, real, and incredibly permanent—just like Jude.

His mouth curved into a half grin as he watched my gaze return to him. *What was he thinking about?* As his eyes dipped to my cleavage, I found myself blushing.

Oh . . . that.

Well, I guessed I would need to thank my good friend Grace for the lingerie.

Pastor Mark began, "Now that Jude and Lailah have given themselves to one another and made promises through the exchange of rings"—Jude squeezed my hand, knowing this was it, and his eyes locked on mine as I bit my lip, trying not to cry—"I am so honored and incredibly happy to pronounce them husband and wife."

We looked to him for permission, the excitement between us nearly causing us to hover off the ground.

Pastor Mark laughed and nodded at Jude. "You may now kiss your bride."

Our eyes met as Jude's cocky grin returned. My heart hammered in my chest. It was as if I'd never been kissed before, as if I'd been waiting for this moment my entire life.

Leaning forward, his fingers found the back of my head, digging into my hair, and he pulled me close. A millisecond before our lips met, he whispered, "Forever," just loud enough for the two of us to hear.

The congregation erupted into cheers and applause as we took our first kiss as husband and wife.

It was magical.

As we pulled back, I looked up to see tears in Jude's eyes. I rose up on my tiptoes and gently wiped them away before we turned toward our family and friends.

"Introducing Mr. and Mrs. Jude Cavanaugh!"

We raised our joined hands in triumph, laughing in joy, and we raced down the aisle to congratulations and applause.

We hadn't been married for more than an hour, and I kind of already wanted to hurt him a little, not a lot—just a small kick to the shin or a tiny shove.

As the guests had all filed out and been whisked away to the beautiful hotel ballroom that was serving as our reception location for cocktails and hors d'oeuvres, we had stayed behind with our small bridal party and family to take photos.

As I dutifully followed directions from our patient and amazing photographer, I felt it—the subtle brush of his fingers across my bare skin, the way his body seemed to hover just a bit closer each time we readjusted our poses. He was doing it on purpose and in front of our family.

And, dang it, I was letting him.

I knew it probably all seemed innocent to anyone nearby—a brush of a hand, a tender kiss. For me, it was anything but. With the raging inferno threatening to burst free from me, desire so fierce pooled deep within that I felt like we might as well be filming a porno right there in front of my mother and father.

"Okay, I think that's enough of the family photos. Everyone but Lailah and Jude can head over to the reception," the photographer announced.

I nearly sighed in relief, and then I saw Jude's mouth twitch beside me.

"Oh, shut up," I muttered.

We got another round of quick congratulations, and then it was just the two of us and the photographer.

But she earned the reputation that had preceded her by managing to fade into the background and letting us do what came naturally—getting caught up in each other. We moved around the church, taking photos in candlelight and near the large arches of the windows. Nothing was posed or stagnant, and it only perpetuated the need to have him more.

After about fifteen minutes, the photographer had gotten everything she needed, and we were let free to join the others at our reception.

"Ready to party, Mrs. Cavanaugh?" Jude asked as he took off his tailored jacket. He placed it on my shoulders right before opening the heavy church door.

"I'd actually rather drive around in the limo for a few hours."

His eyes darkened, and we stepped into the cold winter air. My head tilted upwards, catching tiny snowflakes from the flurries that had begun during the ceremony.

"Snow," he stated, glancing up at the wintery sky.

"Snow," I repeated, remembering my wedding vows from just an hour earlier.

"Let's find that limo," he said.

Scooping me into his arms, he walked down the steps toward the street. I laughed, but it was cut short when I heard him curse.

"What's the matter?" I asked.

"The limo is gone."

"Maybe he's just down the street?" I suggested.

Jude set me down. Romantic moment now over, we looked from one side of the street to the other, but there was no limo in sight.

"I specifically requested that one be left behind for us."

"Well . . . hmm . . ." was all I could offer before adding, "Taxi?"

He turned to me like I'd lost my mind. "In your wedding dress?"

"Well, it's either that, or we walk."

His hand was in the air before I'd even finished the sentence.

Five minutes passed before a taxi was crazy enough to pick us up. Apparently, seeing a bride and a groom in front of a church was just too much drama for most NYC drivers to handle. Luckily, Mo from Queens was feeling a bit adventurous and decided he needed a good laugh as Jude spoke with him through the window before quickly helping me shove the many layers of my designer gown into the shabby backseat.

"You running away?" Mo asked in a heavy accent.

"No! Of course not!" I said adamantly. "Our limo that was supposed to take us to our reception disappeared."

"Limo drivers—can't trust those guys." He laughed. "Well, let's get the king and queen to their party!"

Jude gave him the address, and within fifteen minutes, we arrived fashionably late to our own reception.

"They're here!" Grace yelled, running up to us in her beautiful green satin dress. The way it fit her flattered her figure perfectly, yet it still gave her that frilly feminine look she loved so much.

Even though it wasn't pink, I'd still kept her in mind when picking it out.

"Sorry," we apologized as we walked in. "Our limo was missing."

"What? Well, only one was out there when we left, but I asked him to go back." She was incredibly flustered.

I placed my hand on her shoulder. "It's okay. He probably just didn't understand. We took a cab."

She looked horrified. Her eyes roamed my dress, searching for evidence of our harrowing journey.

"We're fine, really."

"Come on. Let's go enjoy the evening," Jude encouraged, throwing an arm around the both of us.

"Wait!" Grace came to a halt, and she turned. "You guys can't just waltz in. You must be introduced. It's tradition."

We looked at each other and grinned, both realizing we needed to give Grace this moment.

"Okay. We'll wait here then." I said.

"Yes! I'll let the band know. The lead singer will announce you, and then you can have your grand entrance as husband and wife. Very classy."

She flitted off as both of us held our breath, trying to keep from bursting into laughter.

"She's intense. Has she ever considered becoming an event organizer?" Jude asked, a chuckle escaping his throat.

"Or dictator. No one would even know they were being ruled because she's so sweet."

A deep voice came over the microphone, and we scooted closer to the ballroom just in time to hear the magic words. Grace opened the door, her face beaming, as a spotlight hit us square in our faces.

We held hands and made our way through the throng of people clapping and cheering. It was like being a celebrity for a night, and I suddenly realized why movie stars were all so thin. There was no time to eat.

Jude and I had spent a hefty amount of time picking out a beautiful place to have the reception. It needed to be classy enough for his mother's guests and for us. Well, all we'd really cared about was the food. This location had class and great food. Their chef was amazing and managed to make food that was both divine and not overbearing.

But I hadn't had a chance to eat any of it since arriving at our table. Every time I raised my fork to my mouth, someone would tap on my shoulder, ready to congratulate me or offer hugs and kisses. It was lovely and heartfelt, and I adored the attention, but if I didn't get food in my belly soon, people were going to see what a bridezilla truly looked like.

"Miss?" a young waiter said at my side before correcting himself. "I mean, Mrs. Cavanaugh?" His hand covered his mouth as he cleared his throat and blushed, clearly nervous.

I took a moment to glance over at my new husband, who was giving him the evil eye.

"Lailah is fine," I replied sweetly before giving Jude a look that told him to stand down.

"The chef has requested final approval on the cake," he said, his eyes darting toward the kitchen and then back to me.

"Um . . . oh. I'm sure whatever he's done is fine," I said with a wave of my hand.

If there were an award for an easygoing bride, I would win, hands down. No meltdown bridezilla here.

He pulled at the neck of his collar before wiping his palms against his black slacks. "He was quite insistent."

"Oh. Okay." I sighed, not wanting to cause the poor thing any more discomfort.

"Do you want me to accompany you?" Jude offered, rising from his seat to take my hand.

"No, it's all right. I'll be right back. One of us should stay and eat. Save my plate?" I requested, kissing his cheek and he nodded.

I followed the waiter toward the back, waving and smiling as I quickly rushed by. He held the door for me, and I made my way into the kitchen. Quickly remembering the last time I'd been in an industrial kitchen like this, I smiled. Seeing the stainless steel workspaces, memories of pizza dough and marinara sauce flooded my mind. But they were quickly dashed when I saw a single place setting, complete with candles and a cloth napkin waiting for me.

"What is this?" I asked, turning toward the waiter.

"Dinner," he answered. Then, he promptly took his leave through a swinging door, which led further into the depths of the kitchen.

I looked around, searching for answers, and then I found them.

Standing stoically in the corner, he wore his trademark smile and a designer black suit.

"Nice of you to join us," I muttered.

"I've been here the entire time," he answered. "In the background, where I belong . . . on a day such as this," he added.

"You did this?" I asked, not bothering to hide the surprise in my tone.

"Well, we couldn't have the bride fainting on her wedding day, could we?" Roman said, taking a step forward, as his hand slid across the cool steel of the table.

"And what about your brother?" I asked, folding my arms across my chest in defiance.

"Well, someone needs to entertain the masses." His face curled into a wicked grin.

"Why, Roman?" I questioned, taking an angry step toward him. "Why be generous now? After all these months? Don't you see what you've been putting your brother through?"

His features contorted—first with anger and then melting into something closer to pain. He studied the floor, never making eye contact, as he seemed to fight an internal battle for control.

It seemed to be ages before he spoke, "I've been to hundreds of these types of things." Apparently, he decided to entirely skirt around my pointed questions.

"Weddings?" I asked.

"Weddings, fundraisers, galas—they're all the same. Same boring people, same dull food."

I glanced down at my second dinner. It was growing colder by the minute, and I pouted. It wasn't dull. It was beautiful.

"If you stay in New York long enough, you'll realize this. It doesn't matter where you go or what you attend—they all look the same. Pompous old men will brag about their portfolios and riches while their trophy wives will admire each other's gowns and gossip about the latest scandal. It never changes."

"And what would you know about interesting conversations?" I challenged. I eyed my food one more time as my stomach growled.

"Nothing, I'm sure. As always, I'm just here for the booze."

He looked at my untouched plate as he walked up to me. Our shoulders touched for the briefest moment.

"Better eat up, dear sister. They'll start to notice your absence soon."

Then, he was gone.

And I was left wondering just how many sides there were to my strange and mysterious new brother and whether I'd ever figure them all out.

twelve

Perfect Mess

Jude

"DO YOU REMEMBER the first time we danced to this song?" I asked.

Lailah and I slowly swayed back and forth to the haunting lyrics of "All of Me" by John Legend. Everyone was gathered around as we took our first dance as husband and wife.

"How could I forget?" Lailah answered, her warm smile lighting up the room. "You hummed the lyrics in my ear—perfectly in tune, I might add—which only added more proof to the ever growing pile of evidence that you were far too perfect to be real." Her brief laugh interrupted her thoughts. "Then, later that evening, you asked me to move in with you."

My grip tightened around her waist as I pulled her against me, remembering the sheer joy we'd felt that night after discovering that she was being released from the hospital. It was everything we'd hoped for—a start at something real.

"And now? Now that you've peeked behind the curtain and gotten to see the real Jude, am I still perfect?" I asked with a wolfish grin.

"No." She laughed. "You snore when you're sick, and you never put the toilet seat down. And don't get me started on the empty cereal boxes in the pantry."

I chuckled under my breath.

"But I wouldn't want you any other way," she said with sincerity. "Love isn't about perfection. It's a beautiful chaotic mess, and there isn't anyone I'd rather spend my life with than you."

"So, you're saying I'm not perfect anymore?" I grinned down at her.

"Sorry, babe. You're still pretty hot though," she offered with a shrug.

I just shook my head, using the lull in the conversation to step back. I quickly adjusted my feet and hands, and before she even realized what was going on, I had her spinning. She giggled, a young joyful sound, until she fell back into my arms. The guests clapped and hollered as we continued dancing.

She just looked up at me and smiled.

"You know," I began, "you're not perfect anymore either."

"Oh, yeah?"

"The minute I saw those feminine products all over my bathroom, you suddenly became a little less perfect."

She laughed, shaking her head. "Tampons? Really? Holding my hair back in the hospital while I puked my guts out didn't do it?"

"No. That just reminded me how strong you were," I answered honestly. "How strong you still are."

A few glasses clinked together before a few more chimed in, and soon, much like the rest of the evening had gone, the entire ballroom was filled with the sounds of people tapping their glasses with spare utensils.

The wait staff must really hate this wedding ritual.

I didn't know how I'd made it into adulthood without ever knowing of this particular wedding tradition, but I had been well introduced to it now. As the chorus of clinking stemware rose, I looked down at my bride and smiled.

"I guess we should oblige," I said.

"Oh, okay."

A shy grin tugged at the corner of her mouth just before I bent down to capture her lips. The sound of clinking glasses dissolved into cheers as the crowd finally got what they'd asked for—a kiss from the bride and groom.

My finger wove into her hair as I pulled her closer, never breaking the rhythmic sway of our bodies. Her fingers clutched my forearm before sliding around my wrist. Then, I felt her lips curve into a tender smile.

"You wore them."

"Of course I did." I gazed down at my wrist where the cuff link Marcus had given me rested.

It was part of a set, and were a wedding gift from my bride.

"Do you know what they are?" she asked against my ear.

I shook my head, turning my hand to get a better look. The blue-green stone caught the light, illuminating the bright color within. She'd chosen a simple silver setting, which only enhanced the raw edges that the jeweler had left untouched.

"It's sea glass from the beach where we took our first walk through the sand."

My eyes flew up to hers in surprise. "You never cease to amaze me," I managed to say. My voice was rough, and I was fighting back overwhelming emotions.

"As do you."

Our first dance melted into a second and a third until it felt like we'd been dancing for hours. Our family and friends all joined us, and the music picked up as we celebrated the day in style.

About an hour later, the cake was brought out, and we posed in front of it for the photographer.

As we picked up the knife, Lailah eyed me warily. "I won't remind you about how much time I spent getting ready today, Jude," she warned, looking over my shoulder at the tall cake standing behind us.

I smiled mischievously. I had no intention of smashing cake in her face, but that didn't mean I couldn't mess with her.

"Duly noted," I replied, my voice calm and flat.

"Jude."

"Yes, Angel?"

"I'm wearing a thong," she whispered.

Game over.

I looked up at her grinning face and blinked. That was all I could manage—a blank face and an eye blink. Sure, I'd seen a thong or two in my life, but Lailah was different. Lailah was mine, and whatever she did—or wore—was always exclusively mine. I'd never thought I'd be one of those caveman-type males who relished in the thought that my woman would only ever be mine, but I couldn't help it.

Knowing I was the only man who had ever touched her did great things to my male ego. Being full aware that I would be the only one to ever see her in a thong . . . yeah, it rendered me speechless.

"Good. I'm glad we worked that out." She laughed.

I tried unsuccessfully to adjust myself in my pants. I settled on buttoning my jacket instead. I heard Lailah snicker beside me, and I tossed her the evil eye.

Together, we picked up the knife and gently sliced through the bottom tier of the cake as cameras snapped and flashed behind us. Cutting a single piece, we placed it on the porcelain plate the wait staff had provided. I looked up and saw Lailah's eyebrow rise in challenge.

Apparently, I was going first.

I picked up the plate and cut a small piece with the fork. Ever so gently, making sure I kept my thong rights intact, I fed my bride a tiny piece of cake. A bit of triumph swam in those crystal-blue eyes as she took the plate from me and began the same process.

I watched her pick up the piece of chocolate cake with her fingers, just as I had. Amusement painted her porcelain skin as she came toward me, and then shrieks of hysteria were heard throughout the ballroom after she'd shoved the piece of cake in my face, smearing frosting and cake crumbs all over my skin.

I should have known.

My tongue darted out and licked a piece of frosting hanging on the corner of my lip as people giggled.

"Mmm . . . it's good," I said. "Really good. Want to try?" I asked Lailah.

She backed away. "No!" she squealed right before I grabbed her waist.

"Jude!" She laughed as I caught her lips in a sugary-sweet kiss.

"Cheater," I whispered.

"Just keeping you on your toes." She reminded me.

"You always do."

And she always would.

"I about died when your brother caught my garter," Lailah exclaimed, falling back into the corner of the limo with a giggle.

"I don't even think he knew what he was doing over there. He looked completely confused when the little blue lacy thing landed on his head," I replied.

I sipped on a bottle of water as we came to a brief stop.

The wedding was officially over, and we'd just had our grand departure. We could have stayed at the hotel where the reception was held. It was a beautiful and well-known establishment in New York, but for our wedding night, I wanted to be as far away from our friends and family as I could be—or at least as far away as the city would allow.

Tomorrow, we would board a private plane and begin our honeymoon, but tonight, I wanted Lailah to be comfortable and relaxed. I knew the day had probably already drained her. Adding a flight to that was more than I would be willing to risk. Her health was always the most important thing to me. I would never take the chance.

"I have a feeling that Marcus might have had something to do with that," she interjected, lifting her feet up onto my legs.

I slid off her shoes and began rubbing her sore feet. "Oh?"

"Well, I saw them talking minutes before you dived under my dress," she said, giving me a hard stare.

"That is how you're supposed to do it!" I feigned innocence. "I looked it up on the Internet."

"I'm pretty sure you gave some of the old ladies in attendance a heart attack." She laughed.

I shrugged. "I was just doing my job as a new husband."

"Anyway," she went on, "Marcus seemed to be herding Roman in that general direction after I'd tossed the bouquet. He must have decided Roman needed a bit of fun."

"I'm not sure my brother really understands the word unless it involves alcohol and hookers."

"Jude!"

"Come on, Lailah. Why do you keep defending him?"

Her focus shifted to the passing building as we drove down the streets of the city. "I don't know. I guess it's just the fighter in me. I'm hoping that, somewhere deep inside him, there's someone worth saving."

I leaned forward, my thumb grazing her cheek. "How do you always manage to see the good in people?" I asked.

"Because everyone deserves to have someone on their side."

"Even Roman?"

She smiled softly. "Especially him. He's your brother."

"You're entirely too good for this world." I sighed as the car finally pulled up to our destination.

I'd picked one of the oldest, most grand hotels in New York and requested only the best for our wedding night. I wanted her to feel like a princess. In my eyes though, she was a queen.

"Hopefully, not too good," Lailah commented offhandedly as I moved toward to the door.

"Huh?" I turned to see a wicked smile curving around her lips.

"I mean, it is our wedding night. I don't think you want me to be a saint."

She bent forward to crawl toward the car door. It was practically necessary, but the way she did it was not. Slow and sultry, she made the most of whatever was underneath that dress, so deliciously jutting her breasts forward as she squeezed her arms together. It accentuated every deep curve, and I suddenly felt my mouth go dry.

"I think we need to check in—quickly," I said hoarsely.

"Agreed."

All those days so long ago, when I'd walked into a hospital room and met a shy, sweet girl—who later managed to steal my heart with her courageous spirit and zeal for life—I'd never expected to see her blossom into such an amazingly voracious woman. I'd loved her then—when she'd been young and naive about the world around her—and every day since, I'd found new pieces of her to fall for all over again as she took her place in this life she so desperately deserved.

The chauffeur held the car door open for us, and we both stepped out, mindful of the billowing fabric that encompassed Lailah. Every time I looked at her, I still found myself doing a double take. On a normal day, she was lovely, a vision even. But today? I couldn't even find words. I couldn't stop staring at her. I was dumbfounded by the fact that, just mere hours ago, she'd stood in front of a church filled with our family and friends and pledged her life and soul to me.

In all my days, I'd never understand how I deserved so much.

With her hand tightly laced in mine, I tugged her toward the entrance, not bothering to wait for our luggage. The chauffeur knew what to do. I had other things to worry about—like just how many buttons were on the back of that heavenly dress and how long it would take me to get it off her.

Check-in was quick, and within minutes, we were gliding upward in the elevator toward the top floor.

"Oh, no. What have you done this time?" she asked warily as the numbers zoomed by, and we climbed higher and higher.

"Don't fuss. It's our wedding night. I only did what was required for such a monumental occasion."

I didn't miss the slight roll of her eyes, but she didn't say anything further. She must not have noticed the quick swipe of our key across the elevator panel before the doors had closed. Once they opened again, the gasp of surprise that escaped her lips immediately filled the tiny space.

This hotel room wasn't an ordinary room. It was the presidential suite, and it took up the entire top floor. When the doors parted, we were met with dozens of glowing candles lining the private entryway into our suite.

"Jude," she whispered, her hand reaching up to clutch the spot where her heart resided, "it's beautiful."

"Not as beautiful as you."

"Will you let me carry you over the threshold?"

She simply nodded, her eyes dotted with tears. Bending forward, I lifted my bride, my wife, and my reason for breathing, and I carried her over the tiny threshold of the elevator and into our future.

thirteen

Restraint

Lailah

"YOU'RE INSANE!" I exclaimed the minute my feet touched the plush carpet of our suite.

If you could even call it that.

Mini palace stuffed inside the inner workings of a hotel seemed a bit more adequate.

"Maybe a little," he said.

My eyes continued their seemingly endless tour from one side of the living area to the other. Through a slightly open door, I could see another room, which appeared to be a library. It looked to be covered in wood paneling and filled with books.

Our honeymoon suite had a library.

A freaking library.

"A simple bed would have sufficed," I muttered, pulling my eyes away from the books. I tried to hide the drool as I secretly wondered what treasures might lie inside.

He chuckled as our eyes met. "I'll let you dive in there—later," he said, the light green of his irises darkening. "Much later."

My stomach clenched in anticipation. Books, a fancy hotel room, and every other detail that was floating around in my erratic brain suddenly went dormant, except for one—Jude.

There was only him.

And every part of me wanted to melt into his warmth and his unwavering strength and never solidify again.

He must have noticed the change in my tone. One second, he was playfully smiling at me from across the room, and the next, I was in his firm embrace.

"You are my wife now, Lailah," he said softly, the words spoken with such reverence.

My breathing slowed as I inhaled each beautiful word.

"The other half to my soul. The angel I managed to steal from heaven itself." His fingers lifted to brush hair from my eyes. "I didn't think it was possible that I could love you more, but you constantly prove me wrong, each and every day."

I couldn't take any more. *Could a woman's heart actually fail from too much romance?*

Because one more word, and that new ticker of mine might combust.

He was too good. I could spend a lifetime doing nothing but good deeds, and I'd never fully earn the love he believed I was worth. He thought I was the better half of the whole we'd created, but he was so incredibly wrong.

He was my better half in every way, and the fact that he didn't see it proved my point exactly.

Before he had a second longer to utter anything more, I silenced him with a kiss—the kind of kiss that spoke a hundred words and a thousand emotions without a single sound. It spoke of love, commitment, and devotion without syllables or vowels. Poems and stanzas were unnecessary when two mouths moved against each other in perfect synchronization. A sonnet or even the most captivating ballad couldn't surpass the incredible masterpiece that was made when his lips touched mine.

Our kiss never broke as he bent down and lifted me into his arms to carry me to the bedroom. I'd like to say the rest of the grand suite was beautiful and well-appointed, but I honestly didn't look.

I only saw Jude and those amazing green eyes staring back at me.

Quickly kicking off my shoes as we entered the room, it took a moment before I noticed the candles. Much like the entrance, the bedroom was awash with dozens of tiny candles covering nearly every surface. Rose petals adorned the bed, and somewhere, a speaker softly played our song.

He gently set me down and turned me so that I could fully see the room.

"It's gorgeous," I said.

"Mmm," was the only reply I got as his fingers found the top of my zipper.

"Oh, thank God. No buttons," he commented as the sound of my dress being slowly unzipped filled the air.

"I specifically requested that."

I smiled, remembering the way I'd blushed like a fool when I asked for that particular customization on my dress. The original design had tiny pearl buttons down the back, and after one glance, I knew it would drive my impatient new husband insane, so I'd asked if they could add a hidden zipper and faux buttons. As my face had turned beet red, the shop owner laughed, taking my hand into her own.

"Oh, honey," she'd said. "Believe me, you're not the only one who's asked for that specific alteration to a dress. Men"—she'd winked—"are not known for their patience."

As the dress fell to the floor with ease, I was thankful I'd taken the risk and done what I wanted, regardless of the initial embarrassment it had caused me.

I stepped out of the gauzy skirt and turned. Jude's face was worth all the embarrassment in the world, and I was so glad it hadn't taken forever to figure out how to get me out of a dress.

"So, this is what heart failure feels like?" he joked, clutching his chest. "Good to know."

"Is it really that good?" I asked, looking down at the lacy ensemble Grace had picked out. I didn't know much about lingerie, having been too scared to go into a store by myself. Now that I got a good look at myself, I guessed I didn't look that bad, maybe a little hot even.

"Good? That's not even close to the word I'd use to describe what you look like right now."

I took a step forward and saw him blow a ragged breath out

through his lips.

"Today, when I saw you walking down that aisle, you were ethereal, so beautiful that it almost hurt to look at you."

"And now?" I bit down on my bottom lip as he stepped forward.

"Now, you look like the devil incarnate, and all I can think of is throwing you on that bed and burying myself in all that wickedness."

When his fingers touched my bare skin, it felt like a bolt of lightning was igniting every limb, each nerve, and the muscles in my body, awakening the deepest parts of me.

With a single touch, I was his, ready to go wherever he might lead.

It was not like the first time his hand had reached out for mine so many nights ago in that dark hospital room. Somehow, I'd known that my mysterious visitor would one day own my heart. And I, the shy and naive girl, had willingly given it.

But I was not a girl any longer.

"Show me," I whispered.

His hand tightened around my waist, proving just how much he was holding back. Our lovemaking was always passionate, full of the emotions that had set the stage for our breathtaking love story. But I knew he held back. Even after the kitchen had been dusted with flour and he'd taken me against the counter in more ways than one, I had seen it in his eyes—restraint.

In his eyes, I'd always be that girl, lying in the hospital bed, with tubes and wires attached to me, the one with the broken heart he had to care for. As much as I loved him for it, I didn't want to be fragile in the bedroom. I didn't want to be weak when his body moved against mine, and I certainly didn't want to be thought of as a paper doll on the night of my wedding.

Sliding my hands up his chest, I slowly slid the sleeves of his jacket down his shoulders until it fell to the floor. His hooded eyes watched as my fingers worked his tie, pulling it free from his neck, until it joined the growing heap of fabric below. Silently and with slow precision, I bent my head to each cuff link and kissed the turquoise stone before removing them from his crisp white shirt. He said nothing. He just watched with intensity as I undressed him, taking one button at a time, until my hands touched the smooth skin of his chest. Much like his jacket, his shirt dropped from his shoulders and floated like a white dove until it landed softly below us.

If we lived to be a hundred or older, I didn't think I'd ever get used to the sight of him standing before me like this. His height towered over me, and when I collapsed into his arms, I fit perfectly within their embrace, like I had been created to be tucked inside them for safe-keeping. His body was fierce, toned, and physically strong—thanks to years of solitude, which had been spent doing endless hours of jogging and lifting weights. It was something he'd lightened up on since I moved in, choosing time with me rather than an abundance of time spent in the gym, but somehow, the minimal time he put in worked.

Of course, thirty or even fifty years from now, if I were lucky enough to still be walking this earth with him by my side, I wouldn't think any different.

My hands met at the center of his rib cage as he lazily watched my exploration of his body. I caught the small note of surprise the second I pushed him back, pushing his large body onto the bed.

Male laughter followed.

It was not exactly what I was going for.

His eyes glittered with joy and light amusement as I crawled onto the bed to straddle him. I reached behind my back and unhooked my bra, letting it fall to the ground. All laughter and humor died as his eyes suddenly darkened, and I felt his body go rigid. Rotating my hips, I ground myself against his pelvis. A low growl vibrated from his throat.

"What are you doing, Lailah?" he asked, his voice ragged and breathy.

Over the two years we'd been together, I'd mastered the art of flirting. I could flirt my way to the bedroom like a pro. A dirty comment, a sexy move—I had all of that down to an art form. But once we got to the bedroom, it would be all Jude. I'd occasionally have moments of spontaneity, but it was rare. He'd lead the show, and I'd gladly comply. We never talked about it, but we both knew that Jude had the experience, and—well, I didn't. I never asked how many girls he'd been with before Megan, but I imagined it was more than one. I was completely fine with letting him take charge when it came to sex, but sometimes, I wondered if he was.

Did he ever want more?

"Taking what I want," I whispered, hoping I wasn't ruining my wedding night by pushing something that maybe wasn't wanted.

His nostrils flared as his cock twitched between my thighs.

I mentally gave my budding seductress a high five.

I bent forward, taking his mouth in a fevered kiss. Grabbing his hands, I placed each one on my bare breasts. With my small hands over his, I felt as he cupped and rolled my tender peaks, his thumbs rubbing the taut nipples before pinching the tender tips. I'd felt him do this a hundred times, but with my fingers resting over his, it was much more intimate.

Breaking our kiss, I redirected one set of our merged hands over the puckered skin that rested between my breasts. His eyes met mine as his lips found the pink skin of my scar, leaving a trail of kisses. My stomach fluttered, as I watched him lower our hands until they drifted over my belly button. My breath faltered when our fingers slid beneath the lace of my thong and sank into the warm heat of my core.

The invasion sent me skyward, as Jude kept my body pinned against him and slowly worked my clit.

"Oh God," I panted, feeling every move he made as my finger followed his lead.

"Shh . . ." His free hand tenderly touched my chest, pushing me against his raised knees. Removing the scrap of fabric around my waist, he freed me of my thong, never removing our joined fingers. His darkened gaze centered on me. "I'll follow your lead," he said.

I mentally gulped.

I had grown up in a hospital. Most of the time, the door had either been open or ajar. It wasn't until I was over a certain age when I'd demanded more privacy, and even then, I'd still had nurses walking in on my half-dressed body nearly daily. Add in a controlling mother who had barged in on me at home, and it hadn't been the best environment to . . . explore myself.

After I'd met Jude, I hadn't really had a need.

Seriously, he was sex on a stick. *Who needs a vibrator when you have that sleeping next to you every night?*

So, the M word . . . we weren't well acquainted—at all actually.

The brave little seductress cowered in a dark corner of my mind.

I couldn't do this. I'd come so far, so fast, but I'd always be that girl in the hospital—naive, shy, and meek.

I looked up at Jude. His breath was ragged, and his eyes were so intense that they were nearly black.

I'd done that—not the girl or the woman or whatever label I was seeking to place on myself.

Just Lailah, his wife.

My fingers tightened around his, guiding him slightly upward, which sent a zing of fire to my belly. My head fell back, and I moaned.

"Gorgeous," he said.

His praise was exactly the courage I'd needed. Together, I moved our hands, slowly at first, circling my clit, sending shock waves throughout my body. My heart accelerated with each touch, and soon, I was shaking in anticipation.

But it wasn't enough. I wanted more. I wanted more of him.

"Take off your pants," I instructed, rising up on my knees to allow him some room.

He didn't hesitate, unbuckling his belt while still horizontal. His dress pants were now wrinkled and rumpled from our foreplay. I watched as he slid them down, pulling his boxer briefs along, in one fell swoop.

No clothing separated us any longer.

Skin-to-skin, body-to-body—now, we could truly become one.

I took my time exploring him. The pads of my fingers touched nearly every inch of him—from the swirly pattern of ink on his bicep to the outer edge of his ear and down to the defining lines of his stomach. I wanted to take my time loving him tonight.

There would only ever be one wedding night, only one first night as husband and wife.

I wanted it to feel endless.

He threaded his fingers into my long hair, and I instinctively bent toward him, needing the feel of his lips on mine. He grew harder beneath me as I rolled my hips, begging for his body to enter mine.

"Wait," he said breathlessly against my forehead.

I nodded, knowing he'd never let it get past this point without protection. My doctor had given us the okay to go without condoms. I had an IUD. There was no need, but I would never convince Jude. He'd talked about getting a vasectomy, but I'd quickly shut down that idea, telling him it was crazy. *What twenty-eight-year-old male does that?*

So, condoms were still a part of our lives—even on our wedding night.

After everything was taken care of, he returned to the bed. He kissed me with wild abandon, an attempt to forget the minor mood killer.

It worked as I pushed him back, straddling him once more.

Our bodies meshed and moved. Limbs became entwined, and soon, I couldn't tell where one of us started and the other ended. In a move that had my shy little temptress jumping up and down, I slid my hand between our bodies, molding my fingers over his rigid cock.

His breath stopped as his eyes met mine.

I stroked him once, twice, and then I eased my body on his. He let out a guttural moan as his hands clasped my waist. I could see it in his eyes. He wanted nothing more than to slam my body up and down onto his, but he held back.

"Do it," I urged.

His eyebrows furrowed as I circled my hips, causing his eyes to roll back in his sockets. Lifting my body, I nearly came off of him, leaving just the tip, before slamming back down once again.

"Fuck!" he yelled.

"I know you're holding back, Jude," I whispered in his ear after bending down.

My nipples grazed his chest each time he took a breath.

"I want you to let go. I want to see you unleashed."

When I pulled back, his eyes were full of indecision. He searched my features, trying to make sense of what I was asking him.

"I know you need to protect me and keep me safe, and you do. Every day, I'm still here because of you."

I lost his focus as he tried to look away. I grabbed his chin and pulled him back.

"Listen to me. You are my hero—in every way. But here," I said, motioning around the room, "I need you to be my husband and my lover. Stop trying to protect me here." I pointed to the sheets where we lay together. "And love me without inhibition."

He answered by kissing me. His kiss told me without words just how much passion he had chained behind that ironclad resolve of his. I responded immediately, grinding against his body in a way that had him meeting me halfway.

"Yes!" I cried out.

I pulled him closer, wrapping my legs around his body as he came to a sitting position. His hands molded my backside, bouncing me up until I was riding him relentlessly. Our mouths moved as his tongue found mine, never breaking the punishing rhythm of our lovemaking.

"Mine," he growled between frantic kisses.

His possessiveness caused my stomach to tighten as he grabbed the back of my thighs and pushed me back on the mattress. His large body loomed above mine, his breath heavy.

"Yours," I answered.

Braced by his massive arms, he moved, crashing into my body with such passionate force that I senselessly cried out. Adjusting his position, he knelt, pushing my thighs forward toward my head. Suddenly, he was deeper, and I gasped, as he held my knees and drove into me fast and hard.

My body was in overload, feeling everything at once.

His hot breath was against my neck, and his fingers caressed me as they held me. I felt the soft feel of our skin as we slid together, and the fire deep in my belly was begging to consume me. My muscles clenched tightly around him, and I heard his breath falter before he quickened, picking up the pace. My hands tightened around his forearms, feeling his bulging muscles move as he thrust.

God, he was gorgeous.

The first spasm hit me as my body began to shake in the all too familiar way that sent my body into tremors.

"Oh God!" I cried out.

He moaned, grasping my head to pull me into a deep kiss.

We came together, much like everything else in life.

His body shuddered as my legs fell back to the bed like limp spaghetti.

"My wife," he whispered against my cheek.

"My husband," I reciprocated.

His protective warm arms pulled me into the one place where I felt at home, the one place I was meant for.

I winced slightly as I stood, and suddenly, Jude was there, taking my hand.

"Are you sore?"

I blushed, smiling shyly. "It's the good kind of sore, Jude. I've been sore before."

"You have?" he asked, an eyebrow lifting in surprise.

My eyes roamed over his still naked form. "Yes."

"Why have you never said anything?" He tugged on my hand, pulling me toward the bathroom, where he'd just emerged from.

Condoms, with the immediate cleanup they required, always killed the post-sex bliss a bit.

I followed, not a bit ashamed that I was checking out his butt as we went. His round buttocks bounced. They were so tight that I could throw a quarter at them, and it would come back and hit me square in the eye.

I hadn't been in the bathroom yet, and I tried not to gape as we entered. My mother's entire apartment could fit in here—with room to spare.

Okay, maybe not quite, but it would be darn close.

Covered in gray-and-white marble, the shower looked big enough to fit an entire high school football team, and it had enough showerheads to cover each teammate from head to toe. I didn't know exactly why one person would need all that room or showerheads, but I suddenly wanted to find out.

My head turned as we came to a stop in front of a huge porcelain tub. It reminded me of something from another era with its claw-foot bottom and ornate gold finish, but it had modern features, like jets and enough space for two.

Jude bent down and fiddled with the nozzles until he got the temperature to his liking. There were two bottles resting on a fancy towel. He held both out to me. "Which one?"

"Are you going to join me?" I asked, raising an eyebrow in challenge.

"Are you naked?" he replied in question, his eyes twinkling with humor.

I looked down at my lack of clothing, a mischievous smile tugging at my lips, and then I dragged my gaze back up to him.

I laughed briefly, shaking my head at his goofiness. I took a sniff at each bottle. I turned my nose up at the first—a musky rose scent.

The second was more soothing—lavender and a bit of vanilla maybe. Jude dropped a small amount into the bath, and it quickly turned into frothy bubbles. I watched as he stepped in. With his back against the porcelain, he motioned for me to join him. Taking my time so that I wouldn't slip, I placed my foot between his legs and descended into the hot water. My back was against his warm chest, and I felt his hands slowly dripping water down my arms and shoulders.

"Why didn't you tell me that you've been sore before?" he asked softly as his head rested near my ear.

I took a deep breath. "Because I was afraid you'd pull back."

"Pull back how?" He turned my head toward his.

"Tonight, the way you were, you've never been like that, Jude. And I know it's because you're afraid you'll hurt me, that I'll break somehow."

His mouth opened to protest, but I continued, "Let me finish."

He nodded against my cheek.

"I don't blame you, and I don't think less of you or feel dissatisfied. But sometimes, I see you holding back. And I don't want that, Jude. I never want you to feel like you have to tread carefully around me—in the bedroom or anywhere else in our marriage. I want to be your equal—in everything. I'm not fragile anymore."

"I know."

"I know you do, so please stop treating me like I'm made of porcelain. I want all of you—the good, the bad, in sickness and health," I said, quoting the traditional vows we'd decided to forgo but knew still applied.

"Even if it hurts you?" he asked, his hand slipping between my legs where I felt tender from the madness of consummation.

"Yes, especially then. Because those are the times we'll need each other the most."

"Can I ease it? The pain?" he asked, knowing we weren't talking metaphors anymore.

"You can do that? How did you learn to do something like that?"

Why did I ask that?

Don't ask questions you don't want the answers to.

"You ask like it's a superpower. It's just an idea. I'm not sure it will work, but I thought we'd try."

I exhaled, not realizing I'd been holding my breath.

He chuckled a bit behind me.

"Was that a bit of jealousy I sensed?"

I shrugged, and he tilted my head upward to meet his green eyes.

"You are my one and only, Lailah. Never forget that."

My eyes squeezed shut, trying to memorize the moment. I didn't know how many times I'd done this over the past two years, silently trying to time-capsule a memory, a feeling, or an emotion I shared with this man. I didn't want to forget anything.

"Put your legs up on the ledge," he commanded, his voice suddenly deeper.

I loved when his voice dropped and became demanding. I followed his instruction, placing one foot on each side, like I was ready to birth a baby. It was an awkward position, but it pushed my back further into his chest, so it was strangely comfortable.

I felt him adjust, and the jets suddenly came to life around us, the water rumbling and bubbling with life.

"Now, we just need to move slightly until we get the right angle—"

"Holy—" I cried out as a jet came in contact with my core, spread wide and open.

"There we go," he said, pleased with himself.

I had no words. I was reduced to a writhing puddle of gibberish. Every minor movement pushed the pressured water into my sensitive area. I could adjust, sending the most focused area directly where I wanted it. There was no friction, no touch. It was soothing, yet I was careening, sliding, and falling into another orgasm quicker than I could anticipate.

"I'm going to—oh my God," I cried out.

"Let go," Jude encouraged.

My head fell back as a powerful orgasm sent me over the edge. I saw stars as my body floated back to earth.

I curled back into his arms as my heart steadied. Looking up at him, I realized he'd had it all wrong.

He was the angel sent from heaven.

And I was the lucky one who got to sleep within his winged embrace.

fourteen

A Mile High

Jude

I WAITED FOR as long as possible before waking her. The first rays of morning hadn't even begun to break through the clouds, but I knew if we didn't leave soon, we'd miss our flight. Not that I couldn't reschedule, but I wanted her to be able to see our destination as we flew in, and that could only be done if we left well in advance.

I zipped the last of our luggage and dropped it by the door. Returning to the master suite, I knelt beside her slumbering figure on the bed. Her light-blonde hair fell around her face like straw. Tiny puffs of air moved in and out of her perfectly shaped lips.

Sometimes, when work got the best of me and I returned home later than I wished, I would see her like this—in bed, her hands curled around her face that held a look of serene peacefulness. I'd find myself unable to stir her, unwilling to break the calm cadence of her breath or the gentle ease of her slumber. I'd sit across from her, still fully dressed in my suit and tie, and just watch.

Like the peaceful tide rolling in on an ocean breeze, she was my steadfast tranquility in a world that sometimes seemed to be anything but. When days got hectic and the company seemed to take the life out of me, I knew I could return to her, and she'd right all the wrongs of my life.

Hating myself for having to disrupt her sleep, I carefully lifted a hand and gently stroked her face. She stirred slightly, reaching out to touch my hand in her slumber.

"Hey, angel," I whispered.

She moved a bit more. Her eyes fluttered and finally opened, focusing on my features.

She smiled. "Hi," she said hoarsely.

"Good morning, beautiful."

Her lids shut once more, squeezing tight, as she stretched under the covers. "We got married yesterday." She smiled as her gaze returned to mine.

"Yes, we did." I grinned from ear to ear. "And today, we're leaving for our honeymoon."

Her eyes widened in excitement. "Are you finally going to tell me where we're going?"

I laughed. "No."

Her mouth turned upside down into a pout.

"But I'll show you. Get dressed. I put your clothes there." I pointed at the end of the bed. "And I left a toothbrush and your pills out for you."

She sat up, rubbing her eyes, before her hands went to her hair. A frown appeared on her face as she felt the massive rat's nest that we'd managed to create while rolling around the sheets all night.

"Do I get to shower?"

"No. Sorry. But there's a brush in the bathroom."

She looked at me like I was insane.

With the crazy hair and sleepy eyes, it was kind of cute, and I tried to contain my chuckling.

"We'll be late if we don't hurry. I'll make it up to you. I promise!" I exclaimed as a pillow sailed in my direction.

I didn't bother covering up the deep laughter that followed as I watched her stomp, bare ass naked, into the bathroom.

"When you said we needed to hurry so that we wouldn't miss our flight, this isn't what I had in mind," Lailah said. Her mouth nearly dropped to the floor of the stretched limo as we passed the regular airport completely and pulled into a private hangar.

"I didn't say what kind of flight we were trying to make."

"This is . . . I don't even have words." Her head whipped around as she took in the private plane we would soon be boarding.

"See? I told you I'd make it up to you," I said, winking, as I reached for the handle to hop out.

She followed my lead, neither of us bothering to wait for the chauffeur.

"I figured that meant you'd buy me some dry shampoo and a sweatshirt at the airport between flights, not a freaking private plane. Wait . . . does this thing have a shower on it? Is that why you wanted me to skip it?" She walked beside me, grabbing my arm before linking our hands.

"Maybe." I laughed.

Incoherent gibberish followed.

I couldn't tell if she was excited or pissed. Maybe it was a little of both, but she kept a hold of me as we made our way toward the plane.

The presence of money in our relationship still scared the shit out of Lailah. Raised with very little, it was hard for her to see so much of it go to waste. But in my mind, she was priceless. It wasn't about being frivolous or extravagant to me. We had the money, so if I could give her the best of something, why wouldn't I? Why wouldn't any man do that for the woman he loved?

Ready to greet us was our flight attendant, a young brunette who stood a bit straighter when her eyes met mine. Out of the corner of my eye, I saw Lailah reach up and smooth out her hair once again, obviously not happy with her early morning appearance.

I personally thought her hair looked spectacular, but then I was the one who had messed it up.

A sly grin tugged at my lips as visions of our wedding night flooded my brain until an elbow to the ribs brought me back to reality.

"Pervert."

Laughing, I stopped steps away from where we'd board the plane and grabbed her hand. I kissed it, hoping to calm any nervousness she might have. A shy smile surfaced.

"You could have at least given me something better than sweats," she teased, looking up at the flight attendant in her perfectly pressed uniform.

"You are stunning in anything, Mrs. Cavanaugh. Come on. We have places to go—"

"And things to do?" She smirked after finishing my sentence.

"Definitely things to do."

"Race you to the top?" she challenged, a flirtatious grin appearing across her eager face.

As I began to reply, she was already running, racing up the stairs, before I had the chance to form a single word.

"Cheater!" I yelled.

I waved to the woman whose name tag said *Brie.*

It reminded me of cheese, and suddenly, I was starving. I followed my bride up the steps and found her halted at the entrance.

"Have I ever mentioned my concern for your sanity?" she said, her eyes taking in the lavish furnishings and ample space.

"A few times, yes."

"Okay, good. I might again before this flight is over."

"Good to know." I chuckled, wrapping my arms around her waist, and I pushed us forward into the room.

As she looked around, I took a seat. "Are you hungry?"

Her hands flew to her stomach, probably having the same realization as me. "Famished. Please tell me this thing is stocked with food."

I nodded, leaning my head back against the seat, as I watched her walking back and forth, opening doors and checking out buttons.

"Good. Whoa! There's a bed back here!"

I turned and found her blushing. Apparently, she'd just realized all the fun things that we could do with a bed mid-flight.

I felt my body harden at the mere sight of that red stain across her cheeks.

Calm. Must stay calm.

We couldn't be horizontal when the flight took off, and I planned on at least feeding her before fucking her. After last night, we both needed strength.

Good God . . . last night.

Making love with Lailah always filled a dark hole in my heart. Each time our bodies came together, I'd feel whole, alive, and completely connected to her.

There was nothing more I needed. Nothing felt lacking, and until yesterday, I hadn't realized that I'd been holding back. It wasn't that I had been rougher or different with others in the past. It was simply the fact that, with Lailah, I'd always want more because she meant more.

It hurt to admit that to myself, knowing how intensely I'd once loved another. But I knew I couldn't live in the past. I'd never know what my life would have been like if Megan and I hadn't visited Los Angeles and never attended that fateful party. All I knew was, I'd somehow been given a second chance with Lailah, and I'd fallen so deeply in love with her that I couldn't imagine living any other way now.

But seeing her fear that something might be missing between us couldn't be any further from the truth, yet I'd still held back when we made love.

When you'd seen the person you loved nearly die, the feelings, the fear, etched itself permanently in your psyche. Even though I knew logically that she was healthy, even though the doctor had told me she had a clean bill of health, I found myself filled with doubt—doubt that she'd take a turn for the worst, doubt that something would go wrong and she'd leave me much too soon.

As scary as it was to admit, I didn't think I could survive without her.

So, she was correct. I would use caution and act a tad irrationally when it came to her health. I couldn't help it.

But I also wanted to give her everything.

And, fuck, my every fantasy had been wrapped up in a pretty little package while watching her fall apart beneath me as I showed her exactly how little restraint I could have. She was stunning every second of the day, but seeing her like that had been breathtaking. The echoes of her cries as she'd begged for more had been replaying through my head in an endless loop, and I had every intention of recreating that scene in a dozen different places over the next few weeks.

"You've got that dopey, faraway look in your eyes," Lailah said, bending down to catch my gaze.

I smiled, taking in her features, as she stared at me with a goofy grin. Her hair was piled high on her head in a sloppy bun, and not a trace of makeup graced her flawless skin. It was such a stark difference from the woman I'd watched walking down the aisle yesterday, yet it was still so beautiful.

When she was like this, I could see the Lailah I'd fallen in love with. When she'd walked down that aisle yesterday, I had seen the woman she'd become along the way.

"They're just dopey because I'm thinking about you," I answered, tugging on her hand to pull her into the seat next to me.

We were going to take off soon, and I knew we would need to be buckled in.

"Ready to go to . . ." she asked, expectantly looking at me.

"Oh, no. I'm not telling you now. I haven't planned and plotted this long to screw it all up in the last inning."

"Fine." She folded her arms across her chest, and her lips jutted out into a ridiculous pout.

I shook my head, leaning back to close my eyes, as we waited to take off.

She'd forgive me once we landed.

I hoped.

I usually found plane rides uneventful and dull, just endless hours to fill with mindless nothingness. I'd try to work, but I'd never manage to get anything accomplish. I'd pick up a book but get annoyed by the snoopy person next to me who felt the need to read over my shoulder or talk about how he or she had just read and loved something similar. The movie selection was always horrible, and I was a picky sleeper, never able to find the correct position to drift away for a few precious hours of the flight.

But that was all before I'd found the perks of having Lailah with me . . . on a private plane.

Now that I had, I didn't think we'd ever fly commercial again.

Nope, I was officially spoiled.

After a breakfast fit for a king, I proposed we head to the bedroom for a nap. My eyebrows might have suggestively waggled a tad. Lailah looked at me before her eyes quickly darted to the flight attendant as she cleaned up our dishes.

Trained to remain invisible unless acknowledged, Brie was used to attending to rock stars and billionaire businessmen. I was sure the wealth of secrets she had locked away was endless and worth a fortune. But being the professional she was, she remained quiet and courteous, disappearing in the back to finish her duties.

"Oh my gosh! Now, she knows we're going to be in there . . . you know!"

"No, I don't know. Could you be a little more descriptive, Lailah?" I grinned, leaning back in my chair.

"You suck!" she declared, swiftly rising from her seat to pace across the room.

"Oh, come on! She's probably seen it all—and then ten times worse than that. She flies with celebrities. We're probably the most boring flight she's been on in decades. We need to go in there and have loud monkey sex just to liven things up a bit for her."

Lailah turned, blankly looking at me. "You've got to be kidding me."

"About what? The celebrities? No, I'm dead serious. I think Maroon Five was in here last week."

Her mouth gaped for a minute before she shook her head.

"No, you dork! Not the celebrities—although we're coming back to that. You seriously just suggested we have sex . . . for our stewardess?"

I laughed. This was fun. "I don't think the PC term is *stewardess* anymore. I believe they are called *flight attendants* now."

"I'm going to kill you."

"With sex?" I grinned. I jumped from my seat to stalk toward her.

"No, I'm thinking bare hands right now," she answered. She tried to show anger, but all that came through was a dorky smile.

"All I got from that sentence was *bare,* so I'm assuming you agree to the sex."

Her eyes went wide as I stood in front of her. Both of us were primed for attack, but we waited for the other to take the first move.

"What? Jude, no!"

I beat her, bending forward and swiftly hoisting her over my shoulder. It was a bit of a crazy move for a plane in the middle of a flight, but whatever. She was playing difficult, and I had plans—and only four more hours of airtime to execute them.

WELL, *THAT* DEFINITELY hadn't been on my list.

But if it had, I'd be checking *Become a member of the mile-high club* off at this very moment.

I was pretty sure we'd obtained some frequent-flier miles as well.

Wowza.

I shook my head, chuckling under my breath. I shut the water off and stepped out of the shower.

Who takes a shower on a plane?

Well, I just did!

When Jude had woken me up before the crack of dawn this morning, I'd figured it was because we had some ridiculously early commercial flight to catch—probably first-class, knowing Jude. I'd thought I'd be stuck sitting next to some businessman who huffed and puffed every five seconds about one thing or another while the rich kid behind me kicked my chair. I hadn't flown much, but I'd watched a lot of movies and TV, so between my few experiences and vast knowledge of how media depicted airline travel, this was how I'd expected our day to go.

Movies hadn't prepared me for reality.

Heck, reality hadn't prepared me for this.

Who rents a private jet to fly two people to . . . well, wherever we are going?

My husband—that's who.

I'd met him as a nursing assistant who had little to nothing and watched him grow into Jude Cavanaugh, heir to a financial dynasty, yet he hadn't changed—not where it mattered.

Back in the days when he had worn scrubs and checked vitals for a living, he still would have given me anything.

He had actually.

He'd brought me pudding cups during every lunch break he had. When I had been sick, he'd even taken unpaid days off to stay in my room and nurse me back to health even though others had tried to kick him out. And when the insurance company had turned me down, he had given up everything to get my new heart.

Today, he wasn't any different. Money hadn't changed him. I guessed it just allowed him more resources and ways to channel that need to constantly provide. He always said his father had been a great provider. Maybe that was where Jude had gotten the unwavering drive.

I just didn't want to see the money change me. I never wanted to be the type of person to expect a certain way of life. If we were fortunate enough to live like this for the next twenty years, I hoped stepping onto a private plane would always bring a sense of wonder and never dull in my eyes.

I was just finishing blow-drying my hair when a knock came on the bathroom door.

I opened it and found Jude's handsome face staring back at me.

"We're going to land soon. You almost ready?"

Excitement sprang forward as I realized I'd finally discover the spot of our mystery honeymoon location.

"Yes, let me just repack some things."

I turned, but his hand quickly grabbed my wrist, halting me mid-step. Before I had the chance to ask what he was doing, his mouth engulfed mine, quick and hard, before he walked away.

I was nearly dizzy.

I stumbled back into the bathroom before throwing things into my toiletries bag. I brushed through my hair one final time. A quick glance in the mirror told me I looked adequate, so I headed back out and joined Jude.

A sly grin adorned his face as I slid down next to him.

"What?" I asked, wondering why he appeared so smug.

"Remember after the third or fourth orgasm, you said something about being so out of breath that your throat was going dry?"

My mind replayed to our time in the tiny airplane bedroom. He'd tasked himself with determining just how many times I could orgasm in a row. After four, I'd moaned and writhed so much that my throat was nearly raw. He still hadn't shown me mercy.

"Yes," I replied.

He produced a bottle of water from his jacket and handed it to me as I looked at him with questioning eyes.

"It's from Brie, our flight attendant. She told me to give it to you."

Blood rushed up to my cheeks as I contemplated the likelihood of my survival rate if I jumped out of the plane now. I must have sat there too long because Jude finally broke the silence with a boisterous deep laugh.

"I'm kidding. I asked for it before you went into the shower. She'd never do such a thing."

My breath began to return to normal as I shot laser beams into him with my eyes.

"Even if you were louder than a banshee."

"So mean," I said, unable to stop the laughter that was bubbling up.

"So, you forgive me?" he asked, taking my hand in his.

"No."

"What if I told you to turn your head and look out the window?"

My eyes widened, realizing we'd already begun our initial descent while he had been busy with distracting me. It had probably been his plan all along.

As I whipped my head around, I saw it for the first time.

I still had no idea what *it* was, but from above, I was already in love.

Covered in snow and ice, it looked like he'd taken us to the North Pole itself. Tiny colored houses dotted the landscape. It was so unlike anything I'd seen in the US.

"Where are we?" I asked, turning back to see him hunched forward, peering out below.

"Iceland."

"Oh my gosh, Jude!" I hugged him, hating the awkward armrest separating us.

"It's only our first stop—of many," he said against my shoulder.

"There's more?"

"Well, you don't think I'm keeping you here for three weeks? You'd freeze."

I laughed a giddy, happy laugh, nearly clapping my hands together like a child, as I leaned forward to watch the scenery grow bigger and bigger. It was someplace I'd never even imagined going.

"Why Iceland?" I asked, looking out at the vast mountains.

"Well, it's simple really. I used logic when picking all the destinations for this trip. You have your Someday List. You created it and believed that, someday, if you ever got out of the hospital, you'd accomplish all these things to make you *normal,* and I think we've been doing a damn good job of knocking some things off of that list—even if we've waned in our attempt recently. But for this trip, I didn't want you to feel normal. We can go back to finding you a mortgage or flagging down taxis when we get back. There will be nothing normal about this trip. For the next three weeks, we're going crazy."

"Starting with a trip to Iceland," I stated excitedly.

"Yeah. Why not? How many people do you know who have been to Iceland?"

"None."

"Exactly. Get ready, Lailah. For the next few days, we're exploring the land of fire and ice."

Iceland was well named.

As soon as we deplaned, I was slapped in the face with arctic temperatures that New York had yet to reach this winter. It wasn't nearly as cold as I had assumed based on the snowy scenery I saw when flying in. It reminded me of some of the more chilly nights I'd experienced since moving to the East Coast when temperatures had dropped and our heaters had worked overtime. I honestly wouldn't be surprised if the Midwest was just as cold as it was here.

Note to self: Never move to the Midwest.

Jude and I huddled together as our luggage was pulled from below the plane and transferred to the car taking us to the hotel. We had landed in Reykjavík, the capital of Iceland, but Jude said our hotel was a bit farther down the coast, away from the city.

The driver greeted us with a nod and wave before opening the doors, so we could quickly hop inside. He joined us, sitting in the front and sliding down the partition.

"Hello, welcome to Iceland," he greeted in his thick Icelandic accent.

"Thank you!" we both responded.

"Sorry for the cold. It's supposed to warm up tomorrow if you're wishing to explore."

"That's good to hear," I said, rubbing my mittens together as I wondered what *warm* meant to Icelanders.

I'd thought Jude had requested Grace to buy the winter gear as a joke to throw me off from the real destination, but it had turned out that I really needed it after all. Now, I wondered about the bikini. *Was that a ruse? Or would I need that eventually as well?*

Silently, I watched the country pass by as Jude and the driver spoke. I passively listened, hearing their conversation, as the mountains and sea whipped passed my window.

Car rides had been such an infrequent thing for me as a child. I remember spending them with my face glued to the glass, peering out at the world as it whooshed by. At stoplights, I'd see other children, heads down, glued to a portable video game or a book, and I'd wonder why they weren't as interested in what was going on around them.

It wasn't until I was older when I'd realized that, after a while, those kids had grown bored and complacent with what life had to show them through a car window.

So far, I hadn't lost that childlike wonder that I'd so tightly held on to since I was little, and I hoped I never would.

"Be sure you visit the Blue Lagoon," I heard the driver say.

"Like the movie?" I interjected, my mind suddenly filled with visions of a half-naked Brooke Shields stuck on a deserted island.

"It is a natural spa and very good for the skin," he said, patting his cheek to add emphasis to his words.

"Is it outside?" I asked, remembering our brisk walk to the car. Being outside in forty layers of clothing sounded fine. *But a string bikini? Not so much.*

"Yes, but the water is very hot. You must try it."

Jude gave me a challenging look, and I just shrugged.

"You only live once, right?"

He laughed. "That's what all the T-shirts say."

Like everywhere we'd stayed, the hotel was beautiful. Endless coastal views with an upscale-cabin feel reminded me of a secluded mountain lodge. I hoped to spend some time wandering around our suite, admiring the waves as they crashed just outside below our balcony window, but Jude seemed to have other plans.

"We have dinner reservations in an hour," he said, sliding his hands around my waist.

"Really?" I nearly whined. "Can't we just order in?"

"Nope."

Turning, I looked up at him, trying to gauge what was going on in that head of his. "Why?"

"Just because." He shrugged, feigning indifference, but I could see the hint of edginess it carried. "I thought it would be nice to spend the first evening of our honeymoon out. That's all."

Liar.

He was excited and perhaps a bit nervous about something.

Unwilling to foil any plans he might have, I played along. "Okay. I guess I'd better get ready then."

Glad I'd taken a shower on the plane, I grabbed my makeup bag and headed for the bathroom to begin sprucing myself up for an evening out. I unzipped the small case, pulling out foundation and a tube of mascara. Eye shadow and lipstick were set on the counter as well. Like a little girl playing with her mother's makeup for the first time, I always felt a slight thrill whenever I applied it. It was a tiny reminder of independence, of how far my life had come.

I'd never forget.

After fifteen minutes or so, I no longer looked like the tired, jet-lagged version I'd arrived as, and I moved on to tackle my hair. Since I'd blown it dry on the plane, it was mostly straight, hanging down my back with little fuss. Grabbing the curling iron and the wonky plug adaptor, I let it heat up, and I moved to the closet where I'd hung a few dresses after we arrived.

Smiling, I pulled one off the hanger, remembering Grace's reaction when I'd held it out for consideration. Her eyes had bugged out of her head as she held up two thumbs in approval.

It was a bit more risqué than my normal style, but the soft green color was what had initially garnered my attention. After holding it to my body in front of the full-length mirror, I knew it would drive Jude insane.

Nearly skipping back to the bathroom, enthused now by the prospect of Jude seeing me in my devilish dress, I hung it over the shower door and began curling my long locks of hair. The iron was wide, so it left loose wavy tendrils to frame my face and shoulders. Suddenly, my flat, lifeless blonde mass of hair was full and sexy.

Now, all I needed was the dress and a killer pair of shoes.

Shoot, I forgot to grab my shoes.

Still fully dressed in my drab plane clothes, I tiptoed out of the bathroom, hoping I wouldn't see Jude before I had a chance to finish my look. It might be silly, but even after the day most women considered their prettiest day, I still wanted to wow him over and over, and that meant not letting him see me until I was completely ready.

Sexy hair and makeup combined with frumpy clothes wasn't the look I was going for.

Besides, didn't I read somewhere that marriage was all about keeping the spark alive?

Okay, maybe I was jumping ahead of myself, but I still wanted to see his face hit the floor.

I made it to the closet without a hint of my handsome husband. Feeling triumphant, I bent down and picked up a pair of peep-toe nude heels. I turned to make a mad dash back toward the seclusion of the bathroom.

I halted mid-step and froze.

Out of the corner of my eye, I caught a glimpse of him. Obviously still in the middle of getting ready, his shirt was hanging over a nearby chair and he was wearing nothing but a pair of dress pants. He'd casually slung his mint green tie over his neck and was kneeling against the inside railing of the windows overlooking the ocean. With a bottle of water in his hand, he slowly sipped it. He was stoic and calm, peaceful . . . beautiful.

Mine.

The shoes dropped to the floor, and I went to him like a moth to a flame. Suddenly, I didn't care about grand entrances or perfect moments. I just wanted this moment, all the moments.

His breath hitched as my cold fingers touched his bare skin, but he immediately greeted me with his own tender touch.

"What are you doing?" I asked, resting my head against his back.

"Enjoying the view," he answered, turning toward me with a warm grin.

"I love you," I found myself saying, almost as if I needed to hear the words once again.

"I love you, too, more than anything."

"Oh! Oh my gosh! Did you see that?" I exclaimed, my eyes bugging out of my head at the faint green light fluttering over the water.

I jumped, nearly taking off Jude's head, as he turned to see what I was screaming about.

"There it is again!" I yelped, pointing.

He laughed, shaking his head in disbelief. "So much for dinner."

"What? What do you mean?" I asked, unable to take my eyes off of the mesmerizing green-blue pattern swirling across the water.

"I did a crazy amount of research, figuring out when and where the Northern Lights appeared. It's why I chose this hotel. It's supposed to have a great view when the weather and time of year is just right. So, I booked us dinner, hoping it would happen then."

I snickered a bit. "You scheduled our dinner around Mother Nature?"

He laughed. "Okay, when you put it that way, it sounds a bit stupid."

"I was wondering why you were so nervous. You were scared it wouldn't happen."

He nodded.

"You should know, as well as I do, that life is a big box of uncertainties. The best things in life are never planned."

Pulling me into his arms, we looked out into the night sky, watching with wonder.

"You've never been more right."

I didn't know how long we stayed there, admiring nature's magnificent display. Dinner reservations and green dresses had been completely forgotten until my stomach began to rumble.

Jude laughed, turning me slightly so that our eyes met. "Want to order room service?"

"Maybe later," I answered, pulling him closer.

Have you ever made love under the glow of the Northern Lights?

I have.

sixteen

Toes, Sand, and Sea

Jude

NEARLY THREE WEEKS had passed.

Three weeks had been filled with laughter, love, and endless adventures.

Ever since that day in the hospital when Lailah had read to me about wanting to stick her toes in the ocean, I'd known that making every dream and wish on that Someday List of hers come true would become my life mission.

Giving her so much beyond that was just icing on the cake.

We'd spent the last two years of our lives slowly ticking away at that list—from sitting in a parking lot as I'd tried to teach her to drive all the way down to taking a hayride and carving pumpkins. I never wanted her to miss out on life again.

But now, in these few precious weeks, where life had paused and nothing else mattered but the two of us and the new rings on our fingers, I wanted her to know just how extraordinary and big this world was.

We'd started in Iceland, climbing mountains, exploring ice caves, and yes, even swimming in the Blue Lagoon. We'd spent five magical days in the Arctic before packing up and flying south for something a bit warmer.

It was then when I'd introduced her to the secluded Seychelles Islands.

When we'd landed and I'd told her where we were, she'd looked at me, quirked an eyebrow, and said, "Where?"

I'd laughed, loving that I'd finally stumped her.

As her eyes had settled on the heavenly tropical views, she'd suddenly not cared where we were, and she'd just fallen in love. Located in the Indian Ocean, the Seychelles were known for their nearly flawless, untouched beauty. It was exactly the type of place I'd envisioned for our second stop.

We'd spent seven days under the warm heat, lounging on the beach, swimming in the ocean, and enjoying the never-ending views from our private pool. We'd even had our own version of Christmas right there in the middle of nowhere, exchanging gifts, after we'd decorated a tiny palm tree and danced naked to holiday music in our cabana.

It was a hard place to leave. But I believed sheer curiosity had played its part in getting her on the plane that day as we'd said our farewells, and soon, we had been flying to our last destination—Santorini, Greece.

Steeped in history, this hillside city looked like something out of a storybook. Thick white houses made from clay dotted the landscape so perfectly that it was as if someone had come along and painted them there. Every building, it seemed, had sweeping views of the sea, and I just couldn't get enough.

Kneeling against the stucco railing of our balcony, I continued to stare out, watching the sun slowly set beneath the water's edge. I didn't know how long I'd been there, admiring the distant islands and lingering clouds. Every tourist website and travel book had boasted about the beautiful Santorini summers. With clear skies and beautiful beaches, it was a vacationer's paradise, but during the winter, things cooled down, and so did the weather.

To me, the idea of having a little slice of Greece nearly to ourselves sounded like perfection.

And so far, it had been.

"Watching the water again?" she said, seconds before her head gently rested against my shoulder.

"I just can't seem to get enough of it. I think this is my favorite place," I admitted as the pink sky turned purple.

"You've said that about all three," she replied.

I felt her cheek tighten into a smile.

"Really?"

"Yep. Every time I've found you like this, staring out at the waves, you tell me how much you love the view and how it couldn't get better than this."

"Maybe I'm just really good at planning vacations." I smirked.

"I think the water calms you. Is it any wonder you planned an entire honeymoon that revolved around it?"

I opened my mouth but stopped. Turning, I saw her smiling smugly.

"See?"

"Actually," I retorted, "I did do that on purpose but for a completely different reason."

"Oh, and what's that?" she asked, playfully lifting her chin, as she wrapped her small arms around my waist.

"Because I wanted to see you put your toes in the water, again and again, in as many places as possible."

Her eyes went wide. A look of pure adoration swept across her face as she breathed me in.

With a purposeful tug, she pulled me toward the bedroom, and I willingly followed.

"I thought you wanted to take a walk," I reminded her.

"No."

Her body swayed with a sure rhythm to her steps.

"Find a place to eat?" I added.

"Uh-uh," she replied.

Her eyes turned back to mine as we entered the dark room, now filled with nothing but the last lingering rays of daytime.

"You sure?" I asked softly with absolutely no intention of going anywhere.

Stepping in close enough, I could feel her soft breath against my neck, and I let her presence engulf me.

"Yes."

Her lips touched the bare skin of my collarbone as she slowly unbuttoned my shirt, exposing new bits and pieces of me to devour.

I watched her for hours, days, it seemed as she took her time worshiping every inch, kissing and licking a heated path along my flesh that filled me with desire until I was nearly drowning in it.

She'd stripped me bare, in every sense of the word, and now, I planned on returning the favor.

She was wearing a simple sweater and leggings, and I easily undressed her, taking my time with each piece of fabric like I was seeing her for the first time.

Each time felt just like that first time—exhilarating, new, wondrous.

My heart still fluttered and faltered at the mere sight of her naked skin. My chest would constrict whenever I felt our bodies join, and a lump in my throat, heavy with emotions, would form as she called my name over and over, knowing I'd be the only man to ever hear her cries of passion.

Arching her back, I gently lowered her to the bed—kissing her shoulders, stomach, and hips—as I ventured down her lean long body. She squirmed in anticipation, aware the instant my mouth hovered around her upper thighs what my intention was.

"Please," she begged, her voice breathy and low.

"Take control," I urged, loving how fierce she'd been on our wedding night.

"With words?" she asked, sounding a little doubtful.

Bedroom talk always made Lailah a bit squeamish.

"Words work. Hell, you could direct my damn head if you want. It's your rodeo. I just want to see the powerful woman I married. But after this, I'm taking control again," I warned with a cocky grin.

Her indecisiveness turned more and more decisive as the idea developed in her mind. Finally, her expression grew determined as her eyes narrowed in on me like I was her prey for the evening. Her tongue darted out, sweeping across her lips, and sure enough, my cock responded, hardening in length, as I watched.

My palms twitched, and my mouth ached to do something, anything, as I waited for her instructions. I needed to touch her. Every second was agony until her hand finally reached out, grasping my hair to guide me forward.

Knowing the idea of giving instructions probably made her nervous and uncomfortable, I decided to go easy on her. Plus, the idea of holding out any longer was out of the question.

With both hands wrapped around her thighs, I spread her wider as she pulled me closer. With her body opened like a fucking Christmas present, I didn't hold back, knowing exactly how she liked it.

Her cries tore through the silence of the bedroom, spurring my frantic motions further. As her moans grew deeper, my tongue moved faster, harder, sucking and lapping her sweet taste, until she was nearly writhing off the bed. She detonated beneath me, coming apart in pieces, while I felt each quake and tremor of her orgasm against my mouth.

Raw need consumed me as I dragged out each endless spasm to its fatal end, extending her pleasure for as long as possible. I wanted to take her, staking my claim and consuming her, but my need to protect her always outweighed everything else. Rising from the bed, I reached for the nightstand but felt her hand steady me.

"Just one night, please."

My eyebrows furrowed as I stared down at her in the growing moonlight.

"Let me just feel you, feel us, for one night."

My head shook back and forth, giving my answer, before the word even left my lips. "No, Lailah. I can't." I hated denying her anything.

She sat up as she folded her arms across her chest.

Reaching down, I clasped her chin in my palm, tilting her head upward. "I love you, more than anything in this world, Lailah, and as you can see, I would give you anything to make you happy . . . but not this. Please don't ask this of me."

Her eyes rounded as understanding replaced doubt, and finally, she nodded.

Reaching toward the drawer, I pulled out a condom and tore off the wrapper without breaking eye contact. "Let me keep you safe."

Pushing her back on the bed, I knew, no matter what, I'd always keep her safe no matter what life threw at us.

"Do we really have to go back?" Lailah asked.

We packed up the last of the luggage and took one final look at the vibrant blue Aegean Sea. It was a perfect cloudless day, the kind where the view seemed limitless and you could see exactly why mythical creatures and gods had been created in a location like this.

Sometimes, there were places on earth that truly felt divine, where being amongst them felt like we were intruding on someplace above our station. Santorini and every other place we'd visited on this honeymoon were exactly like that. Being there, experiencing it, felt as if a slice of heaven had dropped down to earth, and we had accidentally stumbled upon it.

We were incredibly lucky to have such places around us to discover. I only hoped I would be able to take my own angel to visit each of them.

"I'm afraid so. We have to return to reality sometime." I took her hand and grabbed one of our suitcases.

We turned toward the door, and I saw her take one glance around the room before heading out.

We'd come back. I'd make sure of it.

Her attitude was bleak by the time we arrived at the tarmac and boarded the plane.

The wedding, the honeymoon—all of it was over.

I smiled warmly, realizing it was probably a normal reaction every woman had, and I tried not to take it personally. The last year had been spent getting ready for those precious moments down the aisle, and when those were done, we'd had three weeks of vacation to spend in each other's arms. Now, it was time to go back home, back to school, and back to work.

"Hey, you do remember we still have the holidays to celebrate when we get back, right?" I reminded her, wagering that tidbit of information had gotten lost in her post-honeymoon depression.

Her eyes perked up, and they met mine.

"Oh! I totally forgot about that!"

"And I might have also forgotten to mention that your parents are flying in!"

Her gasp of surprise was followed with a squeal of joy as she threw her arms around me and kissed my cheek.

"That's the best news I've heard all day!"

"Well, it is only ten in the morning," I joked.

"I guess I'd better go Christmas shopping when we get back!" she exclaimed merrily.

And there was my girl again, happy and thrilled to be going home. She'd just needed a jump-start.

Now, I had to make a few calls and figure out how to get her parents on a plane—pronto.

seventeen

A Late Christmas Gift

Lailah

WE'D HIT THE ground running the minute the plane had landed.

School had started back up, business meetings had been scheduled, and family had arrived for our after-Christmas Christmas celebration. As much as I missed the quiet of just the two of us tucked away in our secluded honeymoon hideouts, I had to admit, it had been nice coming home. Five-star luxury just couldn't top the sheer comfort of falling into our own bed again. And even though I hadn't spent as much time with my new husband, there was something to be said about seeing him back in his routine. As much as it sometimes seemed to stress him out , this job—his family's legacy—really was his calling. I could see it in the way he presented himself to employees, the passion he carried in his words, and the details he put into each and every single action.

Plus, the return of his three-piece suit hadn't hurt.

Nope, not at all.

It had taken days, but I'd finally finished unpacking everything from our honeymoon. Clothes had been put away, mementos and trinkets had been stored and put on display, and the few gifts I'd bought had been wrapped and stored under the tree until tonight when we'd leave for Jude's mother's country estate.

The rest of the gifts, I'd purchased earlier in the day, doing a quick after-Christmas splurge.

Last-minute shopper? Me? No way.

Or at least, I usually wasn't, but I'd had this little thing called a wedding—not to mention, four finals, all of which I'd aced—distracting me from the daunting task of buying presents for my now very large family.

It used to be just my mother and me, and now, I had an entire family to buy for.

I smiled, looking down at the large pile of presents under the tree, reminding me of all the people I was blessed to have in my life.

"You ready to go?" Jude called out from the bedroom. Walking down the hallway, he appeared in a pair of dark jeans and a gray sweater.

"Yes, we just need to pack the presents."

He looked down at them—all of them—and huffed, "Okay."

I laughed at his reluctance and bent down to begin helping. A wave of nausea hit me suddenly, and I froze, waiting for it to pass. It was the second occurrence today, and I wondered if I was possibly coming down with something. A couple of students in my morning class had been out, and the teacher had mentioned a bug was going around campus. Luckily, Jude hadn't noticed my misstep, so I proceeded to shuffle packages his way as the queasiness began to fade. I didn't want to miss tonight, especially since my parents had flown in just for it. I could get the stomach flu tomorrow.

Not today. I sent that mental warning to my brain, hoping it would hold things together for at least a few hours so that I could play Santa for my family.

They had graciously held off on celebrating Christmas this year, so Jude and I could extend our honeymoon through the New Year.

"All set?" he asked.

He slung the two large bags over his shoulder like a modern-day Kris Kringle—a really hot one.

I smiled, trying to rid the naughty thoughts from my head, and just nodded.

"You're picturing me as Santa, aren't you?"

"Totally am."

"That's a little creepy."

"You asked." I laughed.

"Come on. Let's go deliver these and see our family."

The drive seemed never-ending as I anxiously sat in the passenger side of the car, watching the busy city slowly give way to rolling hills and sleepy houses. The sky appeared, making its presence known with an abundance of twinkling stars. Stars were such a rarity in the city—always outshined by the bright lights and the tall, towering buildings. Here, in the country, where things were a bit simpler—one could sit back and enjoy what nature had created.

New York was an amazing place to live. Each day was slightly different from the day before even if you'd set out with the intention to do the same dull old thing. That was what I loved about it—the sense of adventure that was always lying in wait, ready to sweep me off my heels and show me something new. It was never dull, never boring.

But there were times when I would grow restless, tired of the noise and the incessant rush.

One day, I knew we'd eventually leave the city and settle someplace less hectic, more peaceful—maybe a place that reminded Jude of the calm quiet of Iceland or the serene beauty of the Seychelles or perhaps somewhere that encompassed the beauty he'd fallen so madly in love with in Santorini.

I'd nearly traveled the world now with Jude by my side. We'd lived on either side of the country—the laid-back beach life of California and the unyielding business world of New York—and it all boiled down to this. It didn't matter where we were, here or across the world in a foreign land.

As long as we were together, we were always home.

The car shifted slightly as Jude pulled off the main road before pushing the code to enter the gate. The first time I'd visited the country estate Jude's family owned, I'd been intimidated, seeing the large wrought iron gate that gave way to a tree-lined pathway. But as we'd driven, Jude had begun telling me stories of his childhood. He'd pointed out the places he used to hide and the gardens he'd helped his mother tend. He'd shared how one summer, long ago, he and Roman had thought it would be a good idea to go bike riding together—using only one bike. He'd gotten paper in a grueling rock-paper-scissors match, and since Roman's scissor had cut his paper, Jude had been the lucky one to ride on the handlebars.

"I would think he would have wanted to do that?" I asked.

"And risk his pretty face? No way," he answered, looking doubtful.

"So, what happened?"

"Well, we were riding up and down this very road, having a blast, until we hit a rock or a ditch. I can't remember. All I know is, we went down—hard. I got road burn like you wouldn't believe. The curse words that flew out of Roman's preadolescent mouth were impressive even then."

I couldn't help but laugh, and I waited for him to continue.

"I tried to get up but realized my foot was wedged in the bicycle spokes. Roman looked down and panicked, screaming that Mom was going to kill us."

"What did he do?" I asked.

"Left me," he answered, a smug grin on his face.

"He did not!"

"Oh, he did. Left me right there in the middle of the road. But to his credit, he went to get help, so I forgave him—for that, at least."

"Boys," I said, shaking my head.

"They're the worst."

After hearing his harrowing stories and adventures here as a boy, the big mountain of a house hadn't felt so dominating anymore, and I'd eased into the warmth and homey-feeling Jude's mother had infused into the dwelling over the years. Even my own mother, who had spent the majority of her life living in apartments less than a thousand square feet, had found the house charming and wonderful.

She was the first person I saw when we entered the living room, and my heart soared. I hadn't realized just how much I'd missed her.

"Hi, Mom," I said softly.

She held out her arms, touching me, as her eyes swept over my features. "You're so tan!" she exclaimed. She sucked in a laugh as she pulled me toward her.

"Not really," I answered. "Maybe a little less pale?"

"Well, you look beautiful, whatever it is."

We finished our reunion, and my attention quickly turned to Marcus, who was patiently waiting his turn. He held up his arm, the sleeve rolled up to his elbow, and he compared our skin tones. His Latino blood mixed with his love for surfing made me look like a ghost.

"See, Mom? Definitely not tan."

We all joined in a round of chuckles as Marcus pulled me into his arms.

"Good to see you, kid. We've missed you."

"Did you get my postcards?" I asked them both.

"Oh, yes. One actually arrived on Christmas Eve, the one from Iceland. Did you really see the Northern Lights?" my mother asked.

We sat down on the couch.

I nodded, catching Jude's grin, as he finished adding our presents to the pile under the massive Christmas tree that was still up just for us. Then, he sat with us on the couch. Jude's mother entered, greeting everyone, and soon, we were all chatting away about the honeymoon adventures abroad.

"Where's Roman?" I asked, realizing I hadn't seen his car out front when we arrived.

"He called and said he was running late, but he should be here in time for desserts and presents," Jude's mother answered.

I saw Jude's face go flat as he tried to restrain his opinion. My hands went to his and squeezed. I knew he was constantly being let down by his brother, but someday, I knew Roman would figure it all out—or at least, I hoped.

"Speaking of desserts, I just need to do a few things in the kitchen to finish up the cake I made," my mom announced, rising from her spot on the couch.

"And I'll work on appetizers," Mrs. Cavanaugh said, following her out.

"Mind if I go help them?" I asked the remaining men.

Jude and Marcus looked longingly at the TV, shaking their heads with enthusiasm, and I tried not to giggle. As I headed off to the kitchen, I heard the TV turn on and then something about a football game and debates on what channel it was on.

Our mothers were in the midst of a pleasant conversation about cooking when I arrived, both of them happily working on their designated tasks.

"Can I help with something?" I asked, looking around as I pushed up my sleeves.

"Sure. Why don't you come over here and help with the appetizers?" Jude's mother suggested, ushering me with a hand motion over to where she was preparing a platter of cheeses and fruits.

My stomach suddenly rolled, and my head spun. I grabbed the edge of the counter to steady myself.

My mom's tender touch was there in seconds. "Lailah, are you all right?" she asked, swiping her hand across my forehead.

Shaking my head to ease her panic, I answered, "I think I'm just coming down with a stomach bug . . . or maybe a mild flu."

"Nothing is mild when it comes to you. Does Jude know?" she asked, taking my hand to guide me toward the breakfast nook.

I took a seat while she went to a cabinet to grab a glass for water.

"No, I haven't told him. I know he wouldn't have let me come tonight, and I didn't want to miss out on anything."

She gave me a stern look. "You know we would have understood."

"But you came so far," I said as guilt washed over me.

Her soft heels clicked as she walked back to me and took the adjacent seat.

Jude's mother joined us as well, her hands wrapped firmly around a cup of tea she'd been nursing. "Keeping you healthy is more important than anything else, Lailah," she said, reaching out with her warm hands.

"And we can't do that if you don't help us," my mother added, scooting the glass of water forward.

I took a small sip, feeling the cool liquid coat my throat, and it eased the tension in my stomach. "You're right. I'm sorry. I'll tell Jude and make an appointment with my doctor first thing in the morning. I just didn't want him to freak out."

His mother smiled softly. "Oh, sweetheart, that's his job."

"Of all the days for my brother to bail on me," Jude huffed, running around the room, trying to get dressed as quickly as possible.

He'd hoped to have a few hours free this morning, so he could be with me for my doctor's appointment.

After telling him on the way home about my less than stellar appetite and the illness that was going around school, he had been ready to swing by the ER on the way to our apartment, but I'd managed to talk him out of it, and we'd both settled on a call to the doctor in the morning as long as he could be in attendance for the appointment.

Just the idea of me being sick made him jumpy, nervous, and downright snippy.

He'd called his secretary moments after my appointment was made, knowing his schedule was fairly clear, to let her know he would be in late, only to find out Roman had called in moments earlier to do the same thing.

Thirteen unanswered calls later, Jude was thrashing around the room, throwing a shirt and tie on, swearing under his breath, and most likely, imagining every way possible to inflict bodily harm to his older brother. He'd even considered taking an elevator ride up to his floor but figured Roman wouldn't answer.

"I can reschedule," I suggested, watching from the bed, as he ran around in frustration.

He stopped dead in his tracks and turned to me, his tie askew, as he was attempting to buckle his pants. "No, absolutely not. I'd rather have the doctor see you as early as possible without me than wait for a later appointment just so I could attend. I'll be fine. I'm more annoyed with Roman than anything."

Placing both feet on the floor, I stood, feeling a little better than I had the night before. I secretly wondered if I even needed to go now that I was feeling fine, but there was no getting out of it since Jude knew.

"You need to let your annoyance with him go," I urged, taking the few steps forward until our bodies met.

"I wish I could."

"You can. Just stop fixating on all his flaws, and focus on the good parts."

"There are good things about Roman?" His eyebrow rose.

"He brought me here, didn't he?" I challenged, sliding my hand up the back of his shirt until I found warm skin.

"Yes, he did. That's a debt I'll never be able to repay." He smiled warily.

"And he didn't leave you in that street all those years ago," I reminded him.

"It wasn't like it was a public street," he retorted, chuckling, before bending down to tenderly kiss my mouth. "Are you sure you're going to be all right without me?" he asked, our lips still nearly touching.

"I'll manage." I said. "Finish getting ready. I'm going to hop in the shower."

"Yet another reason to hate my brother this morning," he said gruffly, watching me, as I turned toward the shower.

"Let it go!" I hollered from the bathroom.

"Are you naked?" he asked.

My nightgown dropped to the floor, and I laughed. "Yes!"

"Then, I still hate him!"

"Go to work!" I yelled, giggling. I turned the faucet toward hot and waited.

Life couldn't get more perfect than this.

The wind hit me like a punch to the face as I exited the cab, making my way into the hospital where my doctor's office was located. When I'd moved from Southern California, Marcus had made sure I would be in good hands. It wasn't quite the same as having my uncle, now stepfather, care for me, but Dr. Hough was a close second.

As I stepped through the glass doors, I suddenly felt uneasy. The familiar scent of bleach and chemicals filled my nostrils, reminding me of my childhood spent in similar washed-out hallways and drab rooms.

I nearly turned around, the single piece of toast I'd managed to eat that morning feeling like a lumpy ball in the pit of my stomach.

Why hadn't I brought someone with me?

Why did I feel like something bad was about to happen?

A nurse walked past me, wheeling a patient in a gurney. An IV was hanging from a pole at the top of the bed, reminding me of the countless surgeries and procedures I'd had over the years. My fingers immediately went to the top of my chest, etching out the scar that I bore from the many hardships I'd endured, the many battles I'd won to get here.

Feeling a bit more confident, I moved swiftly, stepping eagerly toward the elevator that would carry me to the correct floor. I knew every visit to a hospital would bring back memories—good ones and bad ones. Today was just a visit into the dark days, and it was something I needed to move past—quickly.

Nothing is wrong, I reminded myself.

That is all over now, I chanted in my head.

Everything is perfect, I silently screamed.

The elevator dinged, and I nearly jumped. A woman standing next to me held out her hand, urging me to go first. Her warm smile calmed me as I went on my way, down the hall toward the correct suite number. Pushing the door open, I took a deep breath and tried to center myself.

Everything was fine. The air inside was less harsh, giving off a more pleasant aroma, and I felt the muscles in my shoulders relax slightly from just this tiniest adjustment.

Logically, I knew I was still in the hospital, but mentally, it suddenly felt less intimidating. I signed in before relaxing in a comfy chair in the waiting room I'd grown accustomed to, and I pulled out my phone to read, feeling my panic fall away like the leaves on a blustery autumn day.

Soon, I was called back, and after my weight and blood pressure had been checked, the nurse began writing down my other vitals.

"So, what brings you in today, Lailah? We didn't expect you for another few days," she said pleasantly as she cradled my wrist to find my pulse.

"I haven't been feeling all that well for the last two days, and I figured, better safe than sorry, I guess. So, I decided to come in early. I could have gone and seen my primary doctor, but—"

Her hand covered mine. "No need. We're here when you need us. You know that. Now, tell me what kind of symptoms you've been having, and we'll go from there."

I went over the bouts of nausea and the weak and tired feeling I'd been having.

"Classes have started back up, and it's flu season." She sighed. "I'll go check with Dr. Hough, but we'll probably do a few tests to check for a variety of infections."

I nodded as she finished typing a few things into the laptop before making her exit.

My feet dangled beneath me as I shifted around on the uncomfortable exam table. The sound of paper crinkling beneath me took care of the awkward silence as my erratic breath whooshed in and out of my lungs.

Flu. That's not terrible. I could deal with that.

A few missed classes. Maybe a week if it's really bad, and then everything would be back to normal.

My thoughts were interrupted by the sound of a knock. The nurse reappeared with several items in her hands.

"Okay, I managed to catch Dr. Hough in between rooms. He wants me to swab your throat for the flu, and we're also going to do a few blood tests and a urine test just to cover all our bases. We won't get back the results from the blood tests for a few days, but everything else, we'll have immediately."

"Okay," I responded.

She grabbed the giant Q-tip-looking thing and had me open wide before swabbing the very back of my throat. I tried not to gag. My eyes watered and burned, as my throat constricted involuntarily.

"Sorry. So sorry," she apologized, her eyes filled with empathy. She swiftly pulled back and capped the test. "We'll let that sit for about ten minutes. In the meantime," she said, handing me a clear container, "you've got work to do."

I rolled my eyes and hopped off the table, giving a slight smile. She escorted me to the restroom and told me where to put everything when I finished.

After a few minutes and several silent curses, I was done and waiting back in the exam room. I stared at the pictures on the walls, the cartoon-like sketches of hearts and valves, as my own hand reached up to feel the rhythmic beat in my chest. The buzz from the lights became almost hypnotic as I sat there, picking at the leftover nail polish I'd worn for New Year's, a sparkly gold color I'd thought looked festive and bright. A chip fell to the floor, a stark contrast to the dull gray linoleum tile below my feet.

Hours, days even, seemed to float by as I waited. I'd been in this exam room countless times, but it had never seemed this endless. The fear I'd felt when I'd walked through those double doors of the hospital resurfaced. I had this undeniable worry that something was about to happen, something I couldn't control.

The knock on the door caused all the breath in my lungs to falter, and I breathed in, gulping for air, as Dr. Hough entered.

"Hi, Lailah," he greeted, holding out his arms for our usual greeting.

I returned the gesture, hugging him wordlessly, as I tried to regain my composure.

"How are you?" I asked, my voice still slightly hoarse from my startle. "Did you have a nice holiday season?"

"Oh, yes, very nice," he answered rather quickly, taking a seat across from me. His eyes looked heavy, filled with emotions I had yet to sort out.

"You don't have the flu," he simply said, "but we did find something else rather interesting."

Oh God, here it comes—I'm dying.

"You're pregnant."

"That's impossible," the words flew out of my mouth before I even had a chance to realize I'd spoken.

He leaned forward, folding his hands together, as his gaze became intense. "Well, no, actually, since you're sexually active. Surprising maybe, but impossible? No."

My head began shaking from side to side as I rejected his news.

"But how?" I asked.

"Well, the how I can't really answer, which is why I'm having Irene take you over to obstetrics. They're going to give you an exam and an ultrasound to be sure."

"Irene?"

"My nurse," he answered kindly.

"Right."

I sat there in silence, looking down at my wedding ring, a ring I'd worn for barely a month.

"I'm pregnant?" I asked before adding, "Can I survive a pregnancy?"

"I guess the question is, do you want to find out?"

And there it was—my life-altering moment.

eighteen

Fight

Jude

I'D BEEN IN meetings all morning, thanks to Roman.

Every free moment I had, I found myself glancing down to check my phone, but Lailah hadn't sent me anything—not a text, email, or even a voice mail—to let me know how the doctor's appointment had gone.

Is she still there?

Finally, I managed to step out, canceling my lunch meeting, and I left for the day. I was useless to everyone in that office like this. I couldn't think straight, and I definitely wasn't getting anything done.

Not knowing what had transpired with Lailah was driving me crazy.

I tried her cell again on my way down to the lobby, but she didn't pick up.

Damn it all to hell.

Flagging down a cab, I made it back to our apartment rather quickly, deciding to check there first. Showing up at the hospital would be my next step. The elevator was like a slow crawl, moving up the building at a snail's pace, as I tapped my foot restlessly, waiting for our floor to ding. The doors finally opened, and I sped down the hallway, pulling out my keys, ready to unlock the door.

As soon as I bolted into the apartment, I saw her sitting on the sofa, her face turned toward the giant window that overlooked the city.

The blank look on her face stopped me cold.

"Lailah," I called out.

She turned to me with a sudden mixture of emotions moving across her features, kicking my feet into gear.

"What is it? What's wrong?" I knelt by her side, touching her everywhere.

Her shoulders, her heart, were solid and strong. She felt healthy and safe, but her demeanor was saying the exact opposite. It gave me chills.

"I went to the doctor," she started.

"I know. I've been trying to reach you all morning."

"I don't have the flu."

"Okay," I said, pulling a chair toward her and taking a seat. I gripped her hands in mine, willing her to say the words, to tell me what was going on.

Her eyes met mine, and she smiled. "I'm pregnant, Jude."

That finely tuned tightrope I'd been walking since the day she came back into my life—the one I'd kept taking slow, steady steps on each and every time her doctor had told us she was doing great and her heart was healthy—suddenly snapped beneath me.

I felt my stomach hit the floor. My ears rang violently in my head as if my mind was rejecting the very idea because it couldn't possibly be true.

"No," I replied softly. "No," I said again, shaking my head.

"I saw the baby."

From under a blanket, she produced a tiny black-and-white photo. Her name was typed neatly at the top with today's date. Positioned in the center was a tiny black dot. It didn't look like much, but I remembered my secretary had shown me one of her daughter's first ultrasounds, and it looked similar, maybe slightly bigger.

I took the photo as she began to speak, my ears . . . my heart, every damn part of me rejecting everything she was saying.

"Based on the size and the fact that my period is only a few days late, the doctor said we probably conceived around our wedding night. Isn't that crazy?" A laugh laced with tears fell from her lips as she gazed down at the tiny picture in her hands.

"We did everything right." Tears stung my eyes as I looked up at her—my beautiful, gorgeous wife.

"That's what I said, but when the doctor examined me, I guess my IUD had shifted. She said it basically rendered it useless. She had to remove it today so everything will be touch and go for the next few weeks as far as the pregnancy is concerned."

Her expression turned almost mournful—an emotion I couldn't wrap my head around quite just yet. So many emotions, I nearly felt numb.

"But the condoms?" I pressed on as if arguing the matter could overrule the picture I held in my hand.

A late-night *Friends* marathon suddenly flashed through my memory. Lailah and I had been curled up on the couch, and we'd both just finished laughing hysterically as a frantic Ross called the customer-service line on the back of a condom box, outraged that Rachel was pregnant. I'd told her how improbable that was. It turned out, Ross and I weren't that different.

"Dr. Riley—the OB-GYN said it's rare, but these things do happen." That smile returned again as she glanced down at the picture once more.

"They don't, not to you," I said adamantly. "When do we go back to see Dr. Hough?"

"I don't know. I told him I needed to talk to you, and then we'd schedule something."

"I want to see him today." I jumped up, grabbing the phone from my pocket.

"Jude, would you just calm down?" Her hands touched me as she tentatively stood.

"Calm down, Lailah? You're pregnant. This might be a joyous occasion for Bill and Harriet down the hall. But for you?"

"I know!" she screamed, throwing her hands up in the air, as tears melted down her cheeks. "Okay! I get it. But would you just stop for one second and realize that I might be happy about this?"

My hands shook, itching to dial the number I'd pulled up on my phone, but I stopped myself.

I pulled her into my arms as sobs took over, raking through her small frame, while she shook.

"I'm sorry, angel. I'm so sorry."

Hardwired to protect, my first gut reaction was to do just that—protect her by whatever means necessary. But a husband was so much more than that, and a month in, I was still learning.

The emotional grief she'd have from this loss would last far longer than pregnancy.

As her sobs softened, I carried her to the bedroom and gently laid her down. I ran my hands through her hair until her breathing evened out. After I snuck out, I dialed the number that was still up on my cell and made an appointment for the next morning with Dr. Hough.

She needed to hear all sides, learn the risks and deathly consequences she would be dealing with. Once she did, she'd understand and see what we were facing. As much as I'd love to see Lailah as a mother one day, it couldn't be like this, not in a way that would risk her life.

I wouldn't allow it.

Tensions were high the next morning as we worked around each other, showering and getting ready for Lailah's appointment—the one I'd made without consulting her first, the one she'd found out about an hour ago. It had immediately ceased all communication between us.

When I'd slowly grazed my thumb over her cheek and whispered her name, coaxing her from sleep that morning, I'd known my bold move wouldn't go over well. Last night, I'd carried my crying wife to bed as she lay helpless in my arms, and this morning, in her mind, she felt betrayed by my actions.

Honestly, her hurt feelings were okay by me as long as it would get her into that doctor's office.

My fear, the undercurrent running rampant in my system, was that this news would grow. I could see the idea already festering inside her head. Like an infection, it would spread wildly through her thoughts, taking over her ability to think logically.

I needed her clear, focused, and on a truly straight path, the path that would lead to us traveling down a happy life together.

That life could only happen if she was willing to give it a chance.

When I allowed myself to venture down the long winding road where she was round with my child in her belly, it looked bleak, dark, and completely unknown.

Cold, eerie silence followed us as we left the apartment and walked down the hall toward the elevator. I sighed in relief when I reached out to touch her hand and felt her fingers curl around mine. As we entered the elevator, I turned toward her, seeing an entire mountain of emotions sitting on her tiny shoulders.

"I'm sorry about the doctor's appointment," I finally said.

She nodded, stepping forward to burrow her head in my chest.

"I just feel completely out of control, Lailah. It's like our world is spinning on its axis, and you're ready to go along for the ride with no knowledge of what might lie ahead."

Her head turned upward. "I didn't say no to the doctor. I just wish you had allowed me to do it on my own. I've had too many years of people organizing my life."

My eyelids fell in shame. "You're right."

"But none of that matters now," she urged, grasping my face in her palms.

Our eyes met, and in her pale blue irises, I saw everything I felt in that moment, everything I'd been feeling since the moment I walked in that door and the small little planet we called life detonated before my eyes.

She was just as scared as I was, which meant there was still hope.

"Come on. Let's go," she said softly as the elevator doors opened into the lobby.

I let her lead me toward the entrance.

The doorman greeted, "Good morning," to us.

Snow fell lightly on the streets, covering everything in a silvery white glow. It was as if the city had been born anew overnight while I felt drained and dizzy.

I gladly took the doorman's offer to hail us a cab. Wrapping an arm around Lailah, I stood with her under the awning for shelter.

In less than a minute, we were on our way toward the hospital. No words were spoken between us, but our hands clung to each other like an unbreakable chain holding us together, even when it felt like we were oceans apart.

We made our way into the hospital, a united front, moving swiftly from the entrance to the elevators to the floor that held the office suites. Lailah squeezed my hand, a tear trickling down her cheek.

"It's going to be okay. I promise," I said.

She nodded her head, remaining silent, as her gaze stared straight ahead toward the doors as they peeled open. I let her lead once again as we entered the office, and then I held back, allowing her to sign in. It was early, and we were the first to arrive. The smell of coffee lingered in the air, and laughter rang in the distance as coworkers caught up on the latest gossip and discussed TV shows and family. My knee nervously bobbed up and down as I listened to them casually enjoying themselves while I was out here, feeling like my head would implode at any God-given moment.

It was the same exact way I'd felt in the days after I walked away from Lailah. Life had moved on, and people had existed around me, yet I had been left silently screaming in a virtual vacuum of my own demise.

I looked down at Lailah. *Would that be my life again?*

"Lailah Cavanaugh?" the nurse called out.

It was kind of unnecessary, seeing as we were the sole occupants in the waiting room, but it was nice to hear her new name despite the circumstances surrounding it.

We followed the nurse, someone I recognized from prior visits, down the hall and toward the left rather than the right, which led to the exam rooms.

"Dr. Hough thought it might be more comfortable to meet in his office this morning," she offered as an explanation as we stopped.

There, standing behind a large mahogany desk, framed by diplomas and certificates, was the man of the hour, checking charts and signing his name to various letters and statements.

"Doctor, Mr. and Mrs. Cavanaugh are here to see you," the young nurse announced.

"Ah, good. Thank you, Stephanie," he replied, stepping away from the desk to offer me his hand.

I politely took it, giving it a firm shake, even though I felt as weak and thin as the sheets of paper on his desk in front of us. It was then I noticed the woman sitting near him.

For Lailah, he opened his arms and took her in a sweet embrace. They held each other as friends rather than doctor and patient. I could see the hurt and defeat in his eyes. It was as if he wished there were some way he could erase the horrible circumstances of this otherwise joyous news from our lives.

"Please sit," he offered, motioning to the two plush chairs by his desk.

We each took a seat, and I reached out for Lailah's hand. I needed her as much as I hoped she needed me in this moment.

"I hope you don't mind, but I invited Dr. Riley here to offer assistance as well. I know you probably have a ton of questions, so why don't we just start there?" he said, reclining in his chair, trying to give a laid-back, approachable appearance.

"I guess we want to know everything," Lailah said, looking from one doctor to the other. "Our options, the risks, for both me and—"

"The baby," he finished.

She nodded.

"Well, first of all, let me say, the idea of a transplant patient, even one who's undergone something as risky as a heart transplant, can become mothers. It's not totally out of the question these days."

Lailah's hand squeezed mine.

"However," Dr. Riley interjected, "we usually advise patients to do in-depth preconception counseling where we—meaning an OB-GYN and the patient—decide if the patient is healthy enough to tolerate such an ordeal. Pregnancy is hard enough for a completely healthy woman. Add in the complications you face, and . . . well, things become risky quickly."

I took a deep breath, forcing air into my lungs.

Dr. Hough continued, "Unfortunately, we didn't get to do any planning with you, Lailah. The universe had other intentions, and despite all your best efforts, you are pregnant. Now, we just have to figure out what to do from here."

"If we had come to you and asked about becoming parents, would you have given us your blessing?" I asked.

He pursed his lips and sighed loudly. "No, I wouldn't have. It's only been two years since your surgery, Lailah, and with your history . . . well, this is why we had the IUD in the first place."

But the IUD had failed.

"But, she could still miscarry?" I interjected, feeling like we were skirting around a very real possibility.

Dr. Riley nodded, her eyes darted to Lailah. "Yes. Because I had to remove the IUD, there is a very real possibility of miscarriage. But I didn't want to leave it in and run the risk of infection later on in the pregnancy."

When we grew attached. The words hung in the air even though they hadn't been said.

I swallowed a lump in my throat, but it didn't go away. None of this was ever going to go away.

"Tell us about the risks." Lailah's soft voice pushed through the haze of my dark thoughts.

"There's an increased risk of hypertension, infection, and of course, rejection."

My heart faltered at his words. If Lailah's body began rejecting the transplant, there was nothing else that could be done—no magical cures, no last-minute surgeries. Her life would be over.

And so would mine.

The blood hissing through my ears was so loud that it sounded like a freight train. Both doctors went over our options in detail, including genetic testing and when to call as I tried to focus, my eyes blurring in and out as I held back tears.

I didn't remember much of the trip back home, only Lailah's steady hand on mine.

And her eyes—I remembered her vacant, distant eyes. If I had a mirror, I would imagine mine looked much like hers.

The minute the apartment door shut behind me, my legs gave out. The last bit of strength I had been holding on to rushed out of me like a billowing cloud of dust as my back slid against the cold metal behind me. Every emotion and every tear I'd held in check after walking into our apartment the day before and finding her holding that ultrasound picture sprang forward, erupting out of me like a dormant volcano brought back to life.

I sobbed, filled with grief for the life we might never have. I screamed to the heavens for everything they were putting us through, and I doubled over in anguish, secretly wondering if this was all somehow my fault.

I'd always demanded we use condoms. *But did I check them every single time? What if one had a rip or a tear? Was I too rough with her on our wedding night?*

Does it even matter now?

"Jude," a soft voice spoke.

I glanced over to see Lailah hesitantly reaching out toward me. She looked scared, timid, as her hand touched mine.

"It's okay," she soothed.

"How is this fucking okay, Lailah?" I snapped.

I realized my error as she withdrew from me in an instant.

"You don't want to have this baby, do you?" she said softly. Her hands wrapped protectively around her waist as she curled into a sitting position on the couch.

"You can't honestly tell me that you're considering it? You and I were in the same room, weren't we?" I asked, finally standing from my pathetic spot on the floor.

"Don't you see, Jude? Don't you get it? We made a child, a baby, despite our best efforts to do the opposite. It's a gift, Jude. It's a gift," her voice whispered softly.

"It's a death sentence!" I shouted, my hands raking wildly through my hair.

"You don't know that!" she countered, her eyes filling with moisture.

"And you do? What happens when your body starts rejecting the transplant, Lailah? Then, not only do we lose that precious gift of ours, but I lose you," I choked out, my voice hoarse from yelling. "I can't—no, I will not allow it."

The finality of my words cut through the air.

"I think we should talk about this later," she said, taking the sleeve from her hoodie to wipe her swollen eyes.

I could tell by her demeanor that she was done for now, and frankly, so was I. Nothing would be accomplished like this—screaming at the top of our lungs to see which one of us could last the longest.

It was childish and petty.

"I'll head to the office and give you some time alone. I'll be back early this afternoon. Maybe we can talk then?" *When we've had time to cool off.* I didn't say it, but the thought was implied.

"Okay." She nodded.

Reaching down, I kissed her temple, my eyes squeezing shut, as my fingers brushed through her hair. A month ago, we had been nearly drunk on our happiness as our entire lives were spread out before us like the first day of spring. Now? Now, I felt nothing—nothing and everything all at the same time—and I had no idea where any of it would take us.

nineteen

Flight

Lailah

WE'D NEVER FOUGHT like that before.

In all the days and hours we'd been together, I'd never felt such anger and frustration toward him. Even after he'd left, leaving me nothing more than a cowardly note and leading me to falsely believe he couldn't handle my ill-fated future, I hadn't felt a tenth of what I did now—hurt, betrayal, disappointment.

So many emotions were so close to the surface, and I couldn't begin to sort them all out.

Without him here, I thought that maybe I could clear my head, take a walk, or spend some time alone just sorting through everything that was swarming around in my thoughts.

But now, I just felt lost.

During our week in the warm paradise of the Seychelles Islands, we had fallen in love with sunset walks on the beach. It sounded cliché, but when you were in a place like that, you couldn't help but indulge in the dreamy, exotic side of life. As we'd walked, Jude would always point out shells along the water's edge, picking up any he might find interesting. On our last day, as the sun had set behind us, he'd spotted a perfect conch shell among the surf.

"How do you think it made it all the way here, completely untouched?" I asked.

He bent down to pick it up. His hands were now covered in sand as they ran over every edge and groove. "I guess it just drifted, all by itself, until it found its way here," he suggested, a smile radiating through his features as he looked up at me.

"Well, maybe its journey isn't done yet."

We'd left the beautiful conch exactly where we'd found it, hoping it would continue its journey without interruption from us.

I didn't know why, but I found myself thinking about it now. Where might it be? Was it all alone in that big, vast ocean, floating endlessly, until it just happened to hit land again someday? Or did someone else find it, perhaps smuggling it back home as a souvenir, finally ending the traveling days of the conch?

I guessed I felt a strange kinship to the dusty old shell. In many ways, as I continued to wear a path back and forth between our kitchen and living room, I felt like I was adrift, floating between two different decisions that could change my life forever.

The easiest decision was abortion. I knew it was what Jude wanted and what he would fight for. He would always fight to keep me alive even if it meant—

Well, I couldn't even finish that thought.

My heart burned in my chest.

I wandered back toward the kitchen, my feet sweeping the floor, as my thoughts rang loudly in my head. I wondered just how easy either decision would be. No matter what was decided, would our lives ever return to what they had been weeks ago on the sunset shore of that island?

Like a projection screen in my head, my mind moved ahead—one year, two, five—trying to see past the moment of this monumental decision.

Would I get over the grief, the loss? Would I ever forgive him? Would I be around to decide?

Unfortunately, my new heart didn't come with the ability to see the future, and my efforts proved fruitless. I groaned in frustration and decided a light snack might do me some good. Opening the fridge, I looked at the contents, staring at each and every item that sat there, and I felt my stomach lurch.

"Oh God," I managed to get out seconds before turning toward the kitchen sink.

My breakfast—along with every meal I'd eaten for years, it seemed—emptied out of me as I gasped for air, tears streaming down my cheeks. I quickly cleaned up, taking a towel to my face, as my hands shook. The acidic taste lingering in my mouth needed to go before it induced another round of heaving, so I quickly moved through the apartment toward the master bath to brush my teeth.

After brushing and haggling with mouth rinse, twice, I finally felt slightly better.

As my eyes met the mirror, I saw my reflection staring back at me.

A trickle of sweat beaded down my temple, and my eyes were red and swollen from throwing up. I also looked a little green from the nausea.

I'd seen this look many times over the years, but today, it had nothing to do with my heart and everything to do with that new life just beginning inside me.

An unsteady hand moved down to lift my hoodie. I touched my flat belly, and the warmth of my palm cradled the spot where our child grew. I didn't know anything about children. I'd never given much thought to becoming a parent—until this very moment.

How could I choose to put this life before mine? How would I become a mother?

I realized there was only one place to start.

Moving into our bedroom, I collapsed on the bed and pulled out my phone.

My mother answered on the first ring, "Hello?" Her greeting was quickly followed by, "No, sweetheart, don't put your mouth on that."

My eyebrow rose in question. "Hi, Mom," I answered. "Is that how you always talk to Marcus when I'm not around?"

She laughed at my lame attempt at a joke. I was hoping it would cover the anguish in my voice.

"No," she replied. "I took Zander overnight. Brian and Grace needed a date."

"Did you force them out on one?" I asked, already knowing the answer.

"Well, I might have suggested it. Okay, I strongly suggested it. Those two needed some alone time."

"And you needed some Zander time?" I guessed, hearing her make raspberry sounds into the phone. My stomach flip-flopped nervously.

"Well, I'd never turn down time with a handsome man," she joked.

Closing my eyes, my head sank into the pillow as I pictured the two of them, sitting on the balcony of her oceanfront apartment. Marcus had lived alone his entire life, renting an apartment near the hospital for years. When my mother and he had gotten married, they'd decided to splurge, buying a beautiful condo right on the beach, so Marcus could surf whenever he wanted. She'd sit out there, watching him disappear into the waves, as she drank a glass of wine and read. I imagined her doing much the same with Zander—minus the wine. It was still early morning there.

"So, what's up with you? You sound kind of down. There wasn't anything wrong with your doctor's appointment yesterday, was there? I got worried when you didn't call." she said, her tone turning serious.

Taking a deep breath, I answered, "No, Mom. Everything is fine—just a little cold. I didn't want to disturb you on your flights back home. This call was purely selfish. I just wanted to hear your voice."

"Oh, well, that's sweet of you," she said. "And now, you can hear Zander as well," she crooned. Her voice dropped an octave as she began babbling back to him.

I stayed silent for a moment, listening to her, as she fussed over him.

It must have been breakfast time because she shouted, "Don't you dare spit that out!" She laughed and then said, "You little troublemaker!"

Despite my mood, I couldn't help but smile as I listened to my mother interact with Grace's child.

Would Mom's reaction be the same with mine? Or would it be much like Jude's with nothing but fear and panic?

I'd just lied to my mother about my health and the entire experience left me feeling cheated and robbed. Robbed of the happiness and bliss that comes from telling my husband I was expecting our first child. Robbed of that exquisite joy of seeing his eyes flare with pride as he swept me up into his arms, ready to tackle this new journey in life. I felt stripped of those jubilant calls we would make together, huddled around the phone, as we shouted to our friends and relatives that we were pregnant.

That was how all of this was supposed to be.

"Mom," I started, biting my lip to keep the emotions at bay, "what was it like for you when you found out you were pregnant with me?"

The line was silent, and I realized my question might seem out of the blue, so I followed it up in a rush with, "I was just wondering since you had Zander there, and I was thinking about Grace and the day she told me she was expecting."

"Well, it wasn't easy," she answered.

"How so?" I pressed further.

"I was alone, young . . . scared. Your father—the man who donated the sperm," she corrected herself, "bailed and there was just me against the world."

She never liked to refer to him as my father. She never liked to refer to him much at all. To talk about him gave him importance, and in her mind, he didn't deserve any. After the small amount I'd learned, I tended to agree with her.

"How did you make the decision to—"

"Keep you?"

"Yes," I answered.

"I'll be honest. It wasn't easy. I don't envy anyone who has to make that decision. Society has its opinions on it, one way or another, but it truly is a personal decision, and I wouldn't judge anyone who has to make it. I debated it for days until it finally dawned on me."

"What?"

"How many times a day I said the word *me,*" she said. "Every reason and every argument I could think of for ending the pregnancy all boiled down to me, how it would affect my life. Then, I realized how self-centered I sounded. I was balancing the life of a child, a life I'd helped create, all because of me. I decided I'd spent too long focusing on the word *me,* and it was time I started looking out for someone else's well-being first."

A sad smile tugged at my mouth. "And you've been doing so ever since."

"Best decision of my life," she answered.

"Thanks, Mom."

"For what?" she asked. She continued to coo back and forth with Zander.

"For loving me, for choosing me, and for telling me exactly what I needed to hear."

I hung up before she had a chance to respond.

Jumping quickly off the bed, I dialed a new number on my phone and began making plans, ones that would perhaps thin the thread my marriage was dangling on.

But it was time to think beyond the idea of me or even us.

I needed to protect our child.

I needed to become a mother.

twenty

Crossroads

Jude

I'D BEEN STARING at the blank computer screen for what seemed like hours now.

After Googling every possible thing I could think of, trying to figure out anything and everything about Lailah's condition, I was left with more questions than answers.

There was a reason the doctors always warned against the Internet.

A plethora of information could be helpful or turn even the most optimistic person into a crazed hypochondriac.

Right now, I had no what idea what to think.

There were cases, people even, that I'd found online that were similar to Lailah. They had given birth to full-term healthy babies and lived to watch their children grow. But there were also the horror stories, the ones that made my stomach turn from just thinking of the possibilities.

How could we risk it? Why would we want to?

If Lailah wanted to be a mother, there were several other safer options for us. After everything we'd been through to get here, could we really be so careless with her health?

I hadn't gotten a shred of work done in the time I'd been in my office. I had marked myself out that day anyway, so besides my secretary, I wasn't sure anyone really noticed I was here.

It gave me peace and silence, which only made the thoughts in my head that much louder.

Rising from the desk, I stretched out my neck and shoulders and walked toward the large windows overlooking the city below. Whenever I found myself stressed from work or in need of some sort of resolution, I usually found myself here, tracing the steps of my father.

Counting didn't work much for me today, so I focused on Lailah. Thinking of her was my calm in the storm, my anchor when things got to be more than I could handle. But today, her smiling face was replaced with the harsh angry words we'd exchanged and the hurt and betrayal I'd seen in her eyes as she sat across from me, protectively curled around herself.

I felt bitter, useless, and fucking cheated.

What if my interference in her life had just delayed the inevitable? What if, by stepping in and paying for her heart transplant, I'd somehow just altered fate, and now, it was all catching up to us? Was this my punishment—getting her back, only to lose her all over again?

So many thoughts were swimming around in my head that I didn't hear the door swing open or the sound of my brother's voice until he was mere feet from my hunched over frame.

"You look like shit," he said, his dark eyes taking in my appearance.

My eyes followed his gaze downward and nodded in agreement. My shirt was a wrinkled mess, half-untucked. I hadn't shaved, and the cuffs of my sleeves were rolled up in a way that basically said, *Fuck it.*

"Feel like it, too," I replied.

"So, what's up?" he asked, shoving his hands in his pockets, as he began walking around the room. "Newlyweds have a fight?"

"Don't," I warned, my blood turning cold.

"Oh, come on, Jude. You didn't think it was going to be rainbows and unicorns the whole time, did you?"

I gave him a hard stare and watched as he smirked.

"Oh, you did." He shook his head in disbelief. "I would have thought better of you than that, little brother. Marriage is . . . well, marriage is kind of like buying a hot new car. You drive that baby off the lot, take it for a spin, and think life couldn't possibly get any better. But then, your baby needs an oil change and a tire rotation, and suddenly, something is leaking, and it's all demand, demand, demand until you trade her in for a new model. That, or you just never buy in the first place. That's my motto. Much simpler that way."

My feet moved faster than my words, and I found him wedged between my fist and the wall. "Don't ever speak of my marriage! Do you understand?"

Even though my hand was pointed at his face, he just smiled. "Testy today."

My punch sent him to the floor as my lungs burned, and my vision blurred.

"Do you feel better?" he yelled, wiping blood from the corner of his lip. "Or do you need more?"

He stood up and slipped out of his jacket, tossing it to the side. Holding his arms out wide, he said, "Come on, Jude. Hit me again. Will it help? Punching your jackass brother around?"

I didn't know why, but suddenly, Roman became the sole reason for every goddamn problem in my life. No amount of reason or logic could talk me out of my overwhelming need to put him in his place for destroying everything I'd worked so hard to achieve.

He held his own as I tackled him to the ground. I gave him one last punch before he retaliated. I felt a jab to my side as I pummeled his stomach. He got in a few good punches before I had him in a headlock. He was quick, but I was stronger—and fucking pissed.

With a grunt, I pushed him away from me, both of us heaving and gulping in breaths as fast as we could take them. I felt warm liquid trickling down my lip, and my tongue darted out to find the coppery taste of blood. I looked up and found Roman rubbing his side and mumbling under his breath.

"Lailah's pregnant," I said softly, finding a spot on the floor, as I nursed my wounds.

Roman's head whipped around, and our eyes met.

He understood. He might not have been around much, but he was right on point with the risks and the weight of it all.

"What are you going to do?" he asked.

"I have no clue," I answered honestly.

"Does Mom know?" He walked over to the seating area, grabbed a couple of Kleenexes, and handed me one.

I held it to my mouth and felt a slight sting. "No. Please don't tell her—not yet at least."

He nodded silently. "Go home, Jude. You don't belong here right now."

I opened my mouth to protest, a hundred questions ready to fire off all at once.

"I've got it."

I looked at him with a mixture of doubt and surprise.

"I can be a grown-up when I choose to be. Get the fuck out of here, and go be with your wife. This will all be here when you get back."

I rose from my place on the floor, feeling every aching muscle in my body. Roman had been the one in the headlock, but he sure hadn't gone down without a fight.

Grabbing my jacket from the back of my chair, I made my way to the door but stopped short. "Thanks, brother," I said.

He nodded. "We both know I'm not doing this for you."

"Either way, I'm grateful," I replied before making my exit.

Ever since they'd met, Roman had developed a soft spot for my wife. Lailah would play it off and say it was just his budding humanity, but I didn't agree. He had a driving need to protect her just like the rest of us did.

And right now, I needed all the help I could get.

As I stepped into the apartment, I noticed right away how quiet it was.

Too quiet.

"Lailah," I called out.

Nothing.

I looked around, noticing the untouched kitchen and the empty living room. As I padded across the apartment toward the bedroom, I glanced into the office and guest bedrooms.

Nothing.

My stomach began to turn sour.

Crossing the threshold of our bedroom didn't alleviate my nerves as my eyes went from one side to the other, and I still found nothing.

She wasn't here.

I pulled out my cell phone, checking for missed messages, texts, anything that would alert me as to why she wasn't home.

Maybe she'd just gone for a walk or run an errand. She normally had class today, but she'd mentioned she was skipping. She might have changed her mind.

I tried her cell, but it quickly went to voice mail.

Feeling frustrated, I walked into the bathroom, running the tap water waiting for it to turn ice cold. Cupping it in my hands, I splashed my face over and over until I felt my heart calm slightly. Grabbing a clean towel, I held it to my face and breathed slowly, in and out, rationalizing with myself, before I noticed how empty the counter looked.

The towel fell to the floor.

I opened the medicine cabinets and found everything of hers missing. Walking to the shower, I found her shampoo, shave gel, and other toiletries gone.

Running into the bedroom, I pulled open the doors to our closet. Dozens of hangers lie empty. Some were on the floor as if she'd packed quickly for wherever she set off to.

She'd left me.

Oh God, she left me.

My hands shook as I speed-dialed the number on my phone, waiting for Marcus to pick up.

He cheerfully greeted me. "Hey there, J-Man. How's it going?"

"Where is she?" I asked in a rush.

Concern enveloped his tone. "Who? What are you talking about?"

"Lailah. Where the hell is she, Marcus?"

Silence.

"What is going on, Jude? Did you two have some sort of fight?"

"She left me, and the first place she would go is to Molly," I said slowly, my voice gritty and flat.

"Molly spoke with her this morning, but she didn't mention anything about Lailah coming here. What the hell is going on, Jude?"

"She talked with Molly?" I asked, ignoring his last question.

"Yeah. I was out surfing, and I think she called while Molly was feeding Zander. We babysat last night. She said Lailah sounded a little down, but they had a good chat."

"Do you know what they talked about?"

"Motherhood, I guess. She asked what it was like for Molly as a single mother or something like that. Seriously, Jude, you're scaring me. What could possibly have sent her packing?"

My eyes went wide with panic, and I nearly doubled over. "Will you call me, if she contacts you?"

"Jude, will you tell me what's going on?" he pleaded.

"I can't—not yet, not now."

"Okay, son," he answered, sounding defeated. "I'll let you know if we hear anything. Do you need anything?" he offered, his voice warm and sure.

"Just my wife," I answered.

We said our good-byes, and I promised to call in the morning with any updates.

Soon, it quickly became silent again in the apartment. I looked around, feeling swallowed by the square feet of the place. Without her here, the walls suddenly felt large and ominous, growing taller and darker, like a nightmare come to life.

I needed to find her.

Watching the sunset fall across the horizon, I never moved. Feeling paralyzed by my uselessness, I just sat on the edge of the bed and waited for her to come back to me. *Where was she? If she didn't show up in California, how would I even begin to look for her?*

Around eight that night, my phone finally buzzed. I grabbed for it, seeing a single text from Marcus.

She's here, was all it said.

No longer in on hold flux, I had what I'd been waiting for, and I jumped into action. I threw anything I could grab into a suitcase while making flight arrangements on my phone at the same time.

Over the years, I'd been told every marriage, even the good ones, would reach a point where it was time to either fight for the one you wanted or call it a draw and collect your winnings.

It was the great fight or flight of marriage.

I'd known, someday, Lailah and I would have ours. I'd just never expected it to be a month after we'd said our vows.

As I packed the last of my suitcase and locked the apartment, I knew which path I'd chosen, which path I'd always choose.

For Lailah, I'd always fight.

twenty-one

Sea of Emotions

Lailah

LESS THAN TWO days.

Two days of doctor's appointments, arguments, and rushed decisions.

Two days of longing for the way it had once been.

Even though I had made the decision to leave, my heart still bled for the loss. It still reached out for him in the darkness and called out for him in the wee hours of the morning. I hoped we could repair the damage that had been done. I hoped with a bit of time he might see things differently and perhaps warm up to the idea of becoming a father.

Or he'd have to possibly let me go.

My eyes squeezed shut as I listened to the sound of the waves crashing nearby. I pulled my sweater tighter and leaned back into the reclined lounge chair on the deck, admiring the stars I'd missed so much while in the bright lights of the city. The condo was quiet tonight. After my surprise appearance and my rapid meltdown soon after, my parents had helped me settle in, giving me the guest room closest to the ocean. From the bed, I could hear the soothing sounds of the water and feel the heat of the sun as it moved across the sky.

My mother had held me as I cried and told her everything that had happened. The phone call earlier that morning had suddenly made sense to her, and as she'd cradled me in her arms, she'd stroked my hair and told me it would be all right—even though both of us knew better.

We'd faced hardship before.

Marcus had come in after that, wanting to know everything on the medical side of things. Until the next day when I could transfer my records back to his care, all he had was what I could tell him, and unfortunately, it wasn't much.

"We'll get you set up with the best OB in town," he'd promised. "We'll figure it out."

I'd nodded, thanking him for his kindness.

"Hey, you want to order a pizza or something? Watch a movie?" he'd offered. His head had casually leaned against the doorframe, his tanned body turned toward me.

"No, I'm fine. Why don't you two go out or something? You don't need to hang around here just for me."

He must have sensed my need for solitary because he had nodded. "Okay, kid. I'll bring you back something."

"Sounds good."

Now, it was just me and the waves.

"I thought you said watching the water was my thing," a deep voice called out in the darkness.

I turned to see Jude standing in the shadows, holding a suitcase in one hand and the spare key my mother kept hidden in a ceramic frog in the other.

"I figured I'd give it a try," I answered calmly, swallowing the lump in my throat that had just formed at the mere sight of him.

I stood, fiddling with the sleeves of my sweater, as our eyes met. He looked taller and much more formidable as I watched him drop his bag and stalk forward.

"All the way across the country? You know we have oceans on the East Coast?"

"I needed some space," I replied softly.

He closed the distance between us. He was so close I could feel his angry breath on my neck.

"I don't want space, Lailah."

His mouth closed over mine, searing every nerve ending with fire until I was consumed by only him. My hands clung to him, pulling him closer, and his body molded to mine. Every heated, turbulent word and emotion I'd felt over the last two days exploded as I touched him.

I wanted him to feel my pain, my outrage, and torment. I wanted him to understand just how much he'd hurt me by refusing to support me and instead feeling like he could make decisions for me.

It was my life—mine, not his.

I pushed him backward, watching his eyes go wide with shock and a flicker of heat.

"Angry, Lailah?" he asked, the intensity of his face aglow by the distant moonlight. "Good. Me, too."

He grabbed me around the waist and hoisted me over his shoulder. I punched at his back, but he just laughed darkly as he carried me through the apartment.

When he spotted my things in the room toward the back, he lowered me to the bed and shut the door. I watched in stunned silence as his clothes came off, one piece at a time. His eyes never left mine. It was as if I were his hard-earned prize.

He bent down and slowly slipped my sweater off my shoulders. "You always said you wanted all of me, remember?"

My gaze lifted to him, confusion painting my face until I saw his crooked grin.

"Well, I guess you can have your wish now," he said with a hint of sadness.

I wanted to stop him, tell him we didn't have to do this tonight, but before I could, his mouth was on mine once again, and I was lost to the feeling of his naked body pressed against mine. Every article of clothing I wore was shed until skin met skin, and I was drowning in his heat and warmth.

"No more boundaries," he whispered. "No more barriers. Just you, me, and the sea of emotions separating us."

I cried out as his body claimed mine, entering swiftly, and I felt him inside me for the first time without anything between us.

"Fuck," he swore under his breath, his head resting against the curve of my shoulder, as his heart raced against my chest.

"Jude," I softly called.

He answered with a hard thrust that had my body reeling.

"Jude, please . . . look at me."

His eyes finally met mine, and I saw torture and longing, love and sadness, and hope mixed with so much fear.

He stilled as I reached up, pushing back the hair that had fallen in front of his face. Molding my palm against his cheek, I kissed his chin and then his jawline before moving to the outward corner of his lip. I finally pulled him down, fusing our bodies and mouths. Our tears bled together as our souls reunited, reminding us of the never-ending bond we'd pledged to one another.

Love was eternal.

Love was endless, and love would carry us through the storm to the other side—whatever it might be.

I awoke the next morning, alone and disoriented.

My hands reached for him but found nothing but empty cold sheets. As my eyelids cracked open, I searched the room, trying to remember where I was—as anyone might do in new surroundings. Then, the memories of last night flooded my mind.

I bolted upright, looking around the room for something, anything, that would tell me it wasn't a dream.

I found his dress shirt and tie slung over the edge of the bed—a simple sign that he was here, somewhere.

I stumbled out of bed, reaching for a pair of sweats and a hoodie, and I hobbled down the hallway in search of coffee and sustenance. I found my mom at the counter, reading the paper, while she nibbled on a bagel and sipped on a cup of tea.

"Hi," I managed to say, my eyelids barely staying open long enough to find a cup.

"I see your husband arrived last night," she said stoically.

"Yes," I answered. "Do you know where he is?"

"Running," was all she said.

I bit my lip and took a deep breath.

"You two talk?"

"No, but we will," I answered, not offering any more information than that, as I quickly finished buttering a piece of toast and grabbed my coffee.

"Caffeine, dear," my mother stated as she stopped me on my way to the patio.

"What?"

"Pregnant women really shouldn't have caffeine."

I looked down at my steaming cup of coffee, suddenly realizing who I was now.

I was no longer Lailah, the girl with the heart defect. I was Lailah, the mother-to-be.

Priorities shifted. It was a nice change of pace even if it meant giving up my morning cup of Joe.

"Okay," I said, handing her the cup. I went back to the refrigerator for a bottle of orange juice.

I managed to catch the tail end of Jude's marathon run as I settled into the recliner on the patio. His shirt was tucked in the back of his shorts, and as he ran, every fiber of muscle moved with him.

He looked like the same Greek god I'd fallen for in the hallways of that hospital.

Every female head turned to watch him speed by, but his attention was set dead ahead. He swung right and slowed to a walk. His eyes drifted up to the house and caught mine. His gaze intensified and followed me the entire way up the beach until he disappeared below the deck.

The door to the deck slid open about ten minutes later, and I watched him slip into a chair beside me. The smell of soap and freshly washed hair followed him as he moved toward me.

"We need to talk," he said before turning back to the waves as they calmly fell, one after another, like clockwork.

"I can't do what you're asking me to, Jude," I answered softly, my eyes falling to my nervous hands, as my fingers traced my wedding ring.

"I understand that."

"You—what?" I asked, confusion marring my features, as my gaze met his.

"You made that abundantly clear when you left me."

"I-I'm sorry."

"Look," he said, his hands running through his hair, as he bent forward, "I can't make this decision for you. I get that now. But I also can't stand around and watch as you allow yourself to slowly fade away. After everything we've been through, you at least have to know that of me."

I sighed in frustration. "So, where does that leave us?"

"Together, Lailah! Don't you get it by now? Don't you see? The answer will always lie in us figuring things out together. We already tried life apart. It didn't work."

"So, what do you want me to do?" I asked, tears leaking from my eyes.

"Fight, damn it!" he answered loudly. "If we're going to do this, I need you to promise that you won't give up. Fight until your last dying breath. Do everything the doctors tell you to—no exceptions. Take every precaution and promise you won't give up."

He got up from his chair and knelt down in front of me, wiping away the moisture from my cheeks.

"Because I need you—yesterday, now, tomorrow. I'll always need you. And if we're going to be parents, I can't do this alone. You're the better half of this whole, and our child will need you as its mother."

Tears poured down my face.

"You said, *our child.*"

"Yeah, I did. It's kind of strange."

"I don't know what to say," I choked out.

"Say you'll fight for our family."

Nodding wildly, I dived into his arms. "I'll fight. We'll be a family. I promise."

As he held me, I sent a silent prayer to heaven, asking for strength.

This was one promise I never wanted to break.

twenty-two

California Calm

Jude

"SO FAR, SO good," Dr. Garcia said brightly. "I want to see you back here in two weeks, but it looks to me like you've got a fighter. Make sure you keep drinking lots of water, take your prenatal vitamins, keep up on your medications, and call if you have any questions or if there are any changes. Oh, and the nurse will show you the way to your ultrasound appointment."

"Thank you," Lailah said.

I moved to shake her hand. This was our third appointment in a month. Most pregnant women didn't even see the doctor until they reached six weeks, but since Lailah was considered high risk with a high probability of miscarriage, we got the frequent-flyer card and came much more frequently. We'd turned down genetic testing for now, agreeing that the idea of not knowing was less stress and Lailah was convinced it wouldn't change anything.

At this point, I wasn't so sure.

So far, everything was running smoothly, but we still had the ultrasound, and until then, I didn't think I would be able to take a single breath.

"Jude, can you hand me my shoes?" Lailah asked as she threw on her sweater and grabbed her purse.

I helped her into her flats and took her hand as she stepped off the exam table. The nurse was waiting for us, and we followed her down the hall to another wing of the medical office.

The first time we'd arrived at this location, I'd immediately voiced my concern that it wasn't in the hospital. Lailah had laughed, pointing out that it was right next door.

"Yes, but it's not part of the hospital. What if something goes wrong, and you need to be admitted? How long will that take?" I'd questioned.

"Marcus said she's one of the best doctors in obstetrics, as far as he's concerned. I'm in perfectly good hands."

I'd grumbled but relented, agreeing that there was only one doctor in the family and it wasn't me.

We'd decided to stay in California indefinitely.

Right now, we needed calm and serenity. We couldn't get that in New York.

I'd thought Roman's head might explode when I called him and explained I was taking a year off, but he had been surprisingly Zen about the entire thing.

I'd offered to be available for teleconferences and emergencies, but he'd just said, "We got it," and that was it.

I hoped I would have a company to return to next year.

I hoped I would have a lot of things to return to in a year. Lailah and I had agreed to keep the dark thoughts to a minimum, believing that there was no point in mulling over what might be, and instead, we were focusing on the present we still had. But there were times I struggled.

Every time I saw her, I would stare just a bit longer, capturing the way her eyes looked in the warm California sun.

Every time I touched her, I'd linger, memorizing the way her body reacted to mine.

A thousand lifetimes would never be enough. This was true. For now, I'd gladly settle for one.

The nurse finished our quick tour of the office before dropping us off at the ultrasound waiting room. A woman and her husband sat across from us. Her stomach was swelling with their child, and he tenderly rubbed it and spoke in hushed tones. As they were called back by a technician, Lailah looked at me, a nervous halo clouding her normally bright blue eyes.

A quick wink and a nudge to her shoulder earned me a small smile before she tenderly rested her head against me.

"Will you do that?" she asked wistfully.

"What?"

"Rub my belly?"

"Only if you let me rub pudding all over it and lick it off," I said, completely deadpanned.

Her head jerked up to look at me as she tried not to crack a grin. "You're crazy."

"You'd let me do it though, wouldn't you?"

Her name was called before she could answer, but I saw her roll her eyes, and I heard the beautiful sound of her laughter as we made our way down the hallway.

Mission accomplished.

Google and I had become the best of friends over the last month, and I'd learned my fair share about pregnancy, including the importance of stress reduction to the mother.

It was a simple concept—happy mother equaled happy baby. In my world, that meant everything.

We were led to a small room filled with equipment I'd only seen in movies. Lailah was told to strip down, and she was handed a robe. We were given a few minutes of privacy while she shimmied out of her dress and sweater and quickly put on the hospital gown.

"I look hot, huh?" She twirled around once before fastening the ties at the top.

"You forget, I fell in love with you in a hospital."

"Yes." She smiled, taking a seat on the exam table. "But even then, I didn't wear awful hospital robes."

Remembering her affinity for yoga pants even then, I grinned. "No, but it wouldn't have mattered even if you did. It was hopeless. You had me from that very first moment."

"And I, you."

We made idle chitchat until the technician came back, ready to do the ultrasound. My heart took residence in my throat as I watched her help Lailah into the stirrups and gently lean her back. I'd braced myself for the methods used for very early ultrasounds, but nothing could fully prepare me for the massive instrument the technician pulled out.

Lailah choked back a laugh as she saw my eyes go wide, but I refused to say anything, choosing instead to stand by her side and offer moral support.

"This might be slightly uncomfortable," the technician warned as her hand disappeared under the drape of Lailah's robe.

She winced, and I reached out for her hand. The pain must have been brief because she quickly relaxed, her eyes glued to the tiny monitor next to the technician.

"There's your little one," she said, smiling, pointing to a dark peanut-shaped nugget in the center.

I felt the breath rush out of me.

"Is this your first ultrasound?" she asked, looking back at Lailah.

She was busy staring at the screen. "Oh, um . . . no. I had a quick one at four weeks. It was a bit of a surprise, so they wanted to confirm the test."

"Well then, I'm guessing at four weeks, you didn't get to hear the heartbeat then?"

We both turned to her with wide eyes.

"Can we?" Lailah asked.

"Of course. Let me just . . ." She paused mid-sentence, clicking and entering things in on the keyboard.

Within moments, the room was filled with a whooshing sound.

We sat in awe, listening to the heart beating strong and fast, as the technician continued to do her thing. Lailah squeezed my hand, looking up at me, as her eyes filled with tears—happy, joyous tears.

My world doubled in that moment. As I looked into that monitor and listened to the sound of my unborn child, I knew Lailah wasn't the only person I'd lay down my life for.

There were now two.

And now, I had to save them both.

"Maybe a little to the left?" she suggested.

I whipped my head around to give her a hard stare over my shoulder. "That's the exact same spot it was in before," I said, nudging the large framed photo an inch over on the wall.

After weeks of waiting, we were finally in our own place.

Molly and Marcus had been gracious hosts, taking care of us better than I could have ever asked, but we were newlyweds.

We needed space—and plenty of alone time.

It hadn't taken long to find this place. We'd known we wanted to be near the ocean. After our many trips around the world, we'd learned the waves had a certain pull over us both, and I couldn't think of any greater place for Lailah to be than near the calming, healing sound of the ocean water.

We ended up renting a large beachfront house not too far from Molly and Marcus. It was large and bright, and it had endless windows, giving every room a view of the beautiful outdoors.

"It is not. Now, it looks perfect," she answered.

Her head cocked to the side, looking at the portrait I'd been holding against the wall for what seemed like an eternity.

"Are you sure?" I asked, holding up the nail. "Last chance."

"Positive."

Quickly marking the wall, I set the frame down on the sectional sofa I was standing on and positioned the nail.

"Wait!" she called out.

I groaned.

"Maybe just a tad to the right?"

Looking back over my shoulder at her as she sat cross-legged in a chair with a fuzzy blanket spread across her lap, I couldn't help but laugh.

Goddamn, she was adorable. "You're lucky I love you."

"I know." She shrugged.

Moving the nail ever so slightly, I drove it into the wall before she had a chance to change her mind again. As I hung the portrait of us, laughing and looking into each other's eyes during our first dance, I couldn't stop the feeling in my stomach. It was a churning mixture of nostalgia as I remembered that exact moment and a twinge of panic as I worried that days like those might be numbered.

Stay positive, I reminded myself.

"It looks great!" she exclaimed.

"And it only took forty-five minutes!" I answered sarcastically.

Her eyebrow rose as she held a steaming cup of tea to her lips. "Be nice, or I'll make you hang the rest."

"You're giving me a break? What kind of break?" I asked, inching forward, a cocky grin tugging at my lips.

"We're having company," she replied, laughing.

"Not the answer I was hoping for."

"It's good to know you still think I'm sexy," she commented, rising to take her now empty cup to the kitchen.

"Whoa. Hold up." I stopped her dead in her tracks. "Why on earth would I ever not find you sexy?"

"I don't know." She shrugged, looking down at her faded yoga pants and T-shirt. "It's just . . . I've haven't looked the best lately, and I've spent a good majority of time nauseous or throwing up. I feel like we're back to the way it used to be . . . you know, before—"

I clutched her face in my palms, centering her gaze, so I had her attention.

"I understand this is a part of the pregnancy process—issues with body changes—but believe me, Lailah, you couldn't be more beautiful to me if you tried. Nothing will ever change that—not now and not six months from now when you're as round as a house. I'll only see you."

Her eyes watered, and I knew I'd reached her.

"You think I'll be as round as a house?"

"If I have anything to do with it." I grinned just as the doorbell chimed. "You never said who was visiting," I said.

She rushed to the door. It swung open, and I heard Grace's high-pitched squeal.

"Never mind," I uttered to myself.

"I know this isn't permanent, but can I just tell you how much I love being able to see you whenever I want again? It's amazing!"

I watched the two of them hug, giggling like schoolgirls. Lailah helped Grace through the door. Bogged down with a diaper bag and an infant, she looked like her tiny legs might buckle at any moment.

"Here, why don't I take Zander while you give Grace the tour?" I offered.

They both looked at me, wide-eyed, in surprise.

"What?" I asked.

"Well, it's just . . . I don't think you've ever offered to hold him," Grace confessed.

"I have to."

Both females blankly looked at me.

"At least once?"

Two heads shook back and forth simultaneously.

"Okay, fine. Well, there's a first time for everything. I mean, how hard could it be?"

Lailah and Grace gave each other a knowing grin, and I watched Grace drop the diaper bag to the ground.

"He's all yours!" she exclaimed, giving a wink in Lailah's direction. "Let's go take that really lengthy tour."

My hands wrapped around his squishy center as I carefully gripped the tiny human in my arms. Zander had already celebrated his first birthday, so this would be easy. It wasn't like he was fragile anymore. Hell, the kid was practically an adult by now.

I held him out an arm's length, and the two of us stared at one another.

"Hi," I said.

His eyebrows rose, giving me a look that said he clearly knew I had no idea what I was doing.

He'd already figured me out.

Shit, I'm screwed.

I had no idea what to do with him, so I decided we'd take a little walk of our own. Awkwardly, I pulled him closer, feeling his chubby hand grip my tatted forearm.

"You like that?"

His eyes intensely wandered over the black ink while his small fingers scooted along my skin. Finally, he looked back up at me and babbled a string of incoherent baby nonsense.

I laughed. "Oh, yeah? Fond of the ink, huh? I'll keep that between us men. Don't want your mom thinking I've corrupted you already."

Unlocking the sliding door with my free hand, I stepped out on the wide deck, feeling the warm breeze of early spring hit our faces. Zander's finger pointed toward the water, and he clapped in glee.

"I like it, too."

I looked down at him as he took in the view, his big blue eyes darting from left to right. His face lit up when he spotted a dog playing in the water with his owner. My fingers went to his face, brushing against his soft skin, as I inhaled his clean scent.

I'd never given much thought to the possibility of being a father.

When it had been just Megan and me, it had always been something we'd do later, in the future. We were supposed to have forever, so the idea of kids really never came up. I guessed it was just something both of us had figured we'd naturally fall into one day.

When Lailah had come into my life—well, she was all I needed. It wasn't a feeling of losing or giving anything up. When I was with her, I felt complete. But now, there was more, and I still couldn't wrap my mind around the idea that I could possibly deserve it all.

That was why I couldn't shake the nervousness that constantly lingered in the corners of my mind.

When would all of this come crashing down on me like a house of cards?

Would I ever hold my child like this? Cradle him in my arms as we looked out at the ocean, listening to his mother entertain guests?

God, I hoped so.

As the sun began to sink beneath the horizon, the two of us continued to chill out on the deck. We watched surfers as Zander spoke to me about the many adventures he'd been on in his short life—or at least, that was what I assumed he was talking about. He squished my face and laughed.

"Wow, this place is great!" Grace announced, stepping out onto the patio with Lailah.

They both had drinks in their hands, and as they took their seats, Lailah offered me a soda.

"So, how was your alone time with Zander?" she asked before taking a sip of water as she leaned back in her seat.

"Great," I gloated. "This kid loves me."

"Oh, please. He was just being easy on you because he saw newbie written all over your face," Grace replied.

"Nah, we're tight." I gave her a wink, popping the top of my soda.

Zander suspiciously eyed it, licking his lips, as I took my first sip.

"Okay," she simply said.

I saw his hand move a millisecond before soda splattered us both. Both women covered their laughter as Zander burst into tears at the sudden sensation of being drenched by cold liquid.

I wasn't too happy about it either.

"Oh, baby boy!" Grace cooed. "It's okay!"

Her outstretched hands met his, and he reached for her, completely abandoning the mean man who had forgotten about the unwritten rule regarding soda cans and infants.

Apparently, you had to watch both like a hawk, or this would happen.

"I'm going to go change," I announced, standing, as I watched Coke drip down my jeans and into my shoes.

Squeaky-toed, I walked off to the bedroom to grab a new pair of jeans. As I rifled through the drawers of our new dresser, trying to figure out how everything was organized, I found an envelope hidden underneath a drawer stuffed with Lailah's sweaters. Curiously, I pulled it out and found the ultrasound pictures the technician had printed. In addition, the solitary image from her first ultrasound was underneath. I held them side-by-side, amazed by how much our tiny peanut had grown in only four weeks. In the first image, there was nothing really—just a dark circle that showed the place a baby would eventually be. Four weeks later, I could clearly see the progress of growth.

It made me anxious to add to this growing pile. I was hoping, in the visits to come, we'd see more as our child blossomed in Lailah's belly. A month ago, I had argued for abortion, and now, I was staring down at ultrasound pictures with amazement. She'd done that. Lailah had filled me with hope, and I only prayed everything would turn out the way she envisioned it.

I tucked the photos back in their hiding spot, wondering for a moment why they were hiding in the first place, but I quickly reminded myself that I was most likely dripping soda onto the carpet. Throwing on a fresh pair of jeans, I joined everyone back on the deck just in time to hear Grace announce that she'd brought us a gift.

"Well, it's for Lailah mostly," she admitted.

"I'll try not to be offended," I joked.

"Why are you bringing us gifts?" Lailah asked as she bounced a now happy Zander on her knee.

He'd also gone through a wardrobe change, and his mood was much lighter.

"Housewarming gift—of sorts," she said, pulling a flat square package from the large baby bag she'd brought.

"Hey, Mary Poppins, if you dig deep enough in there, can you pull a lamp out as well??" I asked, grinning.

"Very funny," she snorted. "I'll be sure to bank all these funny jokes, so I can remind you of them later when you're carrying a bag just like this on your shoulder a year from now."

Shaking my head, I turned to hand the package to Lailah, who smiled hesitantly back at us.

"What is it?" I asked.

"Nothing, nothing," she answered quickly. "Let's see what this is!"

She pulled a piece of wrapping paper just far enough to intrigue Zander, and he tore the rest. Underneath, the two of them unveiled a beautiful baby book, the front obviously hand-embellished in neutral fabrics and colors.

"Oh, Grace," Lailah sighed appreciatively. "It's gorgeous."

"Yeah? I made it myself. I wanted you to have something special." She leaned forward, opening the book, as it rested in Lailah's lap. "I made sure to include places where you could put baby shower pictures and invitations. There are even spots to write special memories during the pregnancy, like the first time you feel a kick or a flutter and your first pair of maternity clothes."

"Thank you," Lailah said sincerely.

"You're welcome. I can't wait to meet baby Cavanaugh."

With an emotional smile that didn't quite reach her eyes, she answered, "Us either."

A while later, we wished Grace and Zander a good evening and settled into the night with some take-out from around the corner. As I handed her a plateful of salad and pizza, ready to begin our movie selection, I turned to her.

"Can I ask you something?" I said.

She nodded, turning to me in her curled up position on the couch.

"Why did you put the sonogram pictures in a drawer?"

Her eyes went downcast as she worried on her bottom lip. "I'm too afraid to celebrate," she admitted. "It's still so early. What if something happens?"

I grabbed her plate, setting both down on the coffee table in front of us. As I took her hand in mine, she nudged her way into my arms.

"You know something could happen at any moment," I reminded her.

She simply nodded.

"But you know what?"

Her eyes met mine.

"That's true for anyone, Lailah. Sure, our circumstances are unique, but we're still like everyone else—two people preparing for the biggest challenge of our lives. You don't think anyone else worries about things going wrong?"

"But, it's just—"

"I know. It's scary. But if we don't celebrate the good, then the bad will consume us. Don't hide those ultrasound pictures, angel. Frame them. Put them someplace to remind yourself exactly why we're doing this. Fill that baby book with every damn memory you have, so when this is all over with and we're sitting here with our little monster, waiting for him to spill coffee or soda all over me, we can remember every single detail and know that it was worth it. Because we got him."

She smiled a genuine heartfelt smile.

"You think it's a boy?"

"Maybe."

"And what would you name this boy of yours?"

I grinned mischievously. "Zebe."

"No!" She laughed, shaking her head.

"Billy Bob?"

Laughter turned into cackling as I flipped her over on the couch beneath me.

"You don't like my names?"

"Hate them. Try again."

"Could I turn this into a game?"

"You and games. What do you have in mind?" she questioned.

"Every good name gets me an article of clothing?"

"You're on."

I had her naked in two minutes flat.

twenty-three

We're Going to Disneyland

Lailah

"WAKE UP." JUDE nudged me.

My eyes fluttered open. "No." I pouted, pulling the covers back over my head in protest.

"Please?" His hands reached under the sheets, pulling me to him.

I opened my eyes again, focusing on his beaming smile. "Don't want to."

He laughed, his forehead resting against mine, as his sneaky fingers began to wander across my stomach.

"I'm a college student. We're not supposed to wake up before noon. It's a rule."

"Angel?"

"Yeah?"

"You took a year off, remember?"

"Oh," I answered, slumping back on the pillow.

"That means it's time to get up!" he exclaimed, slapping my ass.

I yelped as he stole the comforter from the bed, leaving me in nothing but a sheet to keep me warm.

"What are we getting up for anyway? It's not like either of us has jobs."

"I have a job. It's just very far away," he reminded me with a grin.

A twinge of guilt tried to worm its way into my stomach, knowing that he'd taken an entire year away from the company for me, but I pushed it away. I'd taken a year off of school. We'd both made adjustments for this.

We had to.

"That doesn't answer my question," I reminded him, sitting up to stretch.

"We are going out."

"Out? That's vague. Care to be a little more specific?"

"We're going to Disneyland."

That got my attention. "What?"

"Disneyland," he repeated. "The happiest place on earth. Mickey? Minnie? Any of this ringing a bell?"

"I know what it is, dork! I just don't know why you've suddenly decided to go," I said, looking around, trying to remember what day it was.

Tuesday! It was a Tuesday!

"On a random Tuesday," I finished.

He smiled as he finished putting on his shoes and came to join me on the bed since I still refused to relinquish my warm spot.

"Like you so eloquently stated, neither of us has jobs or school. There are only so many movies I can watch before my brain turns into mush. As lovely as this house is, I'm getting cabin fever, Lailah. We need to get out, and as long as the doctor keeps giving you the thumbs-up, I think we should do just that."

I gave him a suspicious look. "This wouldn't happen to have anything to do with my Someday List, would it?"

His eyes softened. "Do you remember how sad you were that last day of our honeymoon? How you wished we could have more time together just like that?"

I nodded.

"Well, we have it now. It might not be exactly the same, but it's time nonetheless. And I figured if we've been given this uninterrupted time together, where I'm not being called away to meetings and you don't have tests to study for, we should make the most of it."

"By taking me to Disneyland?" I questioned.

"By fulfilling as many of those wishes on that list as possible," he replied.

Because who knows how much time we have?

It wasn't said, but I could see it there, dangling in the air between us. Neither of us wanted to acknowledge the possibility of what could happen if things went badly with my pregnancy, but if they did, he knew we should spend the days leading up to that moment to the fullest.

"Disneyland it is," I said. "But I want Minnie Mouse ears."

His smile grew. "You've got yourself a deal."

I'd lived in Southern California for the majority of my life, and I'd never been to Disneyland.

I never knew it was so big.

People seemed to be everywhere, but we were actually told park attendance was low due to the middle of the week and time of year.

I'd hate to see it during the summer.

"What do you want to do first?" I asked excitedly as I looked around in every direction like a gleeful child.

"This is your day, but we need to go to one place first. Come on," he said, pulling me toward a row of stores.

I laughed when we ended up in front of The Mad Hatter.

"Minnie ears?" I asked.

"Yep, let's go in," he said, taking my hand.

We stepped in and made our way to the many rows of ears I could choose from.

"Okay, wow. I had no idea this would be so difficult."

"I think you should get the ones with sequins," a familiar little voice said.

I turned to see a young girl beaming up at me. Her eyes widened in excitement the moment she saw me, and she threw her arms around my waist.

"Abigail!" I cried out. "Oh my gosh! How are you here? Why are you here? Shouldn't you be in school?"

"We had a teacher workday today, and I have a season pass. Plus a certain someone mentioned you might be here today," she smiled.

I looked up to see her mom standing nearby speaking with Jude. We exchanged waves as I mouthed, *Thank you.*

She nodded, smiling.

"I can't believe you're here!" I said, squeezing her tighter.

"Isn't it going to be great? An entire day together! And I can't believe you've never been here. I'm going to take you everywhere, and we're going to ride every single ride!"

Jude coughed a bit, getting our attention as he joined back in the conversation. "Maybe not every ride?" he suggested.

"Oh, right." She blushed, looking down at my midsection. "Well, most of them," she amended.

To outsiders, I still looked like regular old me. But at nearly three months, when I stared at myself in the mirror, I'd begun to notice the changes, the tiny bulge beginning to form. I'd cup my hand over it, cradling that little bump, hoping it knew I was there, cherishing it.

I grinned down at her. "Want to pick out ears with me?"

"Sure!" she answered cheerfully. "Let me just say bye to my mom." She skipped cheerfully over to her mom, giving her a hug and kiss.

"I'll meet you back here around five?" her mother confirmed with Jude.

He nodded, and they chitchatted a bit more before she headed out.

"This was a very nice thing you did," I said quietly to Jude as Abigail looked through the hats.

"I knew you missed her."

Smiling, I watched her pick up a set of ears with a princess crown. I laughed. "I did—so much."

In the end, Abigail ended up with a sequined set of ears, and after much convincing, both Jude and I walked out of the shop wearing matching bride and groom ears.

We had been Disney-fied to the max.

Abigail had been coming to Disneyland since she was barely able to walk, so she knew the park inside and out. It was like having our own personal tour guide as we strolled down Main Street, looking inside the various shops stuffed full of Disney merchandise.

"Where do you want to go first?" she asked happily, holding my hand.

"How about you pick?" I suggested, not even having a clue where to begin.

"Okay!" She tugged us both to the left through crowds of people standing around, taking pictures of Cinderella's castle.

We continued through the park, walking past the Jungle Cruise and the Indiana Jones Adventure ride.

"This is my favorite ride in the park," she announced as we came to the front entrance of the Pirates of the Caribbean attraction.

Her eyes shifted to Jude. "But it has a bit of a fast part. Do you think she'll be okay?"

He smiled, grabbing my hand, and he brought it to his lips. "Yeah, I think she'll be just fine on this one."

We quickly moved through the line, waiting only about ten minutes, before the three of us stepped into a boat. We wedged Abigail in between us as Jude rested his arm across the back of both of us.

"Do you think I can count this as a roller coaster, so I can scratch off number ten?" I asked.

The attendant pushed the lever to release our boat into the dark water.

"It's your list." Jude shrugged.

"Good," I answered, smiling. "Number ten—done."

Abigail pointed to the right where several people were dining nearby under twinkling lights. "That's the Blue Bayou," she said. "My mom took me there for my tenth birthday, and we sat right by the water and watched everyone float by. I waved." She giggled as she did just that—waved at all the people as they ate.

We passed by the restaurant, and the mood of the ride turned somber.

The music became haunting, and Abigail grabbed my hand. "Are you ready?"

"Ready for wha—"

I screamed as our boat sped down a steep cliff into the caves below. Abigail's laughter sounded in my ear as my shrieks died off, and I joined her.

"Oh my gosh! That was fantastic!" I looked over at Jude.

He was watching me with a happy warm glow. Even in his ridiculous Mickey ears, he was still the sexiest thing I'd ever seen.

The ears might actually have made him even sexier.

I could see why Pirates of the Caribbean—or "Pirates," as Abigail liked to call it—was her all-time favorite. It had everything—thrills, catchy songs, dancing pirates, and even a dash of fright.

I wasn't sure how she was going to top that, but she did. We went from Pirates to the Haunted Mansion, and once again, I found myself laughing hysterically throughout. Even It's a Small World captivated me . . . until I found myself singing the song four hours later.

It really was a hard song to get out of your head.

After several rides, we decided lunch was in order, and we took a break. As Abigail and I rested our feet at an outdoor table, Jude grabbed burgers and fries for everyone.

"So, tell me about you," I said. "What have you been up to? Are you still writing? Reading? Or have boys taken up all your time now?"

She giggled, rolling her eyes. "I still write. I don't think I could stop now. It's something my grandfather is very proud of. He brags about me to all his author friends, says he passed down his talent or something like that." She shrugged.

"He must think you're good at it."

"I just do it because I like it, not because I want anyone to praise me."

"Isn't that the best reason to do anything? Because you enjoy doing it?"

She nodded, her feet swinging back and forth on the bench. "Yeah, it is. So, what about you? Do you still write in your journal?"

I thought back to the days in the hospital when Abigail used to visit me. I'd been vigilant about keeping a journal. In a way, it was my one constant companion. When stuck in a hospital, never knowing if I'd be staying or going, it had been hard to keep friends. That journal had been the one place I could turn to when I needed to purge my emotions. But when I'd left, I guessed I didn't need it as much.

"No, not much anymore," I answered.

"Maybe you should start again," she suggested.

My hand went to my stomach, and my fingers stretched lightly over my tiny baby bump. "Yeah, maybe I should."

This baby had brought Jude and me home, back to where it had all started. We'd reconnected with old friends and family, and now, maybe it was time for me to reconnect with the old part of me I'd so desperately tried to let go of when I walked out of that hospital two years ago.

Maybe there was still something I could learn from that naive young girl who had given all her thoughts to a journal.

twenty-four

"GOD, LAILAH . . . ANYTHING but that one. Please?" I begged.

She smiled up at me from her spot on the sofa. A soft chenille blanket was draped over her now rounded stomach as she glanced down at the tattered old composition book that held the one-hundred-forty-three dreams and wishes on her Someday List.

"You told me to pick whichever one I wanted," she reminded me. "And I choose this one." Her finger tapped the page, signifying the end of our calm existence as I knew it.

I groaned.

"A puppy? Really? You want to adopt a puppy . . . now? Can't we just do something easy, like rake leaves?"

She gave me a doubtful look and laughed. "First of all, we're in California . . . in the springtime. Do you see any leaves, genius?"

My lips curved into a grin at her sarcasm.

"Secondly, I don't see why now isn't the perfect time to get a puppy. It will give us great practice for the baby." She shrugged, placing a hand on her belly. She'd successfully transitioned into her second trimester with little fuss and fanfare.

Well into her fourth month, the pregnancy was going well—too well.

It made me antsy, nervous.

"You want to practice your parenting skills on a puppy? How is that the same?" I argued, knowing it was completely pointless.

"Well, they're both tiny and require constant care and love. And I thought a dog might keep me company when you're gone next week," she added.

Stupid annual board meeting.

Roman had said I didn't need to go, but guilt mixed with doubt that my brother could actually handle everything on his own had me booking a flight and leaving my pregnant wife—something I had sworn I wouldn't do.

"Okay, grab your shoes. Let's go get you a dog," I grumbled.

She jumped up, shrieking and laughing. "You'll be just as excited as I am. Just wait. Once you see all those cute little puppies, you'll turn into a puddle of goo."

I gave her a doubtful sideways glance as she scurried off into the bedroom to find a pair of shoes. Grabbing the journal off the couch, I flipped through the pages, seeing all the numbers we'd managed to cross out over the last two years. It brought back a flood of memories with each scratch of the pen—the day we'd visited the Met or the afternoon we'd spent paddle boating around the lake at Central Park. I smiled as I saw the ones she'd recently drawn a line through as we'd made this book our goal over the last few weeks. My fingers moved from line to line, recalling each moment we had spent together.

It was like a retelling of our love story.

~~72. Have my heart broken.~~

That was one that hurt to see crossed out, knowing I was the reason it had been fulfilled. But it was something I couldn't regret. If I hadn't walked away, she wouldn't be here right now.

Carrying my child.

Possibly facing death—again.

"You ready to go?" Lailah asked, startling me.

"What? Oh, yes, let's go!" I answered, quickly recovering.

Taking her hand, we headed for the car, feeling the crisp ocean breeze blowing through our hair, as we walked down the driveway. I breathed in deeply, letting the smell of the water and air fill my lungs. The smell of the beach was something I'd missed while living in New York, and now that I could simply step out onto my deck and take my fair share whenever I needed, I secretly never wanted to leave. I loved what I did, working for a company that had my family's name on it, but the farther I got from the city, the less and less I wanted to return.

As we settled into the car, I realized I had no idea where we were headed.

"So, where does one go to get a puppy?" I asked, looking over at her for guidance.

She burst into laughter but covered her mouth quickly, trying to stop. "Oh, you really are from a wealthy family, aren't you, babe?"

"What? I mean, do we go to the mall? Petco? Hell, I don't know." I held up my hands in defense.

"We could go to lots of places. But there are animal shelters everywhere. I found one online that looks incredible and has a huge selection right now."

"Okay, lead the way," I instructed, backing out of the driveway.

She began giving directions.

The place wasn't too far away, maybe twenty minutes with traffic. We parked close to the entrance, and as we walked toward the door, I stopped.

Turning to face her, I asked, "You're going to adopt the most pitiful, grungiest-looking puppy in there, aren't you?"

"Why would you say that?"

"Because you have a thing for the underdog."

"You weren't an underdog," she challenged, her hands going to her hips defiantly.

"I wasn't much," I said.

Her hand cupped my cheek. "Looks can be deceiving. And you were more than I could have possibly imagined—even if you didn't have the Cavanaugh last name."

I kissed her forehead and wove my fingers around hers. "Come on. Let's go find a puppy."

I was right.

After an hour of deliberation, she'd settled on a shy, scraggly little fuzzball that looked like he had been eaten alive by all his fur.

"Isn't he the cutest thing in the world?" Lailah crooned, holding him in her lap in the car.

He curled up in her arms, his little nose peeking out just beyond the crook of her arm.

"He's goofy-looking," I replied.

"He's adorable!" she scolded.

I laughed. "Okay, I'll admit, he's kind of cute—in a weird, fluffy sort of way. Can that stuff even be brushed?" I asked, pointing to the sporadic tufts of fur that sprung out in every direction off his body.

"I think he needs a bath. Maybe a trip to a groomer? I don't know. He's perfect just the way he is," she said lovingly.

We stopped at the local pet store, buying everything that was recommended and more. Toys, shampoo, treats, food, and even a comfy dog bed were thrown into the cart.

"We need to get him a tag for his collar," I said, pointing to the engraving machine near the front.

"Oh, okay!" Lailah answered excitedly, holding her new friend close to her chest.

"Angel—"

"Yeah?"

"You need to name him first."

Her eyes went wide, and she stopped mid-aisle. "Oh. I guess we do. Well, hmm . . . what do you think we should name him? You seem to have all sorts of good names in that head of yours," she replied with a knowing grin.

Yeah, that had been a good night.

"Harry?" I suggested, looking down at his wild mane.

Her face scrunched together, and she shook her head. "No, not that."

She held the dog up, getting a good look at his tiny face. His little puppy-dog eyes met hers, and she giggled.

"We should name you after a famous book dog or something."

"There are famous book dogs?" I questioned, leaning against the cart. *This was going to take a while.*

"Of course there are! Bull's-Eye from *Oliver Twist,* Toto from *The Wizard of Oz,* even Clifford from, well, *Clifford.*"

“So, you want to name him Clifford?” I asked, looking at the little runt, thinking he didn’t resemble the gigantic red dog in the least.

“Well, no. But maybe something similar?”

I looked at our crazy-looking mop of a dog, trying to picture him as the hero of some classic tale.

“Sandy?” I suggested. “It’s not exactly from a book, but you love the musical, and he’s kind of a tiny version of the original. And we are New Yorkers after all.”

“That’s perfect!” she exclaimed. “He does look like Sandy!”

The tag was made, making Sandy’s name official. I loaded our loot into the back of the car, rolling my eyes at the amount of stuff required for one five-pound dog. I couldn’t even begin to imagine how much stuff we’d have to start gathering for the baby.

My stomach tightened when I realized neither of us had even talked about it yet.

No nursery had been discussed. No furniture or baby registry had been planned.

Nothing.

We’d decided as a team that we would celebrate everything—every ultrasound, every clean bill of health—and we had. A frame sat by the couch with the latest ultrasound proudly displayed, but it was as if we were unable to move past that point.

We talked about becoming parents all the time. We joked about the lack of sleep and the restless nights, yet neither of us were actually preparing for it.

What were we so scared of?

I awoke, the faint sound of crying ringing in my ears.

“Lailah, the baby is awake,” I whispered, reaching for her across the bed.

But she was nowhere to be found.

Tossing the sheets aside, I stumbled down the hall, covered in darkness, until I saw the sliver of light peeking out the door. Pushing it open with my hand, I stepped forward, following the urgent cries within.

The moonlight cast a light glow upon the crib, and as I looked down, it created almost an angelic halo on his light-blond hair.

"What's the matter?" I asked, reaching down to scoop him up.

My fingers ran through his tiny locks as his light-blue eyes studied me. Bouncing him lightly like I'd done a hundred times, we walked back and forth in front of the window, watching the dark waves crashing into the shoreline in the distance.

Within minutes, he was calm once again, his eyes dropping heavily.

"Want to go see Mommy before you nod off again?" I asked, cradling him to my chest, as I walked down the hall in search of Lailah.

I checked the kitchen first, wondering if maybe she'd decided to grab a late snack, but found nothing. The living room was empty as well.

My heart fluttered as I checked the deck, only to find it bare. My feet carried me back down the hall, checking room after room, until I found myself standing at the foot of our bed, staring at the place where I'd started.

A silver picture frame caught my eye, and I walked toward the nightstand. Picking up the photo, I looked down, tears falling from my face as I stared at the last picture taken of her.

"She's gone," I choked out. "She's gone."

"Sir?" Someone shook me, startling me back to reality. "Sir, we're about to land."

I looked around, taking in my surroundings, as my heart pounded in my chest. The roar of the engine filled my ears as the sound of the landing gear moved into place.

It was just a dream.

Lailah is alive, I chanted. *Lailah is fine.*

The nightmares had started a few weeks ago, a by-product of too much stress. So far, Lailah hadn't noticed when I'd gotten out of bed in the middle of the night to step out onto the deck for air. And I hadn't bothered to tell her.

I still fully believed that the least amount of stress in her life was the way to go. So far, it had worked.

I looked out of the window as the plane closed in on New York. It had been less than two months since I was here, having flown back briefly to pack up things for our new home, but it still felt like eons.

California was like another world compared to New York, and while I'd grown up here, I found myself loving the slow, laid-back life of the beach more and more with each passing day. Unfortunately, my job was here. I didn't know how to change that. I couldn't ask our entire company to relocate just because I liked the beach.

I took a deep breath, trying to relax, as the pilot landed the plane. Within minutes, the flight attendants had the doors open, and I was walking through the airport toward the row of cabs lining the front. My brother, of course, had beat me to it, and as I walked toward baggage claim, I spotted a man dressed in a sharp suit and tie, holding a sign with my last name neatly printed on it.

Shaking my head, I greeted him.

"Isn't this a little beneath you?" I grinned, actually glad to see him for a change.

Roman smirked before quickly turning the sign over.

Welcome home, jackass, it said.

"Now, that's more like it." I laughed.

We shook hands and headed out toward the front. The jet-black car he always had on standby was parked outside, and I quickly put my carryon in the trunk, not bothering to pester the driver with it. My brother fully embraced his wealthy lifestyle while I tended to use it only when it involved spoiling my wife.

"So, why are you picking me up?" I asked as we settled into the backseat.

He reached into a mini cooler and handed me a bottle of water and grabbed another for himself.

"Well, it's been a while since you've been around. Figured I'd give you an update before the meeting."

I was silent for a moment, letting that sink in.

"I told you I could be an adult when I wanted to be," he reminded me.

"I know," I answered. "It's just still hard to see."

His hard eyes stared at me, unblinking.

"Thank you," I responded, not knowing what else to say.

A quick nod was all the acknowledgement I got before he dived into business talk, his mouth moving so fast that I had a hard time keeping up.

I mostly listened, added my two cents here or there, but for the most part, he'd done a stellar job at preparing for our annual meeting. I was actually impressed.

The feeling intensified as the meeting began, and I watched him in action. He'd really gone all in, like he'd said he would, reviewing every aspect until he had it all down pat. There was no cutting corners, no loose ends. He was confident and composed as he spoke to the board, and for once, I believed he really could do it all.

I wasn't a fool. This potential didn't suddenly spring up from nowhere. He'd had it all along—well before I'd left for California.

So, why was he suddenly revealing it now?

If he'd been so capable in the past, why come to me, begging me to come back years ago? Why let the company fall to ruins? Why sit by and let me run the show while he played poster boy for a company he could clearly help lead side by side?

There were so many sides to the Roman puzzle, yet I couldn't figure any of them out.

We ended the annual meeting on a high note, everyone shaking hands, eager for the year ahead. All wished me and Lailah well with the pregnancy, knowing it was a risky one. I thanked everyone and promised to give any updates as they came along. After the room emptied, I turned to Roman, who was loosening his tie, as he flopped into a leather chair, exhausted.

"You did good," I admitted.

"I know." He grinned before taking a large gulp of water from the bottle in front of him.

"Why—" I began.

He cut me off, "You'd better get going. Mom is eager to see you."

"You're not coming?"

He shook his head. "No, I think I've had enough grown-up time for one day. Time to let off a bit of steam." He stood, brushing past me but paused near the entrance. "Good to see you, Jude. Be good to Lailah," he said before disappearing around the corner.

"I've missed you so much!" My mom burst into tears the moment the door opened. "Come in, come in!"

"Kind of hard when you've got me in a vise grip," I said as her slender body held me tightly. My arms folded around her as I smiled.

"Sorry." She laughed. "Just checking to make sure you're really here."

"It hasn't been that long," I said.

She stepped back, taking a good look at me. "It feels like an eternity. And look at that tan!"

I shrugged. "California weather, Mom—it can't be beat. You should try it sometime."

"Well, I don't think I can pull off a tan like that anymore, but I sure wouldn't mind the heat. And I would love to see my daughter-in-law. Tell me, how is she doing?"

She took my coat, and we made our way to the kitchen for drinks. The house felt huge and empty with just Mom in it these days. When I was younger, it had been full of laughter and staff. There never seemed to be a room that wasn't occupied by someone. Now, it just felt drafty and cold. I hated the idea of her spending the rest of her life out here, isolated from everyone. I understood the reasoning. It was our family home, and it had to be preserved, but certainly, other arrangements could be made.

"She's doing great—besides a bit of heartburn," I answered. "She's really good Mom."

"You sound surprised."

"Honestly, I am."

"Why?" she asked, grabbing a Coke from the fridge—the classic kind from the bottle. I'd loved them when I was a child, and ever since, she'd always have them waiting for me whenever I came to visit.

"You're waiting for the anvil to drop?" she asked, knowing my answer.

"Yeah. I know that sounds bad, but I just keep expecting something bad to happen. I've spent hours researching on the Internet. I mean, something has to go wrong, right? So, I just sit around, sucking in my breath, waiting for it to happen."

"And how does Lailah feel about this?" she asked, opening the refrigerator to pull out a casserole she'd made for dinner.

I watched her peel off the layer of plastic wrap off the top and walk it to the oven. Seeing her do such domestic tasks was still so foreign to me. She'd learned to fend for herself so much in the last few years as Dad had grown sick, and they'd cut back staff to hide his illness. Watching her and Molly put together Christmas dinner had been like seeing a rare bird in flight. It wasn't that I didn't think she could cook. I'd just never seen it.

"I don't know. I feel like we're just skimming the surface with our conversations. Neither one of us are willing to delve too deep into the future—too scared by the possibilities and the what-ifs. I'm trying to stay positive, trying to keep things as calm and tranquil for her and the baby as possible . . . but here"—I pointed to my temple—"it's an endless loop of nightmares. I can't stop them. I wake up, drenched in sweat, trembling, night after night. I can't stop thinking about what might go wrong, what could go wrong. Jesus, Mom, I could lose her. I could lose them both." Every emotion I'd kept bottled up for months spilled out of me.

She rushed forward, dinner forgotten, and held me. I purged every worry, every single fear, in the tears that fell onto her shoulders as I clung to her.

Her tears meshed with mine. "Oh, my dear sweet boy. You'll never lose them. They're tied to you forever—whether it's in this life or the next. But I know a thing or two about that girl you married. She's a fighter, Jude. She might look small, but her heart is ten times the size of most. She'll battle to the death for this life she's worked so hard to achieve."

I nodded, knowing she was right.

Lailah was a fighter, strong and willing to stand her ground against any foe—even death.

"You're right, Mom. I'm not giving her enough credit. And I'm jumping to conclusions. We're nearly to five months now, and she's had nothing but good news from the doctor. I just can't stop worrying." I shook my head against her shoulder.

"It's normal," she soothed. "When I was pregnant with you, your father insisted I call the office three times a day to check in."

"Did you?" I asked.

"No." She laughed. "But then, he got sneaky and started having the staff do it for me without my knowledge." Her eyes became glassy as she looked down toward the floor. "He was always one step ahead of me."

"He loved you, more than anything."

"I know he did," she answered, smiling. "Let's get this dinner made." She quickly swiped the tears from her face, moving toward the refrigerator to pull out items for a salad.

I jumped to my feet to help her. Within a few minutes, we were both chopping vegetables and tossing them into a large bowl when my phone rang.

Wiping my hands on a dish towel, I pulled my cell out of my pocket and saw Molly's number flashing on the screen.

"Hello?" I answered, my stomach already clenching.

"Jude," she said, "you need to come home."

Her voice sounded serious, concerned, frightened.

"Molly, what is it? What happened?"

"It's Lailah. She's in the hospital."

The phone fell from my hand.

The anvil had dropped, and all my fears rushed back to haunt me.

twenty-five

Let's Make a Deal

Lailah

DEAR JOURNAL,

Hey, old friend.

Long time, no talk. No write maybe? Well, anyway, it's been a while.

I guess I shouldn't feel bad. You aren't real. But you were there when I needed you.

A friend when there weren't any. A gentle listener when I needed to purge everything in my anxious soul.

Yet I do feel bad—that is, for abandoning you.

As life moved on and the world expanded beyond the tiny scope of this hospital, I kind of forgot about the great friendship I'd developed within the pages of this journal—and the many before it.

Long before pudding or placeholders, you were my rock, the only comfort I knew beyond family. You held me together when all I wanted to do was fall apart.

When nurses or patients left the hospital over the years, promis-

ing to write and keep in touch, I never held any ill will toward them when the letters or the calls began to cease. I knew life was better outside these walls—or at least, I hoped it was. It had to be. Because what else would I be fighting for?

Turns out, it is everything and more.

Love, laughter, passion, frustration, and the freedom to experience a hundred other emotions in a single minute.

The greatest solace and strength of my life.

Now, I know what I'm fighting for, and I've never been more scared, which is why I'm turning to you—my original confidant and friend. Because as much as I love my husband and family, I could never tell them how terrified I am, how every single fear I've imagined took one step closer into reality tonight.

I've allowed myself to dream, to hope, to plan.

As Jude's plane was touching down in New York, I was enjoying a cup of herbal tea on the deck, relaxing with my feet up, thinking how wonderful the sun felt on my skin.

I'd made it nearly halfway through my second trimester without a single issue.

Life was good.

Deciding a little walk might do some good, I grabbed Sandy's leash and headed for the beach. He excitedly jumped up and down the moment my fingers brushed the canvas. The darn thing wasn't even in my hands yet, and somehow, he knew a walk was going to happen.

We took a long leisurely stroll down the beach, waving at runners and happy children playing in the sand. On our way home, I stopped at the mailbox and picked up the mail.

That's when I saw it—a baby catalog.

Somehow, the people in mail land had figured out the impending arrival of our child before I was barely bulging out of my pre-pregnancy jeans.

How did they do that?

I stared at the catalog like it was filled with kryptonite and battery acid as Sandy and I made our way into the house. Setting it down on the counter, I gave him treats and water and made myself a snack, looking at it the entire time out of the corner of my eye.

And then, I swear it moved.

I gripped the counter, shaking my head a little, trying to dislodge any cobwebs or bats . . . because I mean, things were getting a little freaky.

By this time, I was sure I was going crazy.

Maybe I already have. I am a full-grown woman writing in a journal.

Anyway, moving on.

The catalog continued to stare at me through dinner until I finally caved.

Snatching it off the counter, I decided I would just peek.

It couldn't hurt just to see what was out there in the world of babies, right?

So, I opened it, just a little, and immediately, I was sucked in.

Suddenly, I found myself standing at the door of the empty bedroom adjacent from ours, mentally measuring walls for crib space, looking at the windows for types of curtains, and even picking out color palettes.

I'd gone from zero to sixty in the blink of an eye, and it actually felt good.

I wondered what I had been so scared of.

My hand dropped down to my round little belly, the tiny flutter I'd grown accustomed to making its presence known. I smiled, remembering the first time I'd felt it.

It was all real and it was happening.

Jude and I had been tiptoeing around this pregnancy, fearful of everything that went along with it. We both put on positive smiles and charged ahead, but I knew neither one of us was actually taking that fateful first step.

That empty nursery proved just that.

We were two people skating around a frozen pond, just waiting for the center to give in. Take one step too far, and everything would fall into the icy water below.

I decided, in that moment, to be the one to take that first brave step.

Unfortunately, Mother Nature had other plans.

I was so excited in my planning that I hadn't noticed the signs—the dizziness, the blurred vision.

As I look back now, I probably should have, but when focused on a task, especially one that involves a credit card and online ordering,

I tend to push other things aside.

I finally owned up to what was going on internally when I stood and saw stars.

I called my mom, and . . . well, the rest is history.

Here we are.

Sometimes, I feel like life is one giant stage. Just when I think I'm about to hit my high note—the big number that will make me a star—someone comes up behind me with one of those big stage hooks, ready to drag me away.

"Lailah?" Jude burst through the door, his eyes wide and frantic.

He looked like he'd been up all night, and judging by the state of his clothes and the wee hours of the morning, I guessed he probably had been.

"Are you okay? I got here as soon as I could," he rushed out the words. His legs carried him to my side.

I wanted to cry. I wanted to sob, leaking every last tear my body could produce, but I didn't.

I couldn't.

Seeing his worry, his need for everything to be okay, I swallowed every last fear, keeping them at bay, squashing them down for another time.

"I'm fine," I responded. "High blood pressure, that's all. They're discharging me now."

He didn't look convinced.

"I swear, I'm fine." I held my hands up in defense.

"I shouldn't have gone."

"It wouldn't have made a difference. The doctor on call said high blood pressure is a perfectly normal thing for pregnant woman. See? I'm normal," I encouraged.

"I'm not traveling anymore," he replied, completely ignoring my comments.

"Good," I said. "I like having you around." I cupped his face with my hands.

His eyes closed as he melted into my palm. "I'm so sorry I wasn't here."

"But you're here now," I reminded him. "Just in time to bust me out of this place."

"You got it. Let's go home."

"Now, you're talking."

"When you said you ordered a few things while I was gone, did you possibly underestimate that statement a bit?" Jude asked as he carried in what had to be the tenth box in the last two days.

I gave him a sheepish grin. "Maybe?"

"Do you even remember what you ordered?" he asked, looking down at the shipping label with an inquisitive stare.

"Oh, yes," I answered. "Definitely."

"Well, you want to give me a hand then?"

I looked up from the book I was reading. "Right now?"

"Yeah. Why not?" He grinned.

A flutter of excitement mixed with nervousness rushed through my system as I followed him down the hall. I'd ordered every single item in those scattered boxes that lonely night last week with the intention of moving forward with this pregnancy—no more waiting, no more hiding behind fears.

Then, I'd ended up in the hospital, and suddenly, I was back behind that line again, struggling to move past the point where I could tell myself that it was okay to decide on wall colors and baby names. Four months from now, this child growing in my stomach would become a reality.

It wasn't just a fantasy I was trying to will into existence. This was happening.

And the strong-willed fighter I'd become after years and years of battling a diseased heart needed to step up to the plate and realize that.

I placed a hesitant foot into the empty room, taking note of the many boxes neatly stacked in each corner.

"So, where should we start?" I asked him, looking around from one end to the other, as I twisted my hands together.

"Why don't you just take a seat and let me see what we have?"

"But I could help you—"

"Nope," he answered, cutting me off.

"Not even for a little bit?"

"Sorry." He shook his head. "Ass on the floor, Lailah."

I pouted, slumping to the ground. "How am I supposed to help on the floor?"

He took a wide step forward, bending down to capture my lips. "Well, sitting there is helpful on the eyes."

My head cocked to the side, and I gave him an amused stare.

"And . . ." He paused. "You can direct with these lovely little arms of yours. Tell me where to put everything. I'm at your disposal. But no getting up. In fact . . ."

He rushed out of the room and came back with two kitchen chairs. Helping me up, he sat me in one, and after positioning the other across from me, he raised my feet up on the other.

"See? Comfy."

I rolled my eyes.

Using a box cutter, he began pulling everything out.

Okay, so maybe I had forgotten some of the things I'd ordered. That one-click feature should be outlawed.

"So, it looks like I'll be putting together a crib and whatever the hell this is," he said, pointing to the large box in the corner.

"It's a glider," I explained.

"A what?"

"A glider—kind of like a rocking chair but smoother. And it's upholstered."

"So, the La-Z-Boy of baby furniture?" He grinned, looking at the picture on the side.

"It's supposed to be soothing."

"It looks great," he encouraged sweetly, pushing up his sleeves to dive into the assembly. "We're going to do this one first. It will give you a better place to sit."

I giggled as I watched him pull out a million different parts and pieces, never once complaining that we could have easily paid someone to do this for us or just gone to some fancy furniture store where all of this would be preassembled. It felt like a rite of passage—something all parents must do before the birth of their children. For the first time during this pregnancy, I felt normal, extremely mundane and normal. It was as if the fear and anxiety of everything that could happen had been left at the threshold. This was our safe space—where life was planned, not feared.

Eventually, I ordered a pizza and then turned on some music on my phone, and we sat around, eating, laughing and figuring out which side of part A fit into part B. Around two hours later, we had a glider.

"Hey, look at that. It works!" I exclaimed, sitting in it for the first time.

It moved back and forth with little to no effort, and as I perched my feet up onto the matching ottoman, I tried to picture myself here, late at night, with a tiny child in my arms, rocking him back and forth, back and forth.

My eyes closed as the picture formed and blossomed in my head.

Blue eyes to start, but eventually, as he grew, they'd fade into green, soft green eyes like his father.

He'd have his compassion, too, his big heart.

My eyes flashed open as a trickle of fear wormed its way back into my soul.

Dear God, what if he got my heart? A weak, brittle broken little heart.

Thump, thump.

What was that?

My hand flew to my stomach.

"Lailah? What it is?"

I chased the sensation, my hand racing everywhere, as if I were hunting a cell phone signal.

"I think—I mean, I know"—I laughed—"the baby just kicked."

"Different from what you've been experiencing?"

"Oh, yes," I answered. "This wasn't a flutter or a kind of whoosh. This was a solid kick. He—if *he* really is a he—is making his presence known."

Jude rushed to me, kneeling by my side, his eyes staring up at me with an intense sense of wonder on his face. I grabbed his hand, and together, we gripped my stomach, waiting for another moment.

"What were you thinking of when it happened?" he asked, his fingers brushing tenderly along the curve of my belly.

"What he'd look like, the color of his eyes, the—oh! There it is!"

I looked up and knew he'd felt it. Maybe not as strongly as I had, but he'd definitely sensed the slightest bit of movement.

His hand curled around me as he bent down closer. "He's strong. Our little man is healthy and strong."

Tears formed in my eyes as I watched him stare down at my belly in amazement.

Our child was indeed strong. I'd been so scared that I was passing on my diseased genes to him, and in that moment, he'd let us know that he was there, and he was fighting.

Now, I just had to be strong enough to fight alongside him.

"So, care to make a wager?" I challenged.

Our joined hands swung back and forth as we walked down the long hallway.

We'd just finished up another doctor's appointment—twenty-six weeks. Thanks to proper medication and an overbearing husband, I had been given another clean bill of health. I still couldn't believe it.

We were halfway there. Another couple of months, and soon, we'd meet our child.

He squeezed my hand as we made our way toward the ultrasound office.

"A wager?" he asked, his interest piqued.

"Well, we decided today would be the day, so I thought, before we go in there and discover whether this baby you are so determined to call a boy is in fact—"

"In possession of a penis?"

"Jude!" I blurted out, looking around, as my cheeks reddened.

He laughed, "Would you rather me say franks and beans? Twigs and berries?"

"Oh my gosh. You're a child."

"You're the one who cringed when I said penis," he reminded me, making sure to say the P word loud and clear for anyone walking down the hall to hear.

I shook my head, doing my best to ignore him. "Back to the wager."

"Right. So, what do I get when I win?" he asked, opening the glass door for me that led into the small waiting room.

It was empty today, which meant we should hopefully be called back immediately. We'd had several ultrasounds now, due to the high risk of my pregnancy. We could have known the sex of the baby weeks ago, but I'd chosen to wait, wanting to find out around the time when other women did. The wait made everything feel much more normal, and any ounce of normalcy was treasured.

Not that any of this mattered to my husband. He was convinced we were having a boy. There was no changing his mind.

Now, he was eagerly waiting for the proof.

"Who says you're going to win?" I countered, taking a seat near the door.

"You've already called it a boy on multiple occasions!" he exclaimed, crossing his arms in obvious victory.

"Only because you do. And because I hate the idea of calling our child an *it.* That's just wrong."

"So, why not say *she?*"

"You're changing the subject!" I snapped in frustration.

He snorted loudly.

Cocky jerk.

"Okay, fine. If it's a boy, you let me repaint the nursery blue and put up football jerseys."

My eyes narrowed. He knew I hated sports-themed anything.

"Baseballs?"

I gave him a blank stare.

"Um, waves . . . surfers maybe?"

"Better. Go to town with that if you like. Bring in a surfboard for the ceiling for all I care, but no jerseys of any kind—ever."

"Okay, deal."

"And if it's a girl?" he asked, barely paying attention.

So sure of himself.

"I get to pick the name."

His eyes flew up to mine. "But I'm so good at picking names," he reminded me with a wicked grin.

"Ah, yes, I remember. But this is my condition. How sure are you that this is a boy?" I asked, rubbing my belly.

The door creaked open, and my name was called.

We both stood, his hand grasping mine.

As we followed the tech down the hall, I felt his hot breath tickle my ear as he leaned forward to whisper, "You're on."

I smiled, my stomach a flutter of anticipation, as we were escorted to the small room we'd become well acquainted with over the last several months. Luckily, the ultrasounds had become less evasive. No wardrobe changes had been required for some time now.

The technician helped me onto the examination table. Lifting my shirt, she placed white towels at the top and bottom of my clothes. Warm goo was spread across my tummy, and soon, the screen was alive with pictures of our tiny child.

"Do we want to know the sex today?" the technician asked as she plugged away on her keyboard, checking measurements and recording information.

"Yes," we answered in unison.

"Okay, I'll do my best," she replied.

She continued to do her thing, freezing frames as she moved the wand around my growing belly. Lying in the position in this same room several times now, it was easy to see the progression week after week. The first time, it had been hard to believe anything was really different. My stomach had been smooth and flat. Now, there was evidence. Anyone who looked at me could see I was carrying precious cargo, and any second now, I'd know if that tiny kicker I'd grown to love was a boy or a girl.

Each new image the technician showed gave us another glimpse. It was no longer a little lima bean but rather a small baby-shaped blob. She pointed out feet and legs, arms and head. It was crystal clear, but I could see just the outline of everything.

"Okay, are you ready? I'm going to see if I can get a peek between those legs."

Jude gave me a quick glance, his lip turned up in amusement.

"Well . . ." She pondered over that word for a moment or two.

We waited in anticipation.

"Looks like you've got a very unlucky boy or a little girl on your hands!"

"A girl?" Jude said, completely stunned.

"A girl? Really?" I echoed, the words coming out soft and strained.

I looked at the image again—the rounded belly, the two perfect arms, and the beautiful head.

Of course it was a girl.

Jude looked over at me, his eyes brimming with tears, as he mouthed the word, *Angel.*

He squeezed my hand, holding it to his lips, and he placed a gentle kiss in the center.

"Guess I owe you a name?" he said.

"Meara," I simply stated.

He let it hang in the air before smiling. "It's beautiful."

"I remembered seeing it somewhere when we were in Ireland. Maybe a waitress, for all I know, but I looked up the name last week in our baby book because I just couldn't stop thinking about it."

The technician finished up and promised to send everything to the doctor. After I cleaned the goo off my belly and readjusted my shirt, I caught Jude's gaze.

He asked, "And what does it mean? The name?"

"Sea. It means the sea. I thought it was perfect."

He helped me off the table and pulled me into his arms.

"It is. Perfect and beautiful, just like you."

My smiling eyes lifted to his.

"You're going to make me repaint the nursery anyway, aren't you?" he asked, knowing it was coming.

"Well, I mean, a girl does deserve more than just plain old yellow." I shrugged, laughing.

"Slave driver."

"Oh, good. Now that we're talking about it, those curtains really need to be changed, too. I don't know what I was thinking and—"

He just chuckled under his breath the entire way home as I mentally redecorated the entire room we'd just completed.

It didn't matter though because she was healthy. Meara was healthy, and life was perfect.

twenty-six

Tick, Tick . . . Boom

Jude

AS THE WEATHER grew hot and spring turned to summer, we settled into our quiet new life on the coast of California. Long gone were the bright lights of the city, now replaced by lazy evenings nestled around the deck, watching sunsets night after night.

We knew it was temporary. We knew we'd eventually have to go back to a life filled with more—more responsibility, more to do, and more required of both of us.

But for now, we simply just enjoyed each other.

Finally, it wasn't about making up for time lost or trying to cram in as much as possible before some inevitable doomsday occurred. It was only about the present, living in the moment.

Seeing Meara for the first time in that ultrasound, giving her a name after all those weeks of looking at grainy photos up on the screen, had suddenly made something click for both of us.

We were having a child, and yes, a million and a half things could go wrong between now and then. But did either of us want to look back and regret the moments we'd lost while worrying about it? No, we'd want to know we had spent every second making the most of our time together.

So, that was exactly what we'd done over the last few months. We'd slowed down and remembered, rekindling the honeymoon lifestyle we'd fallen in love with before this all began—lazy days on the beach, long nights wrapped in each other by the fire. It was time we would have never gotten otherwise, and we relished in it, drinking in every ounce of each other until there was no beginning and no end. It was one never-ending *baby moon,* as our family called it.

Whatever it was called, it worked. I could see a marked change in Lailah. Her stress level had lessened. Her blood pressure had improved, and so far, everything seemed to be going well.

At least, it had been—until last night.

Just when I'd finally believed we could make it through to the other side without complications, the floor had caved in.

We always knew there was a chance things could go bad.

I'd just never expected this.

I didn't know why I'd awoken.

Maybe I already knew. Somehow, deep down in the marrow of my being, I'd known tonight was the night everything would change. Our extended honeymoon was over, and like the sound of a movie reel settling back into place, our life was restarting.

Whatever the reason, I'd woken up to find Lailah tossing madly. She was in a deep sleep, her eyes moving rapidly, as the moonlight drifted through the window, casting a deep shadow across her tortured face.

"Lailah," I whispered tenderly, caressing the skin across her cheekbone.

She felt warm and sweaty.

"Lailah," I said again, this time with a bit more urgency.

Her eyes opened weakly.

"I don't feel well," she said immediately, grasping her stomach.

"When was the last time you checked your blood pressure?" I asked, my body shifting into high gear.

Ever since her trip to the ER in the spring, she had been put on medication to regulate her blood pressure. She'd also check it once or twice a day, just to be safe.

"Before bed . . . maybe dinner?" she answered sluggishly. "I need to go to the bathroom."

I stood quickly, grabbing her hand, as she swung her feet over the edge of the bed. As she rose, I could see her eyes lose focus, as if the world had just tilted on its axis.

"Lailah?"

"I think we need to go to the hospital," she stated, her voice clear and calm as she gripped her chest.

It was the calm part that made me feel anything but.

I didn't even bother acknowledging her. Rather, I jumped into action. I ran to the closet and dresser, pulling out clothes, anything I could find—jeans and a T-shirt for me, yoga pants and a hoodie for her. Shoes were found, and within three minutes, we were out the door, leaving a very sad and confused puppy behind.

"He'll be fine," I promised as I sped down the highway toward the hospital. "I'll call your mom and Grace the minute you're in a room and have one of them check on him."

"Okay," she answered softly.

I grasped her hand across the seat.

Flying into the parking lot, I stopped in front of the emergency room doors and helped her out. Thankfully, she was wheeled straight back to labor and delivery, and paperwork was put off until things settled down. I didn't think I could even remember my own name right now, let alone be responsible for completing insurance forms.

A nurse helped her strip down as they eased her onto a bed, hooking her up to a fetal monitor. The whooshing sound I'd become familiar with during doctor's visits and ultrasounds gently filled the air. I watched the woman as she wrote numbers down, and she quickly left the room, only to return a moment later with the on-call doctor.

Lailah and I nervously looked at one another, gripping each other for support.

"Hi, I'm Dr. Truman. What seems to be going on tonight?"

Lailah briefly explained waking up, feeling disoriented, her chest burning. The more she spoke, the more anxious I became. Dr. Truman's head bobbed up and down, as if she were neatly fitting all the pieces of a puzzle in her head. It was obvious she already knew what was wrong, and she was just confirming as Lailah spoke.

"And how do you feel now?" the doctor asked.

"Worse. Like I'm crawling out of my skin. My head is pounding, and I feel like I'm going to throw up."

"Well, considering what your blood pressure is, I'm not surprised." Her eyes narrowed. "How do you feel about delivering tonight?"

I could see the panic immediately flare to life in Lailah's expression.

"But I'm barely thirty-one weeks. It's not time." The words rushed out of her mouth. "I'm not due until October. It's not October yet!"

Tears flooded her eyelids as I tried to comfort her even though my own heart was beating in a rapid staccato rhythm that I was finding hard to hide.

Preeclampsia. Maybe worse.

The doctor was sugarcoating everything, trying to keep Lailah's stress to a minimum, but I knew that was what we were facing. They wouldn't be risking a premature birth otherwise.

"It is early," the doctor replied. "But right now, we have to focus on the health of you and the baby, and this is the best option we have."

"We can't just put me on bed rest? Up my medication to lower the blood pressure?"

I could see it in her eyes. She was grasping at straws. She knew as well as I did that this was fruitless, but the idea of seeing our child in the NICU was sending her into mindless hysterics.

"Lailah," I said calmly, pushing back an errant strand of hair from her face, "I think the doctor is right. We need to do what's best for Meara."

The use of her name seemed to calm Lailah instantly, refocusing her priorities and drive. Silently, she nodded, squeezing my hand, as tiny tears fell down her face.

"Okay," she agreed.

"Great. I'm going to go notify the OR, and we'll be back shortly," Dr. Truman said before quickly leaving the room.

The quiet settled around us as Lailah looked out the window. The only sounds were the whir of the machines, Meara's fetal heart monitor, and Lailah's soft sobs leftover from earlier.

"It's going to be okay," I encouraged, grasping her chin in my palm.

I tugged her attention back to me, and her crystal-blue eyes found mine. Doubt, worry, and distress weighed heavily in her soul.

"How do you know?" she asked softly.

"Honestly"—I exhaled, my eyes falling to the floor—"I don't. I don't know, Lailah. But I can't see any other option. Because this," I said, pulling her hand closer to my heart, "us, I can't lose this. So, it has to be okay. Right?"

I met her gaze again just as her arms fell around me.

"Right," she cried.

We held each other, seeking the solid tethered feeling each of us felt when wrapped around each other. I'd always feel whole when she was in my arms.

Suddenly, just as the world was righting itself in her arms and I was beginning to feel like we might be able to conquer whatever might lie ahead that night, alarms sounded, and nurses rushed in, breaking us apart. I stood, stunned and terrified. I stared down at my wife as they began moving cords and IVs, adjusting the bed for transport.

"What's going on?" I shouted.

Lailah eyes rounded in fear.

"The fetus is under distress. We have to get her into the OR now."

She turned to me. Sheer utter terror was written across her face as the room flooded with people. I shook my head, knowing what she was going to say before the words even left her mouth.

"Meara comes first, Jude," she cried out before an oxygen mask went over her head. "Meara comes first!"

I shook my head, unwilling to process what she'd said.

"Her blood pressure is climbing!" someone yelled.

No, no, no. No!

None of this was happening.

They flew down the hall as I ran alongside her. Her eyes never left mine as she silently waited for me to answer her. I couldn't. I wouldn't. No one, not even her, could make me choose between the two of them.

Lailah would always come first.

Always.

But a single word brought me to my knees.

"Please," she said through the mask, tears streaming down her face.

I couldn't form words. It hurt too much. Was I actually going to agree to put the life of our child above hers?

As I nodded, hoping I'd never have to make the choice, I saw her visibly relax. Her hand reached out for mine, but I never got the opportunity to take it.

"Sir, I'm sorry. This is as far as you can go," a nurse said, blocking my way.

Lailah disappeared from my view. I watched the bed roll around a corner, wondering if that would be the last time I saw her . . . alive.

Anger burned through my veins.

"What do you mean?" I spit.

"You're not allowed in the operating room," he simply said.

"I'm her husband, the father. Why am I not allowed to be there during the birth?" I demanded.

"Normally, you would be," he answered, speaking calmly, as if he were talking to a petulant child. "But in emergency deliveries like this, no one is allowed back there since general anesthesia will be administered."

"You're knocking her out?"

"It's the quickest way," he explained, his expression dark and guarded.

The quickest way to ensure the survival—of both of them.

Lailah would never have any memory of those precious first minutes—the first cry, the cutting of the umbilical cord. Neither of us would.

As I slid down the wall and waited next to the entrance of the OR for news, I prayed, prayed to whoever would listen.

Because I needed a miracle, and I needed it fast.

twenty-seven

Lights Out

Lailah

"I DIDN'T GET to say good-bye!" I shouted, stretching my head around, as I tried to will Jude back into existence.

But he was gone, lost behind the double doors that now separated us.

"There's no time, sweetheart," the nurse answered.

I lay there, watching in panic, as they scrambled around me.

Dr. Truman appeared above me, a sympathetic smile on her face. "We're going to administer your anesthesia now, okay?"

"I don't get to be awake?" I cried as I felt a rush of gas flood through the mask over my head.

"I'm sorry, hon. This will all be over soon," a nurse said, appearing by my side. "Do you know what you're having?" She gently smoothed back my hair.

"A girl," I answered, my eyes already drooping.

The background began to fade as the lights dimmed.

"And what is her name?"

"Meara," I answered softly.

"Good. Dream of Meara. And when you awake, this will all be over, and you'll be a mother," she said gently right before my eyes sealed shut, and the world disappeared.

Beep, beep, beep.

My ear registered the familiar sound before my eyelids cracked open. After years of waking up to that particular noise, I knew where I was without having to see it.

"She's awake," my mother said.

The hospital room came into focus.

Stark white walls surrounded me while the buzz of medical equipment whirred around me.

I was back in the hospital, back in the world I'd left behind.

Memories rushed through my mind as pain began to flood every nerve ending in my body.

I remembered rushing to the hospital, alarms, crying as I'd begged Jude to put our baby before me, and then nothing.

"Where is she?" I asked, my voice cracking, the words feeling dry and coarse against my throat.

Marcus and my mother came toward me, warm tender looks of love in their expressions.

Their silence sent icy shivers down my spine.

"No," I responded, shaking my head. "No . . ." I said again.

"She's in the NICU," Marcus finally said.

I froze. "She's alive?"

My mother nodded, a tear escaping down her cheek. "Yes, but it's still touch and go, Lailah. Her lungs . . . well, she's not breathing on her own."

"But"—my lip quivered—"the doctor said it was our only option. She said—" I couldn't finish, my voice trailing off.

She squeezed my hand as Marcus rubbed my shoulder.

"They never know what to expect when delivering a baby early," Marcus interjected. "She was blue when they pulled her out, which means she went without oxygen, and because of her size and age, her lungs aren't fully developed. Right now, we just need to be thankful she's alive."

I tried to adjust in the bed, and I felt a sharp pain shoot through me.

"We're lucky to have you both," he added.

"What do you mean?" I asked.

"Have you heard of the pregnancy complication called the HELLP syndrome?"

I shook my head, feeling dizzy from the wave of information being thrown at me.

"Well, when you came in, Dr. Truman thought you were showing signs of preeclampsia, which is why she moved to do the C-section right away. But when Meara went into fetal distress and your blood pressure kept rising, she knew it was much more serious." He looked down at me, his eyes misting. "You could have died, Lailah."

"But I'm still here," I replied, carefully taking his hand in mine.

He broke down, curling into me, as he cried. My mom joined him, holding her husband, as her arm softly touched my hair.

"I'm right here," I said, knowing they needed to hear it as much as they needed to touch the hair on my head and feel the tears falling down my face.

These two people had nearly watched me die a dozen times over the last twenty-six years. It never got easier, and the fear and worry would never dissipate.

"I'm okay," I reminded them. "But Meara needs us, all of us."

I looked up at the exact moment the door opened. It was as if I'd summoned him from thin air. His hair was a disheveled mess, tousled in every direction, much like his clothes. But none of that mattered as his gaze met mine, and I realized I was still here.

And so was he.

Now, there was only one missing piece of our new little puzzle.

"I'm going to go check for updates in the NICU," Marcus said, adjusting himself.

My mom quickly followed behind. Her hand briefly touched Jude's shoulder before they left, and soon, it was just the two of us.

"I wanted to be here when you woke up," he said.

"You're here now."

Stepping forward, he raised his hand and placed a single cup of pudding on the metal tray beside my bed. "I was running a very important errand."

That single gesture opened the floodgates, and I broke. Every emotion I'd hidden, every fear, every damn scenario I'd envisioned that didn't include me in it suddenly came rushing to the surface, like a hundred-year-old dam breaking in a deadly hurricane.

I just couldn't hold any of it in any longer.

I was in his arms immediately as the tears flowed, and the overwhelming feeling of everything crashing down around me fell to the floor, one tiny drop at a time. When I felt his wet cheek touch mine, I knew he'd been holding back as well.

We'd become experts at our own game. We'd been skating around the icy fear and haunting reality of what might come that neither of us had even realized the true depth our silence had cost us. I'd thought I'd come clean, vowing to live every moment in the present, but really, I had just shoved more and more doubt further down until I was nearly choking on the very idea of what might come.

Now that it was nearly over, now that I was still here, still breathing and clinging to the man I loved, there were no words.

No words but one.

"Meara," I said.

His eyes met mine, red-rimmed and swollen around the edges from the lack of sleep. "She's beautiful," he said softly. "Beautiful, Lailah."

An entirely new set of tears fell from my eyes, but these were happy, thankful tears. "You've seen her?"

He nodded. "Only briefly. She's tiny, just around three pounds. But she's perfect . . . and she's ours."

"I want to see her," I said.

"You will. As soon as the nurse clears you to do so, I promise."

His hand tenderly went to my arm as my eyes traveled to the single cup of pudding he'd set on the tray.

"Do I need to be cleared for that?" I asked.

A small smile tugged at the corner of his lip. "Not if you plan on sharing it." He pulled out two spoons from his pocket and handed me one.

"Deal," I agreed as I watched him peel back the lid of the cup.

Some things never changed.

We'd washed and scrubbed our hands, and as I took a solid deep breath, the nurse wheeled me into the room.

I was meeting my daughter—for the very first time.

It didn't matter that I'd missed out on her first wailing cry as the doctor pulled her from my womb. It didn't matter that circumstances had separated us until this moment.

I was here now.

The room was quiet, and a sense of calm met me as soon as we crossed the threshold. I'd seen NICUs in movies and TV shows but never up close. Nurses and other parents greeted me with a nod, welcoming me into the small club I now belonged to. It was a sudden kinship I never knew I'd have.

A mother sat in a wooden glider, tightly holding a tiny baby against her chest. She lovingly looked down at her son, touching the smooth skin of his face, as she softly sang. In comparison to those in the incubators, he was huge, yet he still looked so fragile.

There were others, too—babies and families that humbled me beyond words. I didn't know what we were going to face, but I knew it would be nothing compared to some of the things I witnessed as I passed by the incubators in that NICU. My heart silently reached out for them as we made our way forward. Jude walked behind my wheelchair as the nurse pushed me forward, his arm firmly linked to my shoulder, as we were escorted to the corner where Meara was.

The first thing I noticed were the wires.

There were so many wires and tubes—in her arms and legs, wrapped around her nose, and taped to her feet. It was horrifying at first. Yet I knew from experience that, sometimes, the road to recovery wasn't pretty, and without it, I also knew she wouldn't be here.

And neither would I.

The second thing I noticed was her face, her little cherub face.

Jude was wrong. She wasn't just beautiful. She was breathtaking—the perfect blending of each of us. As my eyes welled up with tears, I reached toward her, my hands touching the plastic separating us.

Ten tiny toes. Ten perfect fingers.

Somehow, we'd managed to do the impossible.

"Would you like to touch her?" a nurse came over to greet us, her voice calm and soft.

"Can I?" I asked, my eyes never leaving Meara's side.

She was resting on her back, her head cocked to the side. Her little hands lay high above her in a touchdown position. Seeing her like that, in such a baby-like pose, gave me hope that beyond the wires and tubes clinging to her now, I'd see her outside of here—bigger, healthier, and in my arms.

She wasn't even supposed to be here. We'd done everything to prevent this day from occurring. But no form of birth control could stop this little one from making her presence known. She'd come bursting into the world, like a bright white comet careening into our lives, and there was no way she could possibly be leaving as quickly as she'd arrived.

No, she was a fighter.

She'd fought for her place in this world, and now, she'd fight to keep it.

The nurse helped me sit up a bit in my wheelchair and explained what to do. I was nervous. I was so afraid I'd hurt my daughter or upset her. I wanted so badly to touch her, comfort her, and feel that she was really here. The little nudger, who had been kicking me for so many months, was alive. I wasn't awake when she'd been brought into this world, and suddenly, I felt overwhelmed by the fear that I might do something wrong.

I could feel Jude's soothing presence behind me, supporting me.

"Preemies do very well with constant touch," the nurse explained. "She can't be held quite yet, but right now, a gentle warm hand on her stomach will let her know that you're here, that you're both here," she added, looking over to Jude. "And believe me, it will do wonders."

I nodded, still a bit hesitant but now filled with purpose. If my touch could aid her healing, I would be here around the clock if I had to. I put my shaky hand into the plastic holes of the incubator and reached out for her.

The moment my fingers touched the smooth skin of her belly, tears rimmed my eyes.

My little girl.

Every minute of my life, every second spent in this hospital, had been worth it because it'd led up to this precious moment in time. I felt Jude's firm hand grasp my shoulder. With my free hand, I reached up and gripped his fingers.

Now . . . now, my life was complete.

twenty-eight

Jude

THE ELEVATOR DINGED, and I took a brief moment before stepping off.

I'd made my rounds over the past few days as Lailah recovered. I'd picked up pudding at the cafeteria and traded jokes with the staff. I'd even stopped by Human Resources and said hello to Margaret, who had somehow managed to graduate from wool suits to more modern attire. When I had seen the picture frame on her desk of her in the arms of a smiling man, I'd guessed the wool suits had been tossed right around the time the diamond ring on her finger appeared.

Good for her.

I'd visited the cardiology staff and even said hello to some of the ER staff I still knew from my days of working here before switching departments.

Now, there was only one more place to go.

I walked down the familiar hallway, looking left and right, as the memories assailed me. They didn't carry the same punch as they used to, but my chest still ached from the loss. No matter how much I continued to move forward, a part of me would always remember her . . . miss her.

That was why I had to take this journey, this moment, and spend a few minutes alone with Megan.

I'd stopped asking a long time ago why things turned out the way they did, like why Megan's life had ended so abruptly and Lailah's had carried on. I stopped wondering what my life would have been like if Megan and I hadn't gone to that party, and I hadn't played that stupid game with her, allowing her to drive instead of me.

Life wasn't about regret. It was about making the most of it after the dust had settled around your feet.

I looked down at the wooden bench, now marked with the bronze plaque I had installed years earlier.

Life: It goes on.

I breathed out a smile, taking a seat on the bench I'd sat in a thousand times before.

My eyes aligned with the closed door where Megan's last breath had been taken, where I'd thought my life ended.

It was here where I'd begun my self-imposed imprisonment. Little had I known that it would be my road to freedom.

"Hey, Megan," I whispered softly as my head fell to my clasped hands. "I know it's been a while since I was here." A heavy sigh fell from my lips. "But I haven't forgotten . . . about us, about this place."

A nurse walked briskly down the hall, nodding to me, as she passed by. I gathered my thoughts as her footfalls echoed against the floor. I looked up at the door once more.

"I have a wife . . . a child," I said. "Her name is Meara. She's four days old today, and she is just so damn beautiful." My voice cracked as the weight of my words felt heavy around my chest.

"The moment I saw her, I knew I loved her. It was instantaneous, fierce, and staggering. I want to be her everything—her protector, her best friend, and her confidant. I want to be her hero, the one she turns to when she's hurt and the name she cries out in the middle of the night. I felt all that and so much more in a single glance. I never knew fatherhood could be like that."

My hand dropped to touch the smooth wood of the bench, tracing the pattern of the grain, like I'd done so many times before.

"Do you think our fathers felt that the first time they saw us?" I asked the silence, expecting no answer in return.

I hoped so. I looked back to those final moments in this hallway—the battles between Megan's father and me, the tortured pain in his eyes.

Yes, in his world, there was no greater joy than Megan.

And he'd lost her.

There was a time in my life when I'd closed myself off from the world, too scared to risk the possibility of caring for anyone. After losing Megan, I couldn't fathom the idea of putting myself out there again, only to be reduced to ashes once more.

But now, I knew. Love and life—it was all a risk. Shut yourself away from it, and you'd never know what might be waiting for you on the other side of it all.

I stepped into the NICU and spotted Lailah immediately, her eyes alight with warmth and tenderness, as Meara cuddled up to her chest for the first time.

Skin-to-skin—the nurse had said it was called kangaroo care. There were no blankets. It was just flesh against flesh as the baby snuggled under the shirt of the parent. It allowed the baby to stay warm and encouraged bonding.

For Lailah, it appeared to be the most wondrous experience in the world. My hands itched to do the same, but I knew I'd get my chance. For now, I just relished in the sight of my wife and daughter together for the first time.

I thanked God for the many miracles he'd granted in making this possible. The sheer fact that they were allowing Meara to be held meant that she was making serious strides. I knew her hospital time wouldn't be coming to a close for a while, but this small step meant more to us than I could put into words.

Parents celebrated every milestone in their young child's life, and this was just the beginning of ours.

"Isn't it wonderful, Jude?" Lailah said as she saw me approach.

"One of the most amazing things I've ever witnessed," I answered with sincerity, kneeling down in front of her.

"I didn't think she'd be able to be held with the ventilator, but the nurse offered, and—" Her voice cracked.

"You're a natural."

Lailah held her for a few more minutes, enjoying her special time with our daughter, until the nurse placed her back under the warmer. We said our good-byes. It was getting harder and harder to do so, especially knowing Lailah was about to be discharged.

New mothers were supposed to leave with their babies.

I knew the second we left that hospital and arrived home without Meara, things would get worse.

And for once, I didn't have a clue how to make it better.

She didn't say a single word the entire way home.

Every time I opened my mouth to offer up something encouraging, something helpful, the words would get caught midway, and nothing but air would spring forth.

I felt like a failure to her, a traitor to the solid band of love and security woven around my left hand.

I wanted to comfort her, make all her doubts and fears fall away, as I'd done in the past, but in this instance, my own fears were just as overwhelming.

The physical pain I'd felt while walking out of that hospital without Meara consumed me, gnawed at me, until every step I'd taken away from her was like walking through quicksand—nearly impossible.

I didn't know how to be strong for Lailah this time because nothing about this seemed right.

I had so much to be thankful for. Going into that hospital less than a week ago, I'd had no idea what to expect. Would my child take her first breath? Would I ever see my wife alive again?

But somehow, we were all still here yet not fully together.

I knew, deep down, eventually, we would have our day when pictures were taken after baby Meara finally graduated from the NICU to the real world, but for now, it was just the two of us parents returning to an empty house.

As we pulled into the driveway, I noticed a familiar car parked along the curb. As my eyes scanned the street, I spotted another and another. The street seemed to be filled entirely by our friends and family. I looked up at the house and realized it was brightly lit rather than dark and gloomy.

"Did you invite anyone over?" I asked, turning to Lailah.

She hadn't yet looked up.

Her eyes jerked up toward the house in confusion. "No," she answered.

We both jumped out of the car, intrigue now a key distraction for our sadness. We walked up to the front door, finding it unlocked, and we took hesitant steps inside.

"Surprise!" everyone yelled as Sandy bounced up to greet us.

"What in the world?" Lailah gasped, petting her mop of a dog while trying to figure out what was going on.

I held her steady and tried to calm the dog. She and I took a minute to look around the room. Grace, Brian, and little Zander stood by the kitchen. Molly and Marcus sat at the kitchen table beside my mom. Rounding out the group were Nash and Abigail sitting on the couch, smiling at us, as we approached.

"We didn't want you to feel alone," Molly said.

"And we thought you might need some things," Grace added excitedly.

"But you already threw me a shower," Lailah protested. "Besides . . ." She looked around, the obvious missing bundle in her arms weighing heavily on her heart.

Grace stepped forward, taking Lailah's hand. "We know you have diapers and a breast pump and everything else you might need when Meara comes home—and she will come home, Lailah, soon."

Lailah nodded, a deep breath filling her lungs, as I stepped forward to wrap my arm around her waist.

"But I thought you might need other things—for this." Grace pointed to Lailah's heart. "To help make the days more bearable."

With a tug of her hand, Grace pulled Lailah to an open spot on the couch as Sandy followed, placing himself protectively by her side. Grace motioned for me to sit down next to Lailah, so I took a spot on the floor by her feet.

"We all came up with something. I hope you like them," Grace said.

My mom went first, stepping forward with a simple gift basket, accented in pink. I gave it to Lailah to disassemble. Inside was an assortment of bath products and lotions along with some sort of art kit.

"I remember feeling very . . . well, not myself, let's just say," my mom explained, pointing to the bath gel. "I thought these would help you relax when you're not at the hospital. It's not always easy to spring back after giving birth, but a little pampering never hurts."

"And this?" I asked, pointing to the small art kit.

"I had a friend whose granddaughter was in the NICU last year. She told me her daughter made a little name tag for the incubator. It helped make it feel more like home and less like a hospital, I guess. I thought it might be worth a try."

"Thank you, Mom," I said, squeezing Lailah's hand.

I set down the basket in preparation for Grace's gift.

"You know how much I love scrapbooking, photo books, and so on. Well, I thought this would keep you busy for a while, gathering everything, and it'll give you something personal to hang up in her room." Grace stepped forward and held out a large deep frame. "It's a shadow box. You can put everything in it that reminds you of her—announcements, hospital bracelets, pictures. When she gets older, she can look at it and see just how much she was loved from the very beginning."

"I love it," Lailah replied, her fingers slowly tracing the edge of the frame. "It will be perfect in her room."

I heard her take a deep breath behind me, trying desperately to keep her emotions in check. I knew her struggle. I was battling the same internal war myself. With each gift, I felt the lump in my throat grow bigger and bigger.

We'd expected to come home to an empty dark house, and instead, we'd found it full of warmth, love, and family.

I would never be able to repay them for this.

"We're next," Molly said, taking a step forward. Their gift was in a large pink gift bag with matching tissue paper streaming out the top.

Always one to enjoy watching others open gifts more than receiving them myself, I handed it over to Lailah once again and watched her toss pink tissue paper to the floor.

I chuckled in amusement when I saw her face contort into a mixture of horror and bewilderment as she pulled out several large balls of yarn.

"What am I supposed to do with these?" she asked, looking at the soft pink yarn like it was on fire.

"You're going to learn to knit," her mother said simply.

"I am?"

"Yes."

"Do I have a choice?" Lailah looked at the yarn with contempt.

"Well, of course you do. But I think it will be a good hobby to pick up. It's easy to learn and occupies the mind, and when you're done, you'll have a beautiful blanket to keep Meara warm."

I saw her expression soften slightly as she gazed down at the basic with curiosity.

"Okay, deal. But you have to teach me."

"I wouldn't want it any other way." Molly smiled.

Lailah set the yarn aside, and I tried not to laugh. Honestly, I couldn't think of a better gift from her mother. It was thoughtful and caring, and it'd give Lailah a purpose during the time Meara wasn't with us.

A deep voice bit through the lingering laughter. "I guess it's time for my gift," Nash said.

I'd barely had time to greet my old friend since seeing his face as we walked through the door. I was sad to say I hadn't had many opportunities to see him over the last few months, but seeing him here now meant a lot.

"You didn't have to do this," I said, taking the plain brown bag from him with gratitude.

"I know, but I wanted to."

I peeked in the bag and found an empty glass Mason jar. Picking it up, I glanced up at him for hints.

"Look again," he urged.

My eyes fell back to the bag, and there, underneath where the jar had been, was a square pad of paper. Still having no idea where he was going with this gift, I looked up for further instructions.

"Here," he said, pointing to the jar, "is where you will put all your hopes, one for each day she is not here in this house." His accent grew thicker with emotion. "And when she finally comes home, you will seal it up and save it for when she's older and needs it the most."

"Beautiful," Lailah whispered, having little experience with the unwavering romanticism that was Nash Taylor.

He'd won over the hearts of half of America with his overwhelming talent to turn words into melting chocolate with the flick of a wrist. His last stint in the hospital seemed to have tamed him slightly, and he hadn't made a single inappropriate comment since we arrived.

"Me! I'm next! I wanted to go last, and now, it's my turn!" Abigail bounced off the couch and handed Lailah a wrapped present that looked much like a book.

Their eyes met, and I could see this held special importance for Abigail. She watched every movement as Lailah pulled away the wrapping paper, exposing the pink leather below.

She flipped it over in her hands, and her eyes met Abigail's.

"It's a journal. The last time we talked, you mentioned you started writing in yours again, and I thought you could use another one, a nicer one. Also, I thought while the baby is still in the hospital, you could write her a list."

"A list?" Lailah asked.

"Like yours," Abigail said. "A Someday List. It won't be just like yours because she's a baby, but maybe you can add things in there that you guys can do later. I thought it would be cool if you had some things to check off right away, like take a walk on the beach or her first diaper change in her room. You know, things like that."

I got up from my spot on the floor and joined Lailah on the couch, her eyes already misting with fresh tears.

"Thank you, Abigail," she cried, her hands opening wide for the young girl. "I couldn't have asked for a greater gift."

They held each other tightly before we made our rounds, going from person to person, hugging and holding one another. Soon, dinner was ordered, and laughter filled the house.

There were no tears of sadness and no cries of loss, only the sound of hope and the promises of great things to come.

twenty-nine

The New Normal

Lailah

I LOVED SITTING out on the deck early in the morning before the world woke up.

It was quiet, new and fresh with possibilities, and the air clung to my skin, making my steaming cup of coffee taste that much better. Every morning I spent out here, watching the sun rising over the water, felt like a blessing.

Every day felt like a blessing.

I didn't know if there would ever be a point in my life when that feeling would stop.

Did I really want it to?

Did I want to eventually fade into the rest of existence, unimpressed with life and the ways of the world?

No, I didn't.

I loved my life and the constant amazement of it all. I would always be that girl who loved taking taxis just for the thrill of it and who never stopped looking at the ocean because it was too beautiful to turn away.

I would always be that woman who had survived.

The sliding door opened behind me, and I smiled, already knowing who it was.

"Look who beat us awake again this morning," Jude said in that voice he'd adopted ever since the moment he first held her.

His dad voice, I called it. It wasn't nearly as sexy as the voice he'd use in the bedroom, but it still gave me chills and goose bumps.

I looked up at them, my beautiful family.

Through it all, I would always be theirs.

Jude's wife and Meara's mother—nothing could get any better than that.

Having a child in the NICU was something you could never fully prepare for. It was something you could never explain to another who hadn't experienced it either. Even after coming home from the hospital alone on that first day, we'd Googled and read everything we could, trying to make sure we were up on every piece of equipment she was hooked up to and medication she was on. We'd stayed in touch with doctors around the clock and planned our schedules around hers. Still, nothing could have ever prepared us for the grueling days of waiting for our child to finally come home.

Our family had helped in so many ways. They'd arranged meals, even come and cleaned for us, but nothing could bring Meara home faster. Only time and patience could do that.

We'd ended up seeking out those like us, the ones who were still waiting and those who'd finally made it out. Making friends with parents of preemies was probably the best thing either one of us could have done. It'd opened our world of support and given us people to talk to. They'd completely understood every emotion because they, too, had suffered through them all.

Forty-one days—that was how many days Meara had spent in the NICU. It was forty-one days until we had our celebration day and finally taken her home with us.

It was a day I'd never be able to forget.

I didn't think I'd slept a single second that night. I'd just lain there, watching her in her bassinet by our bed, amazed and terrified at the same time. I had been so scared she'd somehow stop breathing, and we'd end up back in the hospital.

But she hadn't, and now, two months later, she was still thriving.

And we were getting ready to say good-bye to our California home.

Our year on the beach had come to an end.

"What are you thinking about?" Jude asked as he and Meara settled in on the chaise next to me.

I turned to kiss each of them, a tiny smooch on Meara's nose and a lingering long kiss for Jude.

"How much I'm going to miss this view," I admitted, placing my head on his shoulder.

Meara rested on his chest, and her fingers reached out for a strand of my hair.

"Me, too," he sighed.

"But I don't mind New York either," I said, trying to rally up some encouragement.

"We can introduce Meara to all our favorite restaurants when she gets a bit older," he offered.

I didn't respond as my head tried to envision our new life back in our old one. We'd once been happy in the city. We could be again. It would just be a readjustment. Lots of people raised families in big cities. We would, too.

"Hey, I know we still need to pack some things, but I want to take you somewhere this morning. Do you think you could go get ready real quick?" he asked before adding, "I'll throw in breakfast afterward."

"Well, only because you're feeding me," I said with a grin.

I raced down the hall before taking a quick shower and tossing on a pair of jeans and a blouse. My hair was thrown into a casual bun, and within a few more minutes, I was ready to go. He was already jiggling the keys by the door, and he had Meara in her car seat.

"No chance I can talk you into running by Dunkin' Donuts beforehand?" I begged, rubbing my grumbling stomach.

"Sorry, no. We have an appointment. And we're going to be late if we don't leave now."

"Well, you could have let me know sooner!" I announced.

We raced down the walkway and into the car. Of course that took time now as well. With a baby, we couldn't just run out the door like we use to. Diaper bag had to be packed, bottles made . . . it was a lengthy process.

After quickly clicking Meara's car seat into place, we were ready to go.

"So, any clues as to where we are going?" I asked, looking over to him, as he raced down the road.

"Nope." He just grinned.

It didn't take long to reach our destination, and as my eyes wandered around the construction site, I began to get suspicious.

"What are we doing here?" I questioned. I took a step out of the car.

"Just wait a second, and I'll explain everything."

I pulled Meara out of her car seat and held her to my chest. She hated being trapped in that thing, and if the car wasn't moving, she would demand to be freed from it. As I walked around, I noticed the expansive ocean view immediately. It was endless and uninhibited to whatever they were building since it was the only house around.

I turned just in time to see Jude returning side by side with another man wearing a hard hat and vest.

"Lailah, this is Jim Duncan. He's the lead on this project, our project."

My eyes flashed back to the building, looking from one end to the other. "Ours?"

His grin widened as he nodded. "Yep. Ours."

"Is it an investment property?" I said, trying to figure out just what was going on.

There were boxes all over my house that were going to New York at the end of the week. We were moving to New York. That was what he'd said.

"We're not moving back to New York—ever."

"We're not?"

"No." He laughed.

"I don't understand."

He looked over to Jim, and some sort of understanding was struck between the two of them. Jim gave a nod. As Jude took my hand, we walked up the stone path leading to the front door. Landscaping hadn't been done yet, but mostly everything appeared to be finished. A large Spanish-style door greeted us, and we entered. The entire back wall was completely made of glass, giving a surrounding view of the sandy beach beyond.

The Spanish theme continued inside. Rustic colors of deep orange, yellow, and various shades of tans moved throughout the kitchen and living room. No furniture yet, but it already felt warm and inviting just standing there.

"I couldn't let us leave," he finally said, turning toward me, as we stood together in what would be our family room.

"But what about the company? Your job?"

He smiled. "Part two of our stops for the day. We're opening a West Coast division. Expansion seemed like a good move, and several of the New Yorkers were looking for a change of scenery. When I suggested it to the board, they wholeheartedly agreed. Roman about croaked, but he'll get over it. He once told me he could be a grown up when he wanted to, so now he'll just have to make good on that promise—permanently." He shrugged. "So, here we are." He opened his arms out wide.

"We don't have to move?"

He laughed, pulling me close. "Well, we do but not cross-country. And not away from that," he said, pointing toward the ocean.

I looked around at this amazing house he'd built and then back to him. "It's breathtaking."

"And so are you."

There were still a hundred boxes scattered everywhere, but we were finally here, in our very own house.

Home—it had a nice ring to it.

Over the last year, I'd become quite attached to the house we rented on the beach, but there was always a part of me that knew it wasn't permanent. It wasn't ours. It had been a temporary solution, and I'd thought, eventually, we'd move away, back to New York, so I'd never allowed myself to get too attached to it.

But here, within these walls, I could finally find peace.

As I settled into the glider with Meara that night, taking a deep breath as she nuzzled up to my breast, I knew I was home.

Feeding an infant gave me a lot of quiet downtime.

I couldn't recall a time in my life, except for maybe long silent hours spent in the hospital, when I'd just simply sat and thought. These special moments with Meara had given me much needed time to process everything that had happened over the last year . . . and even beyond that.

I'd thought the moment I'd met Jude, I'd begun maturing, growing from the small naive girl I had been into the woman I was meant to become. By the time I'd followed him to New York, I had truly believed the process was nearly complete. It was a bold move after all.

But really, I'd been blossoming into myself every day since then. Maybe I always would be.

As my hand gently stroked the tiny hairs on Meara's head, I smiled, remembering how boring I'd thought life was within that drab hospital room.

Little had I known what was waiting for me beyond it.

When my mom and I had driven by people standing on the street corner, holding their coffees and bagels, I'd thought about how glamorous their lives looked, how normal it must feel to be late to work or to cross a street. I had envied them, envied the normal.

When I'd finally gotten the opportunity to do the same, those little things in life did feel glamorous to me because nothing about this life of mine would ever feel normal.

No matter how many lines I crossed off that Someday List, I would never feel like everyone else.

And I no longer wanted to.

Life was extraordinary, and there was nothing normal about that.

epilogue

Eighteen Years Later . . .

Meara

"MEARA! GRANDPA IS here with his truck ready to load up!" Mom hollered from downstairs.

"Okay. Just give me a minute, and I'll be right down!"

Rising from my bed, I took a look around, realizing how empty everything appeared. It was the little things really—the missing slippers at the end of the bed, the random collection of makeup that used to reside on my dresser, and the ever present laundry basket of clothes I never managed to put away.

All of it was gone, reminding me of one very obvious fact.

I was going away to college today.

Granted, UCLA was barely considered going away, but a dorm room wasn't down the hall from my parents, and I'd be sharing a bathroom with an entire floor—including boys.

I tried not to think about that vital piece of information more than I had to.

I could have gone nearly anywhere. With stellar grades and amazing SAT scores, I had my pick of some of the top schools—Stanford, NYU, even Chicago—but when it had all come down to that final decision, I'd known I couldn't tread too far away from home.

I was, and forever would be, a homebody.

When raised on the beautiful coast of California, who could really blame me?

And with parents like mine, it wasn't hard to want to stay as close to home as possible. Some of my friends had helicopters for parents—who hovered and overreacted over everything. Others wondered if their mom and dad even knew they existed. Mine—well, they were a perfect blend of awesome—always there when I needed them, but yet always aware of when I needed space to grow and develop on my own.

Shifting around the room, I looked at the various pictures on the walls. From my first birthday to my graduation, this room held so many memories. There was a framed picture on my dresser from the day we met my adopted brother Ian. I'd been so excited to finally have a baby brother. I'd skipped down the halls, singing and clapping my hands—I was two, but when I got there I realized he wasn't as little as I expected. I guess my toddler mind expected a cabbage patch doll I could play dress up with—not a six month old baby who cried and pooped. I was not impressed. I got used to him though, and eventually I grew to like him. Okay, I loved him. He was a great brother and really completed our family. Who knew the little poop factory could be such a blessing.

As my eyes roamed further down the line of photos, I glimpsed a picture of Ian and me, wrapped around our Uncle Roman and his wife—taken several years ago during one of our yearly trips back east. We were on a boat after spending the day out in the sun and we all looked happy and carefree.

I had so many treasured memories.

"Are you hiding in here?" Dad asked, peeking his head into my room.

"No, just saying good-bye," I said sadly.

"Not good-bye. Just—"

I smiled, shaking my head. "See you later?"

"I've said that one before?"

"A few times, Dad."

"I need better lines." He laughed. He came up to me, his arm wrapping around my shoulder. "We're only a short drive away. Besides, you'll need someplace to do your laundry, I'm sure."

"I'll come home for more than just laundry," I assured him.

"My charming wit?" he guessed.

"Definitely."

"I knew it. Now, come on. Save the waterworks for later. We've got a truck to load, and if we don't hurry, Grandpa's going to throw his back out from trying to do it all himself. Ian and I keep trying to help, but you know your Grandpa . . ."

"Okay. One more minute?" I asked.

He nodded, placing a soft kiss on my forehead. "Okay."

I heard his footfalls trail down the hallway as I took one last look around the room. My eyes settled on a tattered old journal of my mom's. It was something I'd found the other day while going through her nightstand in search of a bottle of lotion.

She'd told me stories of her Someday List over the years, and she'd even shown it to me when I was younger. It had been years since I last saw it, and when I'd found it again, I'd secretly taken it from its spot and brought it back to my room to look at it.

Opening it once more, I looked through the pages of wishes and dreams she'd once had, all crossed out throughout the years. Some remained—"*A life still being lived,*" she'd once explained—but it amazed me how many she and my father had managed to make come true since her years in the hospital.

As my eyes settled on one left untouched, I thought about my birth story—how I'd come to be, how they'd risked everything to make sure I had my place in this world. She should have put herself first, after everything she'd gone through in life. She'd deserved it after all. But my mother had never taken the easy way and because of this . . . here I stood.

With a shaky hand, I grabbed a pen off my clean desk and crossed off one of the last remaining wishes on my mother's Someday List.

~~Save someone's life.~~

A small smile tugged at the corner of my mouth as I quietly placed the journal back in the drawer. With one last glance toward the bedroom that had kept me safe for the last eighteen years, I took the first step into my future.

My parents had always taught me life is what you make of it—you just have to be brave enough to spread your wings and fly.

So here goes nothing.

You've fallen for one Cavanaugh . . . but are you sure you can handle another?

It's time for Roman turn in the spotlight . . .

Behind Closed Doors

Coming early 2016 from USA Today Bestselling Author J.L. Berg

Waves—Mr Probz

It's Always You—Kris Allen

Maps—Maroon 5

Ghosts That We Knew—Mumfor & Sons

(Everything I Do) I Do It For You—Bryan Adams

Thinking Out Loud—Ed Sheeran

How Long Will I love You—Ellie Goulding

Not About Angels—Birdy

Doesn't Mean Goodbye—John McLaughlin

Wave—Beck

At Last—Ella James

It's Your Love—Time McGraw

Hey Jude—Paul McCartney

All of Me—John Legend

I Lived—OneRepublic

acknowledgements

This book would have never become a reality if it weren't for my amazing readers. Because of your loud, demanding love for Lailah and Jude, here we are and what a wonderful journey it has been. I only hope I've given you the ending you always hoped for. So first and foremost, I must thank you-my wonderful readers. I love each and every one of you.

Secondly, I must thank my husband and family. I don't know how I got so lucky to included in such a rad weird bunch of people, but I'll be eternally grateful.

Leslie: You are that friend. The irreplaceable kind. Thanks for being you. Oh, and for getting knocked up with an IUD . . . that really helped with my storyline.

Melissa & Carey—I lurve you. Always.

Beta Readers—Thank you for working with my crazy quick time crunch. I know, I'm demanding.

Junkies—You guys rock! Thanks for your constant support and love.

Bloggers—Thank you for loving and supporting authors like me.

Kelsey—I'm running out of ways to tell you how awesome you are. So just look at the cover and nod. Yep, you did that.

Elizabeth and Grant—Thank you for bring Lailah and Jude to life. I don't think a day has gone by that I haven't looked at this cover in awe. It's breathtaking.

Sarah—This cover is so fetch. Oh, and XOXO because I know you hate that.

Stacey—Thank you once again for making the inside of this book as pretty as the outside. You are amazing.

Jill Sava—What did I do before you? I'm pretty sure it involved rocking back and forth in a corner while Facebook notifications chimed in my ear. Thanks for keeping me on point!

Jill Marsal—Thank you for everything you do. When I started this venture two years ago, I would have never guessed my books would soon be translated into other languages and I'd be signing deals with major publishers. I owe so much to you.

Tara (and the rest of my InkSlingers Family)—You are all amazing. That is all. Oh, and I love you.

J.L. Berg is the USA Today bestselling author of the Ready Series. She is a California native living in the beautiful state of historic Virginia. Married to her high school sweetheart, they have two beautiful girls that drive them batty on a daily basis. When she's not writing, you will find her with her nose stuck in a romance novel, in a yoga studio or devouring anything chocolate. J.L. Berg is represented by Jill Marsal of Marsal Lyon Literary Agency, LLC.